WATCHING THE DETECTIVES

Watching the Detectives

Essays on Crime Fiction

Edited by

IAN A. BELL
Lecturer in English
The University College of Wales, Aberystwyth

and

GRAHAM DALDRY
Copywriter
McCormick Publicis (Advertising), Manchester

St. Martin's Press   New York

First published in the United States of America in 1990

Printed in Hong Kong

ISBN 0–312–04068–7

Library of Congress Cataloging-in-Publication Data
Watching the detectives: essays on crime fiction / edited by Ian A.
    Bell and Graham Daldry.
        p.   cm.
    ISBN 0–312–04068–7
    1. Detective and mystery stories, English—History and criticism.
    2. Detective and mystery stories, American—History and criticism.   3.Crime
in literature.   I. Bell, Ian A.   II. Daldry, Graham.
    PR830.D4W27 1990
    823'.087209—dc20   89-24158
                                                                        CIP

To the memory of Raymond Williams, 1921–88

Contents

Preface

Crime fiction in all its various forms is one of the most visible and popular kinds of literature today. According to recent market research, crime titles account for at least 10 per cent of all paperbacks sold in Britain, and their share of the market is growing. Although part of this can be attributed to the popularity of individual authors, specifically P. D. James, Ruth Rendell and Ellis Peters, it bespeaks a more generalised interest in the literature of crime in all its aspects. Some publishers have sought to exploit this interest by offering specialised imprints for crime, such as Arrow's Mysterious Press or Collins Classic Crime, whereas other publishers have signalled the allegiances by conventionalising their covers, from the donnish sobriety of the old green Penguins to the more lurid iconography of death, sex and guns on recent books. Bookshops almost invariably set aside separate sections for crime, prominently displaying titles by currently popular authors or works recently adapted for television or film. For the reading public, it seems, crime fiction is identifiable and attractive.

The immediate problem for anyone wishing to offer commentary on this form is that its apparent homogeneity and recognisability begins to disappear once examined. On these separate 'Crime' shelves, you will find James Hadley Chase alongside G. K. Chesterton, Deighton next to Doyle, Simenon flanked by Sayers and Spillane. If you actually get beyond the miscellaneous titles to the covers, you will find an extraordinary range of styles and forms all comfortably inhabiting the same area. Whodunits and procedurals and psychological thrillers and memoirs of pathologists and all sorts of things get lumped together under the general category. In terms of meaning and ideology too, the range is immense, from the classic, conservative validation of the legal process to feminist reappraisals of violence to radical deconstructions of authority. And all of these are offered to while away the time. . . .

Only a few literary critics have thought this immensely popular form worth serious attention, and the work done so far has been extremely selective. Most of it relies heavily on the notion of 'genre', a way of intervening between the general category of literature and the specificity of individual texts. Whereas most traditional literary criticism concentrates on those features that individuate a work, that make it unique, genre criticism concentrates upon representative features. 'Genre' then becomes a kind of grid through which individual works are seen and appraised. Inevitably such criticism covertly devalues the works it articulates, turning them into versions of some recurrent ideal, and leaving the critic with little to do other than to survey the range of variations available. Such surveys of crime fiction do exist, from the entertainingly anecdotal Julian Symons with *Bloody Murder* (1972) to the instructive H. R. F. Keating and *Writing Crime Fiction* (1986) to Ernest Mandel's tendentious and purposeful *Delightful Murder* (1984). There are also more abstract typological works, such as John G. Cawelti's *Adventure, Mystery and Romance* (1976) or Tzvetan Todorov's important essay 'The Typology of Detective Fiction' (1962), which try to detect the basic formulae that are variously combined in crime fiction. These efforts are interesting, but seem to present the works simply as exercises in reformulation, in rule-following. They rely in part on the notion that the fundamental elements of crime fiction can be identified – as they were by S. S. Van Dine in 1928 in his twenty rules for detective writing – and that their combinations can be articulated.

This is a seductive idea, but it leaves out far too much. The important thing about so much crime writing, like similar science-fiction work, is the way it responds to, parodies and explores its own conventions. Crime fiction does not simply reiterate its previous forms. Rather, it regroups them, explores their congruities and incongruities and refers allusively to parallel texts. An obvious example of this would be Umberto Eco's *The Name of the Rose* (1984), where the central investigating figure is defined in terms of Sherlock Holmes, and the whole process of detection is used to examine the conflict between rationality and faith. Eco's novel is highly artful and 'literary', and might be thought to transcend generic conventions. In fact, however, it is to be read as a crime novel amongst other crime novels, drawing on and examining its own conventions. The reader who arrives at Eco's book through Conan Doyle and, say, Ellis Peters, is more ably equipped to assimilate it than the reader ignorant of patterns of such fiction.

So some kind of generic competence is required for readers of crime fiction, some recognition, however subliminal, of the rules of the game. Typological studies and general surveys may provide this, but what they are less able to do is yield the meanings of such works. Cawelti, it is true, does try to establish the meaning of crime writing in its archetypal substructure, but as with all archetypal studies, his argument is heavily rhetorical and loosely universalist. A more fruitful approach is followed by Stephen Knight in his *Form and Ideology in Crime Fiction* (1980), where the forms of crime writing are seen as vehicles of meaning rather than simply identifiable structures. Knight, then, is able to move beyond taxonomy to more assertive speculation about what crime fiction can convey, what it disseminates and contests. This notion of ideological critique, which can also be seen in Jerry Palmer's *Thrillers* (1976) and Colin Watson's *Snobbery with Violence* (1971), is fundamental to the present project. Although we offer attention to the forms and construction of crime writing, we are ultimately concerned with the ideological problems of voice, gender and authority that such writing dramatises.

Accordingly, we have organised the book in four sections. The first part, comprising the first four essays, looks at authors who have attracted very little critical attention, who are at the forefront of the form today (Highsmith, Higgins, McIlvanney, Wings, Wilson). The essays explore the various ways of reading these books, and provide the context for a way of reading crime fiction in general. The next two essays innovatively look at the relationship between 'factual' and fictional accounts of crime. Richard Ireland looks at the ways a popular text can contest the prevailing ideas of criminology, and John Simons shows how even 'factual' accounts of crime are conducted through fictional forms. The next four essays reappraise those authors who are as near to 'canonical' as crime writing gets – Poe, Chandler, Christie, and le Carré. By paying attention to the formal construction of these texts, their cultural role and their inherently unstable forms, our contributors hope to allow a discussion of crime fiction to be carried on at a level every bit as sophisticated as that of more orthodox literary criticism. Finally, we offer a speculative overview by Stephen Knight, in which the inherently radical nature of this popular form is explored and validated.

The volume is thus deliberately eclectic in scope and approach. We hope to initiate and stimulate discussion, rather than to provide a textbook, or to say the last word on these matters. We hope to demonstrate the complexity of these popular forms, which are so pervasive as to be almost invisible. In this project, as in so much else, we have to acknowledge our debt to the late Raymond

Williams. In May 1987, Raymond Williams gave a lecture on 'Secret Agents since Conrad' at the University College of Wales, Aberystwyth, where he was Honorary Professorial Fellow. It was a typical Williams piece, in its willingness to challenge assumptions, to take on the most important matters through a reading of popular texts. It was this occasion that stimulated us to begin the project that has culminated in this volume. Professor Williams had agreed to give us a finalised version of his paper for inclusion, but his untimely death prevented him from finishing it. We have not replaced his proposed contribution, as a mark of respect, and we wish to dedicate the book to his memory. In our contributors' willingness to take seriously something that is part of the fabric of many people's lives, and in our collective desire to cross the boundaries of conventional literary criticism, we wish to carry on his work.

Acknowledgements

The editors and contributors would like to acknowledge the help given to them by Christine Christie, Helen Cox, Suzanne Daldry, T. B. James, Morfydd Radford, Joan Rowlands, Kate Simons and Joy Williams, who made useful suggestions, gave secretarial assistance, lent us books, and were generally supportive. Conrad Goulden of Arrow Books and Graham Nelson of W. H. Smith were very co-operative in telling us about sales and audiences. In particular, we must thank Brian P. Carter of the Black Lion, Llanbadarn Fawr, who generously gave us as much time as we needed to consider the project to begin with, and we must pay tribute to the effervescent presence of the Law Librarian, Bill Hines, whose unfailing zest for life kept us going throughout.

Notes on the Contributors

Tony Barley is lecturer in English at the University of Liverpool. His study of the novels of John le Carré, *Taking Sides*, was published in 1985.

Ian A. Bell was educated at the universities of Glasgow and Edinburgh, and at present works in the English Department at the University College of Wales, Aberystwyth. He is author of *Defoe's Fiction* (1985) and *Literature and Crime in Augustan England* (forthcoming) and a number of articles on eighteenth-century topics and Scottish writing.

Graham Daldry was educated at Selwyn College, Cambridge, and the University of Liverpool. From 1986 to 1988 he was University Research Fellow at the University College of Wales, Aberystwyth. He is the author of *Charles Dickens and the Form of the Novel* (1986) and articles on Wordsworth and Shelley. At present, he is a copywriter with a Manchester advertising agency.

Simon Dentith is lecturer in English at the University of Liverpool. He has published *George Eliot* (1985) and a number of articles on mainly nineteenth-century topics.

Richard W. Ireland teaches Legal History and Jurisprudence in the Law Faculty at the University College of Wales, Aberystwyth. He has published articles in the UK and USA on the history of crime and criminal procedure. He is co-author of *Imprisonment in England and Wales: A Concise History* (1985) and *Punishment: Rhetoric, Rule, Practice* (1989).

Stephen Knight has worked at Sydney University and the Australian National University Canberra. He is Professor of English at the University of Melbourne. His many publications include *The Structure of Thomas Malory's Arthuriad, Rhymyng Craftily: Meaning in Chaucer's Poetry* and *Form and Ideology in Crime Fiction*.

Ffrangcon C. Lewis is a lecturer in American Literature in the English Department, the University College of Wales,

Aberystwyth, having previously taught in further education. He is currently at work on a study of stories by Melville and Hawthorne.

Maldwyn Mills was educated at University College, Cardiff, and Jesus College, Oxford. He now holds a personal chair in the English Department, the University College of Wales, Aberystwyth, and has published extensively in the field of medieval romance.

Lyn Pykett was educated at the University of London, and is now lecturer in English at the University College of Wales, Aberystwyth. She has published articles on the Victorian periodical press, nineteenth- and twentieth-century fiction, and is currently completing a study of Emily Brontë.

John Simons was educated at the University College of Wales, Aberystwyth and the University of Exeter. He has published mainly on medieval topics, and is currently lecturer at King Alfred's College, Winchester.

Anna-Marie Taylor was educated at the universities of Bristol and Lancaster. She has worked in the Communications Department of Bristol Polytechnic and is currently in the Drama Department of the University College of Wales, Aberystwyth. She is working on a study of German drama in Britain since 1945.

1

Irony and Justice in Patricia Highsmith

IAN A. BELL

Let other pens dwell on guilt and misery
Jane Austen

It is the crime writer's peculiar vocation to dwell on guilt and misery; to invent, articulate and linger over acts of violence, hatred and sudden unnatural death. And it is the crime reader's peculiar pleasure to participate vicariously in these inventions. Look around any train compartment or waiting-room, and you will see the most mild-looking people engrossed in the most lurid titles. What kind of pleasure does crime fiction offer? We may feel comfortably superior to those eighteenth-century voyeurs who enjoyed regular visits to Bedlam to be amused by the antics of those confined, but perhaps the satisfaction of the detective novel is a vestigial performance of the triumph of sanity over deviance. For the conventional crime novel not only dwells on guilt and misery, it isolates and seeks to dispel the guilty and the miserable. Crime fiction does more than simply display its deviants. It presents a world in which crime is identifiable, soluble and explicable. Crime may not be preventable, but the damage it causes can be limited. The world is thus packaged into the two exclusive bundles of the normal innocents and the deviant guilty, and readers can be reassured about their own status and safety.

In this caricature form, then, the detective novel engages with violence to show that, despite appearances, we live in a just and well-regulated world. Just think how regularly Perry Mason's skill saves the innocent from wrongful accusation, or Steve Carella's integrity brings the fugitive villain to justice. The 'message' of these fictions is that the social institutions of law enforcement, though clearly flawed, are as good as we are likely to get, and that the intelligence and integrity of the officers of justice are more than good enough to compensate for any failings in the system. By emphasising the salutory powers of intelligence, intuition, dedication and perseverance, both Erle Stanley Gardner and Ed McBain,

1

amongst many other writers, validate the institutions of legality and the customary practices of these institutions.

However, there are crime writers whose engagement with guilt and misery is more disturbing than this, and the most interesting of them is Patricia Highsmith. Highsmith has been an active and prolific writer for forty years, producing an enormous number of novels and short stories. Although she is uneasy about the 'crime fiction' label, preferring to see herself as a writer of 'suspense fiction', her work is fully engaged with guilt, violence and unnatural death. What makes her work remarkable, however, is its fastidious dismantling of the conventional categories of guilt and justice. Although very diverse in setting and action, her fiction sustains an ironic inquiry into the possibilities of justice and the ramifications of guilt. The violent acts that do occur (and some of her works have only the suspicion of violence in them) are neither the instigation nor the climax of the novels. In fact, she has so little interest in the practice of detection that she abandons the hermeneutic aspect of crime fiction altogether. The crimes perpetrated or suspected are of secondary importance in comparison with the very deliberate construction of environment and atmosphere, and the distanced, ironic presentation of character. Her treatment of her subjects is best illustrated by an analogy from her own work. In this extract, a character called Peter Knoppert is enjoying his hobby, snail-watching:

> He spent all his evenings with his snails in the room that was no longer a study but a kind of aquarium. He loved to strew the tanks with fresh lettuce and pieces of boiled potato and beet, then turn on the sprinkler system that he had installed in the tanks to simulate rainfall. Then all the snails would liven up and begin eating, mating, or merely gliding through the shallow water with obvious pleasure. Mr Knoppert often let a snail crawl onto his forefinger – he fancied his snails enjoyed this human contact – and he would feed it a piece of lettuce by hand, would observe the snail from all sides, finding as much aesthetic satisfaction as another man might from contemplating a Japanese print.[1]

Eventually, Mr Knoppert's fascination with his snails becomes overpowering, literally, and he is smothered by them. This is characteristic Highsmith in its presentation of the quiet obsessions in 'ordinary' life, and in its macabre ending. However, it is also a miniature image of her own practice in creating an environment for her own specimens, caring for them and watching with distanced pleasure as they go about their business. Both Highsmith and Knoppert might be called, in different ways, naturalists.

Highsmith herself seems heiress of the naturalist legacy, setting up quasi-scientific studies of individual behaviour in specific environments. The environments vary from Italy to North Africa to East Anglia to Pennsylvania to the Mid-West, and the pressures exerted on characters differ accordingly. However, what remains constant is Highsmith's pretence of objectivity. Although she is setting up and orchestrating the events, she strives to appear unobtrusive and uninvolved. Unlike so many other crime writers, she refuses to accept the responsibilities of judgement or adjudication:

> Creative people do not pass moral judgements – at least not at once – on what meets their eye. There is time for that later in what they create, if they are so inclined, but art has nothing to do with morality, convention or moralizing.[2]

Paradoxical though it may sound, it is this aloofness, this impersonality that is most characteristic of her writing. The refusal to judge her characters is most obvious in the unapologetic, yet unsupportive presentation of the pitiless and calculating killer Ripley, her only recurrent character, who has so far appeared in a number of different novels. Similarly, her reluctance to commandeer her fictions can be seen in her most characteristic plot device, which is to demonstrate (not initiate) the unavoidable and grim consequences of an apparently trivial accident. In her first novel, *Strangers on a Train* (1950), the entire grotesque adventure is contingent upon the chance meeting of two people on a train. In her most recent, *Found in the Street* (1986), the disastrous ending is impelled by the chance discovery of a lost wallet. By erecting all the complexities of plot on these apparently insignificant events, Highsmith is resisting the overly dramatic, and simultaneously showing the persistent proximity of extraordinary events to 'ordinary' life. The potential for violence is *already* written into the fabric of things.

By these ironic exposures, Highsmith is showing the fragility of any secure life. The characters who fall into disaster in her books come almost entirely from the established professional classes, leading the most organised lives. She shows the disruption that a chance encounter can create, but more regularly shows how a prosperous, steady, middle-class life contains within itself tensions and stresses that lead to its eventual catastrophic collapse. Her characters all live respectable white-collar existences, working as publishers, illustrators, architects or engineers, or even having private incomes. They are surrounded by a ritualised life of cocktail parties, dinners and all sorts of social responsibilities, encumbered by property, and often trapped in intensely habituated and unsatisfying marriages. The humdrum, regulated nature of their lives is well summed-up by the list of hobbies of Victor Van Allen, the strange central figure from *Deep Water* (1957):

> in a casual way he was interested in a great many things – printing and bookbinding, bee culture, cheese making, carpentry, music and painting (good music and good painting), in star-gazing, for which he had a fine telescope, and in gardening. (p. 23)

These lives seem at once orderly and aimless, lacking any drama or sense of climax. In this sense, the transmutation of Guy Haines from respectable architect to celebrity tennis pro in Hitchcock's film of *Strangers on a Train* (1951) distorted and sensationalised the tale. It is important for the stealthy development of Highsmith's plots that a monotonous existence is either gradually or explosively infiltrated by obsession and madness. After all, even Tom Ripley is seen to be a caring and meticulous gardener.

While Highsmith does not go so far as to suggest that an interest in gardening (or bee keeping, or snails, or whatever) is a morbid symptom, she uses these peripheral activities to show how close to obsession any interest can become, and how hard it can be to distinguish between the two. She repeatedly shows how an idea can cease to fulfil any rational purpose, and can take over its creator. In *The Blunderer* (1956), for example, Walter Stackhouse incriminates himself in his wife's accidental death by repeatedly visiting a man who murdered his own wife in a similar fashion. Stackhouse's desire to see Kimmel, and to participate vicariously in murder, eventually causes the collapse of his career and his security. An even more graphic example comes in *The Tremor of Forgery* (1969) when Howard Ingham, a New Yorker, is so disorientated in Tunisia that he becomes obsessed by his possible guilt in the death of an

Arab. In an ironic reversal of Camus, Highsmith makes it impossible to be certain whether there is any dead Arab, and she makes the whole episode more absurd by grounding Ingham's fears in his bizarre act of throwing a typewriter at an intruder in the night. Appropriate or not, Ingham's guilt is circumstantially plausible to others, and seems to be an admission of certainty in a very nebulous scene.

The peculiar merging of fantasy and fact is prominent throughout Highsmith's writing. Dreams, however, are seen as dangerous delusions, obsessions and signs of mental collapse. She engages with all aspects of the irrational, the dark and threatening concealed side of modern life. What makes her writing so chilling is that the irrational is conducted with all the appearances of lucidity and calm. Van Allen, in *Deep Water*, accurately describes his own mental condition in a disturbingly clear fashion:

> Schizophrenia, hon, means a split personality. It is a mental disease characterized by a loss of contact with one's environment and by dissolution of the personality. There. Understand? And it looks like your old Daddy's got it.   (p. 160)

Irrational desires and beliefs are seen to lie at the heart of society, and neurosis is commonplace. Communities, even the Enlightenment community of the USA, are not rational congresses between rational, free individuals, but claustrophobic gatherings of obsessed and sordid fantasists. Highsmith deliberately and repeatedly denies the distinction between the normal and the deviant. Her 'normal' people behave in the most irrational ways, and her 'deviants' carry out their schemes meticulously and rationally. After all, the swopping of murders that Bruno suggests to Guy Haines in *Strangers on a Train* is a sublimely *rational* plan. The result of this confusing of categories is that the reader's confidence in the rational ordering of the world is disturbed. The presentation of the neurotic is so powerful that it carries over into the other figures. As Erich Fromm puts it in a pertinent analysis:

> The phenomena which we observe in the neurotic person are in principle not different from those we find in the normal. They are only more accentuated, clear-cut, and frequently more accessible to the awareness of the neurotic person than they are in the normal who is not aware of any problem which warrants study.[3]

Highsmith's presentation of the neurotic confirms this diagnosis, and, as we shall see, it is by this kind of social psychology that she introduces further radical themes.

Of course, Highsmith is not the only writer to see crime as neurosis, or to see it as widespread. Georges Simenon has a comparable interest in the psychologies of his characters, and a similar sense of the virtual universality of insanity. So too Ed McBain's 87th Precinct is densely populated with psychopaths. However, each of these writers builds a little enclave of sanity and security in his mad world. Inspector Maigret can go home to the comfortable flat he shares with his wife, whom even he describes as 'Mme Maigret'. Steve Carella has a refuge of cloying sentimentality with his significantly dumb wife and his children. In Highsmith, there is no such retreat. Domesticity, in her work, is an arena of tension, not a haven of security. And although it may be individual transgressions that motivate the action in her novels, these individual passions are understood as part of the fabric of the societies they inhabit and disrupt. In his consideration of crime fiction in general, Ernest Mandel gives the following description:

> Disorder being brought into order, order falling back into disorder; irrationality upsetting rationality, rationality restored after irrational upheavals: that is what the ideology of the crime novel is all about.[4]

It may well be, but it is not what Patricia Highsmith is 'all about'. It is virtually impossible to find any confidence in the restoration of order or rationality in her fiction, but the vision of order falling back into disorder is recurrent and intensely presented.

The endings of the Highsmith novels are irresolute. Order is not restored, and right and wrong are not clearly identified. More typically, the novels end with the protagonist sunk in a hopeless morass of confusions, which intensify the moral uncertainties that the narrative has created. The ending of *The Cry of the Owl* (1962) is a representative example:

> Robert took his hands down. He started to go to the door, to go out, but the sunlight blinded him and he stopped. He did not look again at Nickie, but the white of her shirt, the dark of her slacks, stayed like a pattern in the corner of his eyes, wherever he looked. The knife was at his feet, not a bloodstain on it that he

could see. He bent to pick it up, then stopped. Don't touch it, he
thought, don't touch it.　(p. 250)

The violence in this ending is haphazard and grotesque. The central
character seems caught up in actions which he may partly have
instigated but which have taken on a force beyond his control. In
this case, Highsmith is exploiting the strange psychology of Robert
Forester to sustain an oblique examination of bourgeois codes of
justice and morality. Elsewhere in her fiction, she interrogates such
bourgeois ideals in a fastidious, disconcerting way. In particular,
the institutions of legality and the courts are treated with disdain
and scepticism.

Despite the propensity to violence of Highsmith's figures, her
novels offer little in the way of solution. As she says:

> I find the public passion for justice quite boring and artificial, for
> neither life nor nature cares if justice is ever done or not. The
> public wants to see the law triumph, or at least the general public
> does, though at the same time the public likes brutality. The
> brutality must be on the right side, however. Sleuth-heroes can
> be brutal, sexually unscrupulous, kickers of women, and still be
> popular heroes, because they are chasing something worse than
> themselves, presumably.[5]

She herself does not introduce any of these brutal 'sleuth-heroes'
(by whom I take it she means someone like Spillane's Mike
Hammer), and her boredom with the notion of justice is expressed
differently. It appears in her cynical treatment of the police and the
officers of official justice. Although only a few of her novels have
any investigators in them, and more often than not these investigators are peripheral to the events, when they do appear, they are
seen as just as obsessed and misguided as the 'criminals'. In *The
Blunderer*, Walter Stackhouse comes under suspicion in the
mysterious death of his wife. He is hounded by an Inspector Corby
(= corbeau?), who *idée fixe* is that Stackhouse is guilty. Although
there are circumstantial grounds for thinking that he might be, he is
not, but Corby cannot let doubt enter his mind. Corby is equally
convinced (rightly this time) that a man called Kimmel has
murdered his wife. He tries to extort confessions from each by, on
the one hand, a campaign of psychological pressure, and on the
other, by overt physical violence and brutality. Each suspect

regards him differently. For Stackhouse, the whole business is a
weird battle of wits:

> It's all a jolly game, Walter thought. Cops and robbers. It must
> take a mind that's nasty or twisted somewhere, he thought, to
> devote itself exclusively to homicide, especially with the gleeful
> zest that Corby showed.   (p. 159)

For Kimmel, however, the game is graver and the stakes are higher:

> Kimmel had felt until Corby came that he had enjoyed a
> supernatural immunity, and now Corby himself seemed pos-
> sessed of supernatural powers, like a Nemesis. Corby was not
> fair. His methods were not those commonly associated with
> justice, and yet he enjoyed the immunity that official uniformed
> justice gave him.   (p. 209)

In fact, Corby's methods in dealing with Stackhouse are those of the
sleuth. His gradual building up of pressure on the suspect is
reminiscent of the procedural novel, and is complicated only by the
fact that Stackhouse is innocent.

His collapse into brutality in his treatment of Kimmel is a
different matter, and one that Highsmith uncharacteristically
defended. In trying to have *The Blunderer* accepted for serial
publication, Highsmith encountered some resistance to its stark
treatment of the police. She tried to persuade editors of its
acceptability by verifying it:

> I had spoken earlier to a detective of the homicide squad in Fort
> Worth, Texas. . . . I asked him if the police used physical force –
> blows and truncheons – and I told him exactly how far police
> brutality went in my book. He endorsed what I had written,
> saying, with a big smile in which I could see a certain relish, 'If we
> get a guy we have good reason to think is guilty, *we don't hesitate* to
> work him over.' But I went . . . to a police station in Lower
> Manhattan that I was referred to and put the question to a police
> official. He also corroborated what I told him I had written.[6]

Highsmith's evidence here may be unsupported and anecdotal, but
it reveals a deeply ironic view of police behaviour. She is not
content to rely on the metropolitan prejudices that lie at the heart of

much American 'liberal' crime fiction, such as John Ball's Virgil Tibbs series. Rather, she sees the proximity of criminal and juridicial behaviour to be inevitable, and seems to think that the drive for justice is only the craving for satisfaction or revenge given some spurious social sanction.

Her scepticism is more vehemently articulated in one of her most hectic novels, *The Glass Cell* (1964). Again, the failure of the law to secure justice is not attributed to the accidental presence of evil or incompetent executives. Rather, the disastrous miscarriage of justice that motivates the narrative is ironically embedded in the judicial process itself. Philip Carter, the central figure, is in prison as the novel opens. He has been a civil engineer, who has casually accepted the delivery of materials he did not know to be sub-standard. When the swindle of substituting cheap goods for more expensive ones comes out, he is the only person who might legitimately be punished. The real culprit is dead, but someone must pay. In prison, he is grotesquely mistreated, being strung up by the thumbs for long periods. Given morphine to kill the pain in his hands, he becomes addicted to it. The prison scenes are handled with that heightened documentary style associated with the Warner Brothers' 'Big House' films of the 1930s, revealing the awful conditions within institutions designed to dispirit and humiliate rather than reform. But unlike those films, Highsmith's novel is not crusading for better conditions of incarceration. Instead, she recounts the hardening process of imprisonment, and shows how it disables Carter from living a thoughtful life on release, but at no point does she point her moral or adorn her tale. Carter's case is not a cautionary tale, or a dire warning, but rather a potent example of the contradictions involved in the institutional implementation of justice. Being convicted does not make Carter face up to his criminality: it turns him into a criminal.

Highsmith's treatment of prisons is interestingly different from that in the 'Big House' films, and in the analogous 'prisoner of war' genre. In those cases, the incarceration serves only to intensify character, and is often at the service of the heroic myth of individual integrity. The innocent convict, or, to take the most intense form, the prisoner of war, triumphs over his environment by retaining his dignity and his sense of justice and duty, despite the potentially brutalising circumstances. In Highsmith, the grim environment exerts such pressures on the inmates that all pretensions to heroism are destroyed. Survival takes precedence over any system of values.

This is most marked in her presentation of prison, but is more widely applicable to her vision of the modern city. In *Found in the Street* (1986), the isolated and disturbed Ralph Linderman sees his environment as an example of the collapse of standards in the modern world:

> New York for the most part was a sordid town. You had only to look around you at the littered streets to realize that people weren't pulling together, kids learning early that it was all right to toss paper cups right on the sidewalk, nuts of all kinds walking around muttering to themselves, usually obscenities and curses against their fellow men. Sick people and unhappy people! Then there were the muggers, one of them grabbing your arms from behind, the other fishing for your wallet, fleet of foot they were too. That had happened to Ralph once, coming home from work at around 5 in the morning. A curse upon *them*, muggers, the scum of the earth!   (p. 2)

Even if Ralph is one of the 'nuts' himself, his vision is a disturbingly grim one, and one that Highsmith's narrative does not deny. The characters she puts into this New York are shallow, unstable people, both too innocent and too guilty to forge purposeful relationships with one another.

Highsmith then expresses sustained scepticism about the efficacy of both the officers and the institutions of justice, and the frightening triumph of environment over character. It is frightening because the environments are so empty, so devoid of meaning. The urban world is lacking in sense, but when its inhabitants are taken from it and forced to confront themselves, as happens in *The Tremor of Forgery*, they break down. The only character capable of survival in a variety of environments, and the only one who is truly cosmopolitan, is the guiltless Tom Ripley. Her criminals then are not scoundrels, but transgressors, and the most radical edge of her writing can be seen in the way she cuts up all notions of guilt and innocence.

Within the bourgeois, socialised notion of justice, a clear distinction between innocence and guilt is essential. The function of justice is to apprehend the guilty and punish them, either as simple retribution or as a way of bringing them to a sense of their own wrongdoing. In Highsmith's fiction, however, this unitary notion of 'guilt' is never sustained. She shows all the possible combinations of feeling guilty, being guilty and being found guilty, and shows the impossibility of the clear-cut, absolute condition that the institutional code of legality requires. As I said above, Howard Ingham in Tunisia, beset by self-recrimination about the possible death of an Arab, suffers from intense feelings of guilt without any certain basis. On the other hand, Victor Van Allen, in *Deep Water*, commits terrible crimes without a pang. After drowning his wife's lover, and being loudly accused of the deed by his wife, Vic seems to get along without undue anxiety: 'Vic's guilt did not materialise. Perhaps it was because there were so many other things to think about and take care of' (p. 112). Vic never really gets round to guilt, and, in fact, the murder of De Lisle seems to have bucked him up considerably. Taking these two cases together shows that Highsmith has no confidence in the coincidence of being and feeling guilty. Similarly, *The Glass Cell* and the Ripley novels show that there is no necessary connection between wrong-doing and apprehension, and *The Blunderer* problematises the issue yet further.

It is worth dwelling on this point, because it shows Highsmith's inversion of the conventional forms of crime and detective writing. In the whodunit, for instance, the identity of the guilty party is made difficult to detect, but only so that it may eventually *be* detected. It is hidden so that it may be found, albeit by a sleuth more adept at that sort of thing than the reader. The quest for a *name* is the central issue, not the complex nature of culpability. Suspects may be interrogated; concepts are not. Once the culprit has been named, the narrative can very briskly be tied up, and the process of detection is that of individuation – the guilty party is incriminated by the discovery of traces that only he or she could have left behind. Detective fiction, like the bourgeois institution of justice itself 'exists expressly to dispel the doubt that guilt might be impersonal, and therefore collective and social'.[7] If that is true, then Highsmith's fiction reintroduces such doubt, and raises all the social questions about guilt that most crime writing is designed to suppress or redirect.

In her more recent novels, Highsmith makes a great deal of the social contexts of her plots, and in so doing she is able to explore the social and political issues that are embedded in them. One of the most impressive and sophisticated novels is *Edith's Diary* (1977). Here the narrative ranges over twenty years in the life of Edith Howland, recording her decline into a kind of schizophrenia. At the

beginning of the book, she is just about to move to a new house in
Pennsylvania with her husband and ten-year-old son. Her marriage seems secure and her family life supportive. She and her
husband set up and write a liberal newspaper called *The Bugle,* and
feel themselves to be politically and socially alert people. Then
everything starts to go wrong. Edith's husband invites his Uncle
George to live with them. Uncle George is semi-senile, tetchy and
incontinent. Then the husband leaves her for a younger woman.
Her son, Cliffie, grows up to be a wastrel, who may be responsible
for the deliberate killing of Uncle George. Edith retreats into a kind
of madness by writing a fantasy version of her life in her diary,
where Cliffie is transformed into an ideal son, happily married to a
successful woman, and her husband is loyal and supportive. She
also becomes increasingly obsessed by the encroaching authori-
tarianism of American society, and writes increasingly strident
editorials for her paper.

If this was all there was to the book, it would simply be another
claustrophobic study of ordinary madness, albeit an intense and
powerful one. However, what is most interesting about the
narrative is the way Highsmith uses this plot to sustain a critique of
American political life over this twenty-year period and the
inability of liberal ideology to cope with the transformations. As
always, the novel interrogates the idea of family, but this tale
situates its drama in the confrontation between the life of the
Howlands and the life of American society as a whole. Edith's diary
is a pathetic fantasy of a wholesome life, a symbol of her dislocation
from her environment. But her private history is an intensification
of a public history. Her fiction starts just at the point when
President Johnson starts talking about the 'advisors' he is sending
to Vietnam, and Highsmith juxtaposes these distortions of the truth
to show the neurosis of political life, the grotesquely defensive
postures it is taking up. The interpenetration of public and private
becomes more apparent later, when Bobby Kennedy is assasinated.
Edith's reflections indicate a sense of overpowering madness in
public life, intensified in her own home:

> Only now was Bobby Kennedy's possible death sinking in. And
> the insanity, the wrongness that had inspired that bullet! And
> Tricky Dick was the Republican candidate. What a world! What
> an America! California, the state with the most nuts, everyone
> said, full of cults, mostly destructive – they couldn't even try to

conserve trees without being maniacal about it. John Kennedy, however, had been shot in Dallas. Where was the enemy? Who was it? It was right here in the house, Edith thought. (p. 160)

Edith sees her private life invaded by the values of public life, and these are the values of mendacity and betrayal. As she puts it in a brief, late moment of lucidity, 'this is a political world. . . . You're all playing rotten politics – squirming, delaying, anything to avoid stating plain truths!' (p. 301).

In *Edith's Diary*, then, Highsmith is using the central figure of the neurotic heroine to examine wider issues, to support a critique of the bourgeois world. What Edith sees at the moment of her death as 'the crazy, complex injustice of the Viet Nam situation' (p. 316) is reflected in her personal life where nothing seems fair. The failure of institutional justice in her more orthodox crime novels is here transformed into the absence of any notion of desert or fairness in the world at large. Edith does not deserve her fraught life of domestic imprisonment (as it seems to her), entrapped with her useless son and her ex-husband's dribbling uncle. But that is the life she gets, and she has to try to come to terms with it. Highsmith shows that Edith's resort to fantasy is both inevitable and destructive, and shows that the wider reality in which Edith is caught is a profoundly squalid and crazy one. Edith ends up as a pathetic figure, trying to hold on to the ideals of Tom Paine in the world of Richard Nixon, a task she does not have the domestic security to carry out. The only survivors in this novel are the complacent or the apathetic, a pitilessly ironic final vision in a troubling tale.

Equally powerful, and even more fully infiltrated by social and political themes, is *People Who Knock on the Door* (1983). This novel signals its affiliations by being dedicated to 'the courage of the Palestinian people', although the author adds that this book 'has nothing to do with their problems' (p. 5). In fact, it is a complex narrative, where the ostensible main plot, of adolescent love and loss, is a way of examining the awful consequences of the fundamentalist revival. The central figure is Arthur Alderman, an unexceptional teenager, whose life is profoundly disturbed when his father, an insurance salesman, takes up a strident and irrational fundamentalist religious position. Arthur is trying to conduct a love-affair with Maggie, a girl of slightly higher social position than himself, and it is as messy and inconclusive as these things usually are in Highsmith. Arthur's father becomes increasingly authoritarian and dogmatic, taking on board all the moral and political aspects of his self-righteous born-again state. The other son, Robbie, is more drastically affected by his father's conversion, and takes refuge in a curious kind of combative maleness and toughness. When it is apparent that Richard Alderman has failed to live up to his own strict standards of personal morality in his dealings with the fallen woman Irene, Robbie kills him. The bizarre sense of retributive justice that Richard has advocated catches up with him, and the novel ends by showing how little such a violent action solves.

The novel is another intense study of family relationships, with some extraordinary scenes of awkwardness and embarrassment – there is a wonderfully awful family Christmas dinner at the Aldermans' with Irene and her obese sister Louise which has all the macabre and absurd atmosphere that is peculiarly Highsmith. But as well as being a tragedy of manners, the book takes on a number of central issues. The workings of the plot centre round abortion, with Arthur's girl-friend having one and Irene not. The complexities of this issue are carefully elaborated, partly to reveal the irrational hypocrisy of Richard, but less functionally to introduce a highly charged social and political issue into the narrative. Similarly, the novel develops an analysis of guilt, showing that Arthur suffers badly from it, as a relic of his liberal conscience, whereas his brother does not. The psychiatrist's report on Robbie remarks 'absence of guilt-feeling notable' (p. 310). But although these are extremely important features of the text, they are used to sustain an analysis of Reagan's America and the irrational values it exploits. Regularly throughout the narrative the wider political context is indicated. During a particularly nasty hellfire sermon, Arthur thinks about the congregation:

> What was going on in the heads of the people around him? Arthur saw only the backs of heads and washed necks in clean shirts, a few fresh haircuts, most of the women in hats. Were they as bored as he, daydreaming too? They weren't all elderly, lots were under thirty. Most if not all had voted for Reagan, Arthur thought.   (p. 164)

The fervour of the fundamentalists is related to the Puritan inheritance of Cotton Mather, and likened to the extremism of Nietzsche, but takes on a frightening political life of its own: 'The news was on, and it was about Reagan's big budget demands for armaments, defence. Arthur had heard it before, and it seemed to get bigger every time he heard it' (p. 264). Reagan's passion for weaponry is figured in the novel by Robbie's 'manly' interest in guns and knives, and although the novel could be read as a self-contained study of internal family volatility, it demands to be seen as a much wider, much more suggestive articulation of national political psychology.

Highsmith's naturalism, then, uses domestic locations to show all the tensions latent in liberal notions of guilt and justice, and to provide a forum for her ironic rendering of family life. More than that, though, it gives her an opportunity to dissect the collapse of liberalism and the rise of authoritarian thinking. In this project, she is interestingly related to the school of 'dirty realists', like Raymond Carver and Jayne Anne Phillips, who use a very spare style and deal with the lives of the aimless to show 'how things fall apart and what is left when they do'.[8] However, Highsmith's recent fiction has been more aggressive in its treatment of politics than those related writers, and she has been less oblique in her presentation of the structure of feeling they inhabit. It could be argued indeed that in Highsmith, as in George V. Higgins and Elmore Leonard, we see a fiction that directly confronts political issues through the received forms of thrillers and detective stories. Higgins's treatment of civic corruption, Leonard's concern with American foreign policy and Highsmith's perception of the tensions and contradictions within her society all give their fiction a resonance and intensity that is vainly striven for by the more portentous writers of 'serious' novels like Mailer or Vidal. In fact, rather than aligning Highsmith to the 'dirty realists', I would prefer to set her in a different perspective. Here is Engels setting forth his ideas on the 'socialist problem novel':

the solution of the problem must become manifest from the situation and the action themselves without being expressly pointed out and . . . the author is not obliged to serve the reader on a platter the future historical resolution of the social conflicts he describes. To this must be added that under our conditions novels are mostly addressed to readers from bourgeois circles. . . . Thus the socialist problem novel in my opinion fully carries out its mission if by a faithful portrayal of the real relations it dispels the dominant conventional illusions concerning these relations,

shakes the optimism of the bourgeois world, and inevitably
instils doubt as to the eternal validity of that which exists,
without itself offering a direct solution of the problem involved,
even without at times ostensibly taking sides.[9]

Highsmith's irony gives her this appearance of neutrality, and her
work clearly seeks to dismantle any lingering confidence in the
most hallowed bourgeois institutions of justice and the family. Her
scepticism is such that readers are given no obvious hints about
how things might be improved, if they ever could be, and there may
be more fatalism in Highsmith than Engels would have accepted.
However, her work remains as one of the most radical and
persuasive accounts of the shallow foundations of bourgeois
thinking, and the fragility of social coherence.

   Like Jane Austen, Highsmith may restrict herself to her favoured
recurrent themes. However, the development in her work which
this chapter has been concerned with has been to move away from
the schematic reformulation of the notions of irony, guilt and
misery towards a more purposeful articulation of them. She uses
her central ideas in her more recent novels to look at a variety of
political (and, even more recently, ecological) issues. Upon the
basis of the domestic murder story, she builds an ironic vision of
American political life from McCarthy to Reagan. Unlike the
eventually comforting vision of comparable popular writers such as
Stephen King, Highsmith displays no confidence in the triumph of
good or the efficacy of justice. In her most recent novel, *Found in the
Street*, the nutty Ralph Linderman compares what is happening
around him in New York to 'the dreary Lebanon situation' (p. 122).
He finds it incredible that anyone believes what Reagan is telling
them: 'Ralph liked to think that American public opinion would not
have stood for any more rubbish, any more lies as to objectives.
Ralph still had faith' (p. 122). Highsmith, however, does not share
this faith. Her fiction dismantles any lingering confidence in liberal
attitudes, and shows how far irrationality and absurdity have
penetrated. Reading her work is disquieting and disconcerting,
since she seems to offer no easy solution to the problems raised, but
her engagement with the most important issues is one of the
salutary pleasures of contemporary writing.

Notes

1. Patricia Highsmith, 'The Snail-Watcher', in *Eleven* (London: William Heinemann, 1970; Harmondsworth, Middx.: Penguin, 1972) p. 17. Further references to Highsmith's fiction will be to the Penguin reprints of William Heinemann editions, and will be incorporated in the text.

2. Patricia Highsmith, *Plotting and Writing Suspense Fiction* (London: Poplar Press, 1983) p. 24.

3. Erich Fromm, *The Fear of Freedom* (1942; London: Routledge and Kegan Paul, 1960) p. 118.

4. Ernest Mandel, *Bloody Murder: A Social History of the Crime Story* (London: Pluto Press, 1984) p. 44.

5. Highsmith, *Plotting and Writing Suspense Fiction*, p. 56.

6. Ibid., p. 104.

7. Franco Moretti, 'Clues', in *Signs Taken for Wonders: Essays in the Sociology of Literary Forms*, trans. Susan Fischer (London: Verso Press, 1983) p. 135.

8. The words are Jayne Anne Phillips', as quoted by Bill Buford, 'Editorial', *Granta*, 8 (1983) p. 5.

9. Friedrich Engels, 'Letter to Minna Kautsky', 26 November 1885, quoted in David Craig (ed.), *Marxists on Literature* (Harmondsworth, Middx.: Penguin, 1975) p. 268.

2

'This Shitty Urban Machine Humanised': The Urban Crime Novel and the Novels of William McIlvanney

SIMON DENTITH

I

My topic is the urban crime novel and in particular the two crime novels of William McIlvanney, *Laidlaw* and *The Papers of Tony Veitch*.[1] I want to approach McIlvanney's writing by way of a discussion of 'wise guy' or 'hard-boiled' style, and its possible take-up in British writing. But I shall begin by juxtaposing two ways of understanding genre, as a means of demonstrating what is at stake in the following discussion; namely what meanings are generated by, and can be carried by, urban crime writing.

My first way of understanding genre comes from Jameson's *The Political Unconscious*. Attempting to explain the persistent interest of medieval romance as a genre, he writes:

> To limit ourselves to generic problems, what this model implies is that in its emergent, strong form a genre is essentially a socio-symbolic message, or in other terms, that form is immanently and intrinsically an ideology in its own right. When such forms are reappropriated and refashioned in quite different social and cultural contexts, this message persists and must be functionally reckoned into the new form. The history of music provides the most dramatic examples of the process, wherein folk dances are transformed into aristocratic forms like the minuet (as with the pastoral in literature), only then to be reappropriated for new ideological (and nationalizing) purposes in romantic music; or even more decisively when an older polyphony, now coded as archaic, breaks through the harmonic system of high roman-ticism. The ideology of the form itself, thus sedimented, persists

18

into the later, more complex structure as a generic message which coexists – either as a contradiction or, on the other hand, as a mediatory or harmonizing mechanism – with elements from later stages.[2]

In this account, genre carries with it indelible traces of its originating social context, traces that speak of the structure of social relationships out of which the genre emerges and to which it is addressed; and these traces persist in the multifarious different contexts in which the genre is used and reused. By contrast, Stuart Hall has insisted on the essentially open nature of form; he writes, in an essay on popular culture, as follows:

That is to say, the structuring principle of 'the popular' in this sense is the tensions and oppositions between what belongs to the central domain of elite or dominant culture and the culture of the 'periphery'. It is this opposition which constantly structures the domain of culture into the 'popular' and the 'non-popular'. But you cannot construct these oppositions in a purely descriptive way. For, from period to period, the contents of each category changes. Popular forms become enhanced in cultural value, go up the cultural escalator – and find themselves on the opposite side. Others things cease to have high cultural value, and are appropriated into the popular, becoming transformed in the process. The structuring principle does not consist of the contents of each category which, I insist, will alter from one period to another. Rather it consists of the forces and relations which sustain the distinction, the difference: roughly, between what, at any time, counts as an elite cultural activity or form, and what does not. These categories remain, though the inventories change.[3]

Here, the forms of popular culture are to be understood as plastic, taking on meanings and valuations from the shifting relations of popular and élite cultural forms. I hope it does not sound as though I am trying to square the circle if I say that both positions are useful in understanding the history and significance of urban crime writing. I shall be arguing here that crime writing can be seen both as a specific way of comprehending the realities of urban life, in direct line of descent from an identifiable mid-nineteenth-century social situation; and that such writing is an open form, capable of being inflected in many different ideological and indeed more narrowly political directions. It is in the context of this argument that William McIlvanney's work seems to me so important, for he provides one of the most striking examples of the many contemporary attempts to inflect the form of crime writing in radical or leftward directions.

A useful starting-point for understanding the way in which crime stories negotiate the realities of urban life – in the spirit of Jameson's understanding of genre – is provided by Peter Brooks's account of Eugene Sue's *Mystères de Paris* (and the account would probably serve as well for English Newgate novels as it does for Reynolds's *The Mysteries of London*, a direct imitation of Sue's massive work).[4] For Brooks, crime in Sue becomes a way of unlocking the otherwise mysterious depths of Paris; the mystery of the big city is made narratable, its story can be told because of the aberrant nature of crime – the transgression, indeed, providing the opportunity for narrative. Brooks suggests, in fact, that *Mystères de Paris* provides an example of a particular aesthetic, a way of negotiating the alienated and class-divided realities of the modern city that combines crime, narratability, sexuality (the central female figure is a prostitute) and the rendering of accounts – drawing on the double force of that expression. I am impressed by this way of understanding the continuing appeal of specifically urban crime fiction, though I recognise – indeed I shall be stressing – that this is scarcely the dominant tradition of the English detective story. If we wish to provide a genealogy of the urban crime novel, we could do worse than trace it back to Sue, where the mysterious realities of urban life are made paradoxically more comprehensible by unlocking them through aberrant narratives of crime.

However, though in *English* writing there is a line of descent that draws on this aesthetic (in addition to such obvious candidates as *Oliver Twist* one could mention perhaps Arthur Morrison, or indeed Margery Allingham in such a novel as *The Tiger in the Smoke*), it is evident that the most important twentieth-century models for British writing have been American, in particular Raymond Chandler and Dashiell Hammett. Ken Worpole, in his outstanding essay on these writers in *Dockers and Detectives*, has suggested that their appeal to working-class British readers was that they provided a style more relevant to their experience of urban life than anything in contemporary British writing – crime fiction or otherwise.[5] In particular, Worpole stresses the attractiveness of the hard-boiled style to urban, working-class and male readers; its actual closeness to some urban demotic verbal styles, of London, Liverpool or

Glasgow, makes it especially attractive to such readers, offering them a way of negotiating the realities of their own lives, and their places in the city, which at once legitimises and reinforces their own hard-won and highly prized attitudes.

This seems to me a compelling argument, though it needs qualification. Stephen Knight is surely right, for example, to stress the aestheticising impulse in Chandler's style, seeing it as drawing on aesthetic resources a long way from urban demotic.[6] Nevertheless Worpole's emphasis on the appeal of this style is evidently the correct one; he provides an argument that is concerned to stress the use that readers make of their reading, and does not simply forget the readership as though writing issued into a vacuum.

Though I am persuaded by this argument, it remains a surprise how little take-up there has been in British writing of the hard-boiled style. I want to stress this question of style as crucially significant in carrying meanings; style rather than the simple presence or absence of the tough guy/private eye figure. That is obviously important too, and it is evidently the case that a culture delighting in Lord Peter Wimsey might find it difficult to adjust to Philip Marlowe, or readily find his British equivalent. Moreover on both sides of the Atlantic there has been a move away from private eye novels to police novels, though numerous American examples suggest that it is possible to sustain the tradition of Chandler and Hammett into the late twentieth century, and use it to deal with new social, political and cultural realities. The fact remains – at least, so my researches in W. H. Smith's and station bookstalls suggest – that the dominant tradition of British crime writing remains the one established by Agatha Christie and Dorothy L. Sayers, and that few novels written in English by British writers have successfully taken up the hard-boiled style and used it as a way of exploring the contemporary city.

This is less surprising when you consider some of the difficulties, suggested, for example, in the work of Peter Lovesey, whose novel *Rough Cider* ('Grips like an Apple Press') draws on the figure of the reluctant amateur detective – in this case, he is an academic. Give such a figure a hard-boiled style and the result just tends to sound peevish:

> We were on the A4, heading west to Somerset.
> Surprised?
> By now you must have got me down as a hard-nosed

opportunist, so I won't blame you for assuming I reneged on the deal after Alice made an idiot of me over the gun. Only I didn't.

I'd like you to believe it was because after all I'm a man of integrity. Duke's daughter had asked me to show her the place where the tragedy was enacted, and I was uniquely fitted to act as guide. It was a small repayment on my debt of gratitude to Duke.

I'd like you to believe all that, but you're sharp enough to see that she still had me by the short and curlies while Digby Watmore was in attendance. Who wants to feature in the *Life on Sunday*?[7]

This passage is a version of the 'bottom-line' moments that feature in many crime novels, which I will be discussing shortly; here, however, I merely want to suggest the difficulty of grafting a hard-boiled style onto the English amateur. It is not only that such a figure lacks the appropriate dignity; just as importantly as Worpole's suggested link between what he calls 'masculine' style and urban demotic indicates, a style is not like a coat, which you can put on or take off, but issues from and speaks to a particular linguistic hierarchy. The populist strain in American culture simply awards a much higher prestige to versions of popular speech than in the more evidently formal and class-obsessed linguistic situation in Britain.

Even without these kinds of difficulty, created by the distances that divide American and British culture, there are real dangers of pastiche and cultural nostalgia involved in the attempt to carry forward once-powerful forms. The widespread use of the style in parody and allusion, from *Gumshoe* to *Shoestring* to *The Singing Detective*, suggests how hard it is to use the form 'straight'. The following passage suggests some of the dangers:

The heat was exhausting, the Tigers had been humiliated by the Cardinals; and my rent, like the Vets Bonus, was long overdue. Otherwise everything was hunkey dory.

I was doing laps in the pools of my own perspiration when I heard a faint tapping on my office door. I didn't care for the interruption, but I was in a business that depended almost exclusively on tapping doors. I drew in a mouthful of stale air and acknowledged the tapper. . . .

The door opened and in glided a hundred-and five pounds of the slickest gift-wrapped frail my tired, wet eyes had seen since Hector was a pup. She was a tall job with plenty of fahrenheit.[8]

This is taken from the first page of a novel called *October Heat* published in the Pluto Crime Series in England, but first published in America in 1979. However, the novel is actually set in the 1930s, and aims to expose dirty tricks played on Upton Sinclair's campaign for the California governorship. This seems a somewhat misplaced ambition anyway – surely there are fresher political fish to fry – but quite apart from the danger of nostalgia, the pastiche of Chandler here is simply too evident to carry conviction. The last paragraph of my quotation, for instance, with its unrelenting and compacted use of the Chandlerian code, gives more the impression of alluding to past masters than using their example to effective contemporary advantage.

The possibility of taking up hard-boiled style, then, is not necessarily easy; and the pioneer in this area is undoubtedly television, where series like *The Sweeney* do offer an authentic, English, televisual equivalent. This matter of style is especially important, because it is at the level of style that the rhetorical appeal of writing becomes most apparent. To use Althusserian vocabulary, style interpellates the reader, hails him or her in specific ways, constructs him or her as a subject for this text. The moment in the extract from *Rough Cider* contains an especially evident interpellation, when as readers we are told that 'you're sharp enough to see'. This is a characteristic interpellation of crime fiction, across a wide variety of its different versions; the classic whodunit as much as *The Maltese Falcon* invites the reader to adopt a position of superior knowingness. Yet hard-boilded style, as we shall see, makes a very much more specific interpellation than this.

The precise nature of the stylistic interpellation is especially important for those writers who wish to appropriate the form to make it carry democratic or socialist meanings. This is not confined to the current generation of writers engaged on this enterprise. We could compare the attempts made by G. D. H. and Margaret Cole, working in the 'Golden Age' of the English detective story, the 1920s, to make use of this form for socialist – or at least anti-capitalist purposes. In *The Death of a Millionaire* (first published in 1925), they write in a matter-of-fact, explanatory, even rather flat, prose style, which explicity addresses us as 'stout-hearted, democratic reader';[9] it's a brave effort, but in my judgement it simply does not have the allure of, say, the following:

'You're Marlowe?'
I nodded.

'I'm a little disappointed', he said. 'I rather expected something
with dirty fingernails.'
'Come inside', I said, 'and you can be witty sitting down.'[10]

Here, though not specifically addressed, the text is working no less
hard to interpellate the reader. It is not only that Marlowe is offered
as a model of laconic and successful repartee, but also that the
reader's admiration for his success is necessary for the success of
the book. Marlowe – more wise guy here than tough or hard-boiled
– offers the reader the satisfactions of the successful comeback, the
unshakeable confidence of the never-failing witty rejoinder. The
satisfactions offered by being the 'stout-hearted, democratic
reader' are just not in the same league.

Style hails the reader in a variety of other ways, of course. One
characteristic feature of urban crime writing is that it tends to be
specific in its use of brand names. The élite hard-backed novel, like
presenters on the BBC, tends to be coy about such matters as make
of car, or clothes, or radios. Crime writing has no such inhibitions,
using brand names as a readily available way of indicating class,
style, prestige. Certainly, this can amount to no more than capitula-
tion to the exploitative codes that advertising and marketing have
attached to the commodity system; but it can be other than this, a
way of negotiating these codes, getting them to serve as a way of
unlocking a social landscape:

> Jacob ushered me through a foyer flanked by a mahogany
> staircase, down a corridor, and into a den that looked rather like a
> fifties furniture showroom. . . . Sitting in that room was like
> sitting in an Edsel, an experience vaguely embarrassing and
> borderline funny.[11]

It is very important for crime writing to get such details right,
because throughout the novels the textual surface is continuously
significant, loaded with information that locates the reader with
respect to the places and people of the story.

This is connected to another characteristic of urban crime
writing, which is that the cities that their private eyes or policemen
inhabit are particular cities – Los Angeles, Cincinnati, London,
Glasgow – and not 'representative' ones. When travelling from one
side of the city to the other, the characters go down named streets
and pass real public buildings. This is not just a matter of

authenticity, even if understood in Barthesian terms as an *effet du réel*. It is also a question of offering the reader a very particular kind of knowledge. Evidently this will alter if you actually know the city or not, and that is very important for a writer like McIlvanney with his specifically west of Scotland and Glaswegian loyalties and affiliations. But even if the towns and their street-names are unfamiliar, these allusions do give you a kind of *ad hoc* or instrumental knowledge. Granted, street maps do not provide the kind of scientific knowledge of political economy, or a Venn diagram of unemployment ratios; but then street maps have their uses too, as any stranger to a city knows. At its best, this kind of writing too can be used as a way of providing a social landscape, as another quotation from Jonathan Valin's *Final Notice*, set in Cincinnati, demonstrates:

I drove west down Erie, that stately street full of red brick colonials and towering oaks, to Madison, where I turned south past the high-rises and the old yellow-brick apartments that are set above the boulevard on grassy slopes. . . .
     What they're doing to this city is a crime. The downtown money-men, I mean. With those magic wands that marbelize everything, turning good red brick into skyscrapers of polished stone and plate glass. Or maybe it isn't a crime. Maybe you're just getting old, I thought, and need something to feel bitter-sweet about on this fine fall day. Feeling nostalgic for demi-Gothic buildings and WPA frescoes didn't quite fit the bill. But, just the same, I was glad I was headed for the old Court House on the north side of town, well away from the part of the inner city that's been torn down and rebuilt.[12]

Or, to take an example from McIlvanney's work, here is his description of Glasgow's Albany Hotel:

Milligan climbed the hill to where, overlooking what had been Anderston, now redeveloped into anonymity, the Albany Hotel stood. He had parked in Waterloo Street. The Albany is a huge glass-and-concrete fortress to the good life. The drawbridge is money. It's where a lot of the famous stay when they come to Glasgow. It's maybe as near as the city gets publicly to those embassies of privilege by which the rich reduce the world to one place, although in Glasgow few public places would have the

nerve obtrusively to discourage certain clients. They merely give
discreet financial hints.   (*The Papers of Tony Veitch*, p. 120)

The point of these examples is not only that they provide good
descriptions of the urban landscape, but that these descriptions are
worked into a rhetoric, where the descriptions provide the prag-
matic grounding for some of the fundamental interpellations made
by the texts. Descriptions such as these provide the reader with a
rhetoric that encourages him or her to negotiate the realities of the
city, puts him or her in a position of confident knowledge with
respect to the city.

Indeed, this position of privileged knowledge offered to the
reader is perhaps the fundamental interpellation that the crime
novel makes. It is difficult not to sound scathing about this; indeed,
the very point of Althusser's word interpellation is that it is an
ideological mechanism, not a characteristic of knowledge. But
while indeed recognising that the knowledge of *crime* offered by
crime writing is, at a certain level, illusory (the burden of some of
Stephen Knight's book[13]), to say this is perhaps to concede too
much. The gist of what I have been saying about style can be
summarised by saying that style provides knowingness rather than
knowledge – if 'knowingness' can possibly carry non-pejorative
connotations. The urban crime novel draws on, recycles and represents a shared set of attitudes, responses and scattered shards of
knowledge, together constituting a way of negotiating city life. You
can recognise such styles in any major city, at once abrasive and
reductive, defensive, hospitable and naïve. Verbally inventive,
given to tall stories, anecdotes and downright lies, such styles can
be sharp and impatient. But they provide you with a way of getting
through the day with your self-esteem intact.

William McIlvanney's novels draw very heavily on Glasgow
speech, to the point where at times it is pointless to distinguish
between a post-Hammett hard-boiled style and a version of the
city's verbal style. This can be disconcerting; *The Papers of Tony
Veitch* opens with a chapter written from the point of view of Micky
Ballater, a Glaswegian hard man; yet some of his insights into
Glasgow are allowed to stand. But it is not the 'hard' or aggressive
aspects of Glaswegian verbal style that attract McIlvanney; in fact
he has written a fine tribute to Glasgow speech which, very
appropriately for this chapter, sees it as both springing from and
addressing a particular social-historical situation:

Glasgow speech, that aspect of the city in which I see most hope for the survival of its identity undiluted. For Glasgow's soul is in its mouth. . . .

Even a cursory acquaintance with that speech will reveal that it is not merely a collection of slightly different words. It is the expression of a coherent attitude to life, a series of verbal stances as ritualised as one of the martial arts. But it is also continuingly inventive, an established style within which individual creativity can flourish.

The salient features of that style emerged directly from the hardness of life in the streets of a major industrial city. . . . The core of its style is two main qualities: deflation of pomposity and humour. It's hard to be pompous when you have a geggie for a mouth and a bahookie for a posterior. The humour takes many forms but I believe that the commonest of these is the humour of disgruntlement – that central source of laughter to which we have been led by such practitioners as Evelyn Waugh, Groucho Marx and Woody Allen. So much of Glasgow humour is disbelief under anaesthetic. It is anger with the fuse snuffed but still burning.

Glasgow speech, like so much of Glasgow itself, expresses partly incredulity at what life offers, partly a way to make the best of things, partly an invitation to seize the moment and to hell with the formalities.[14]

There might be some sentimentality in this, but this passage nevertheless eloquently evokes many of the characteristics of Glasgow speech that feed into McIlvanney's own writing and provide it with some of its particular force.

McIlvanney is the only one of the crime writers that I have discussed who is explicit in his admiration for an urban demotic style. But 'knowingness' is a characteristic of all of them, and characteristically it issues in the frequent use of the exotic and reductive simile. Chandler's writing, so widely parodied, is often like this: 'The whole face was a trained face, a face that would know how to keep a secret, a face that held the effortless composure of a corpse in a morgue'.[15] It is a pigeon-holing style, especially fond of the construction 'the xxx of a xxx'. It is what Barthes in *S/Z* calls the cultural code, the code of knowledgeable reference to the everyday world, a code of shared knowledge that assigns objects and individuals to classes.[16] Here is an example from a contemporary English novel: 'He had a harrassed expression and a smile that was meant to be nice. He produced it with the practised ease of a conjuror'.[17] Of course, the categories are made up as you go along – how many of us actually recognise the 'effortless composure of a corpse in a morgue'? But it certainly provides a sense that the narrative voice has got the capacity to place people, to see through them, to get them into the appropriate category, even if, in Chandler, this voice is so often betrayed. By a paradoxical movement, this is a style that at once provides pleasure for readers in the unlikeliness of the comparison, and tames the city for them, suggesting that it can be held in a network of knowable comparisons.

These meanings, then, are carried by the local texture of the prose, in the insistent and nearly exclusive use of the cultural code. The openness of the genre in part depends on this, and this is worth insisting on if only because of the widespread temptation, since *S/Z*, to see the detective story as the purest example of the hermeneutic code, the code of enigmas.[18] It seems to me that the ideological meanings carried by crime writing can be seen to be much wider – you can acknowledge their real diversity – if you are not locked into the evidently ideological mechanism suggested by the (illusory) solution of mysteries.

A tough and reductive style, one that cannot be phased, has its own dangers, in particular the danger, suggested in my quotation from *Rough Cider*, that the protagonist's motives will appear as poor or as readily seen through as everybody else's. More acutely, there is the difficulty of finding any kind of heroic language, or vocabulary for values, that will not sound simply absurd in the stylistic context I have outlined. This is the problem that I earlier referred to as that of 'bottom-line' moments – those moments in the text when the hero indicates just where the bottom line is for him, just where it is that, despite his acceptance of so much that is bad about the world, he is prepared to act. Here is one such moment, again from Jonathan Valin's novel, *Final Notice*:

I've learned to suspend my disbelief about what other human beings are capable of doing in anger or in despair, although a part of me – the Cincinnati moralist side of Harry Stoner – can still get mightily outraged when appearances and realities drift too far apart. When they lose their bearings entirely, I become just as devoted to the cosmetics of the established order as the most pious burgher. Sometimes it's useful to pretend that the world ought to be a better place than it is, even if it is an imperative founded exclusively on schoolboy good wishes and the quirks of the subjunctive mood.[19]

The self-disparagment of the final sentence is a characteristic strategy of the bottom-line moment: 'I recognise that you may find this silly, but nevertheless . . .'. A variant of the same moment comes in police novels, where the policeman hero has to differentiate himself from his brutal, or careerist, or just plain stupid colleagues:

'You really want to stay a sergeant, don't you?' he said.
'I like to see justice.'
'Justice? You're a berk', said Bowman. 'You're forty, you're a sergeant, and you actually despise promotion.'[20]

Here, of course, the minimal commitment – justice – is actually rather a large one, and it is arguable whether the text carries it successfully (that is, without embarrassment). Most urban crime novels, however, need some such moment, when despite the discounting or scepticism of valuations upon which the hard-boiled style habitually insists, some other, minimal, valuation is offered.

I hope that I have said enough to show that it is useful to think of urban crime writing generically, in the way that Jameson suggests: as a genre that is in a real sense ideological. Crime writing is a genre that emerges from the alienations of the modern city and is addressed to those alienations, offering its readers an imaginary way of negotiating the realities of urban life; in its hard-boiled form, drawing on and re-presenting the sharp and abrasive demotics of modern city life. Yet this understanding of genre need not tie us to believing that genre has a fixed ideological meaning, as though in a stripped-down version of themselves all crime novels somehow emitted the same message. Hard-boiled style can be inflected in different ways, to yield radically different social landscapes or to suggest unlikely bottom-line valuations. Evidently also, the various *actants* in the narrative of crime can be identified with different figures to yield very different meanings; a lot hangs on whether the villain is a small-time hood (*The Papers of Tony Veitch*), a CIA agent (Hannah Wakefield, *The Price You Pay*), a sexually inadequate pair of psychopaths (*He Died With His Eyes*

Open) or the boss of a capitalist corporation (Ernest Larsen in *Not a Through Street*)[21] – though even here these identifications do not yield self-evident meanings, but have to be worked at and glossed in specific ways. So while it is true that the form of crime writing entails definite meanings, it is also true that these meanings are not fixed, but can be inflected in different ways and appropriated for different purposes. Here, then, are the dangers and the opportunities for those who wish to take over the form for democratic or socialist purposes. What social landscapes can the form offer? Who will speak that knowledgeable patter, and what kind of knowledge will it presuppose and seek to extend? Who will the novel identify as the criminal? What kind of valuation will emerge as the bottom line? The form is certainly not neutral, but it is open to different uses; with that formulation, which I hope provides a genuine distinction and is not merely a compromise, I turn more particularly to the crime novels of William McIlvanney.

II

Why single out the work of McIlvanney when so many other writers, more explicitly socialist or feminist, have attempted to appropriate the form of the crime novel? (My local radical bookshop has a section devoted to 'radical thrillers'.) At least three important characteristics distinguish his two crime novels. McIlvanney has not tried to take over the form simply by setting the novels in a radical milieu, but determinedly uses the form to explore large sections of contemporary Glasgow. Second, the novels delight in urban demotic speech, as I have already suggested; though the elaboration of that speech is more complicated in the actuality of the novels than McIlvanney's account of 'Glasgow speech', quoted earlier, might suggest. Finally, and in some ways this is the most important difference, the novels are published by a straight commercial publisher (Coronet, an imprint of Hodder and Stoughton), and so do not immediately come bracketed in the way that publication by Pluto Press or The Women's Press entails. This is crucial when you are dealing with an attempt to use a popular form, part of whose very meaning emerges from the fact that it is not 'art', and is available at the local supermarket or station bookstore, and not the local bookseller. These are not simply extrinsic matters but determine the kind of significance that any piece of writing carries.

It is evident also that McIlvanney is not engaged in any simple business of pastiche, the dangers of which we saw evidenced, in some of the attempts to appropriate the form. Indeed, the hard-boiled style is only one of the stylistic registers that McIlvanney draws on in *Laidlaw* and *The Papers of Tony Veitch*, though he draws on it rather more heavily in the later book. He can also use a more mediative and exploratory style, not unlike the style that he uses in his other novels. Here is a moment reminiscent of his genre models, however:

> Laidlaw opened the door. The room was well carpeted, nicely furnished. Opposite them, behind a desk, a young man was sitting in a swivel-chair. He was sallow-faced and his lank hair had more grease than a chip-pan. A black leather jacket sat on his body like a suit of armour. His calf-length boots rested on top of the desk. He was cleaning his fingernails with an ornamental knife.
> 'Aye, whit's the gemme?'
> 'We'd like to see Mr Rayburn', Laidlaw said.
> 'Ye got an appointment?'
> 'What is he?', Laidlaw said. 'A dentist?'
> The young man was concentrating on looking very tough.
> 'Put your sneer away', Laidlaw said. 'It's getting faded. Keep it for a good thing.'   (*Laidlaw*, p. 81)

One immediate difference of this from most novels in the 'masculine' style, of course, is that it is not written in the first person. In fact, relatively little of *Laidlaw* is narrated from Laidlaw's point of view, and the multiplicity of narrative viewpoints helps to make Laidlaw himself the site of contradictions rather than a solution to them. In the extract I have just quoted it is also worth noting how a tough-guy style has itself entered self-consciously into the characters' consciousness; the 'young man' of the extract is an apprentice hood whose fantasy life is filled with imagining himself tough in the authentic style.

The use of hard-boiled style is thus a complex matter in these novels, and can be used to disconcerting affect. The opening of *The Papers of Tony Veitch* is a case in point:

> It was Glasgow on a Friday night, the city of the stare. Getting off the train in Central Station, Mickey Ballatar had a sense not only of having come north but of having gone back into his own past.

Coming out on to the concourse, he paused briefly like an expert reminding himself of the fauna special to this area.

Yet there was nothing he couldn't have seen anywhere else. He was caught momentarily in the difficulty of isolating the sense of the place. Cities may all say essentially the same thing but the intonations are different. He was trying to re-attune himself to Glasgow's.   (p. 15)

This (and the chapter it introduces) is disconcerting, as I suggested earlier, because Mickey Ballater will turn out to be one of the nastier characters in the novel, yet we do not realise this at first and his insights are allowed to stand. The use of free indirect style, here and throughout the novels, might, of course, be used for ironic effect; the alignment of a hard-boiled perspective with aspects of Glasgow critical demotic might be used to suggest the inadequacy of both. But it is not; Mickey Ballater has a valid and indeed memorable perspective, and that striking opening sentence – 'Glasgow on a Friday night, the city of the stare' – is 'Ballater's', formally speaking. It is surely one of the finest opening sentences in crime fiction, evoking succinctly the rituals of the working-class week and the implicit threat posed by 'looking' in male working-class culture, and placing Glasgow by virtue of these evocations. McIlvanney's decision to 'share out' the narrative point of view certainly offers us, as readers, the pleasures of the 'knowingness' provided here, but it relativises these pleasures and makes them provisional.

The fact that McIlvanney draws on other stylistic registers should also remind us that there is no absolute dividing line between crime novels and other kinds of novel. This is especially evident in McIlvanney's case, since after writing *The Papers of Tony Veitch* he published *The Big Man*, not a crime novel, but one that shares many of its underworld characters with the two crime novels, and in which Laidlaw himself makes a brief appearance.[22] Indeed, the three novels can be thought of as making up a *roman fleuve* for Glasgow and the west of Scotland. Furthermore, in *The Big Man* McIlvanney goes down the route that he actually avoids in the two crime novels; he makes the relationship between the 'big man' of the title and the hoodlum who employs him a metaphor of exploitative class relations more generally. In *Laidlaw* and *The Papers of Tony Veitch*, by contrast, little significance is attached to the identity of the murderers, and they are not identified in class terms. In fact, in the earlier novel the reader is aware of the identity of the murderer from the beginning of the novel and the narrative excitement is created by knowing that there are several attempts to find him and kill him, and being uncertain whether Laidlaw will get there first. In short, in the crime novels McIlvanney avoids any easy short cuts to radical meanings, preferring instead to take the stereotypical meanings of popular culture (the sex-murderer of *Laidlaw* is a repressed homosexual) and to try to stretch them and redefine them against themselves.

One of the main concerns of this *roman fleuve* is the problematic persistence of working-class decencies in the devastated social landscapes of the 1970s and 1980s. In many ways these novels are a celebration of Glaswegian working-class style, full of cameos in which unexpected wit, humour, generosity or hospitality suddenly materialise. But they do not baulk the question of working-class violence, even if the texts are finally ambivalent about this. On one level such violence – the almost ritualised conflict of the pub confrontation, for example – is seen as a matter of honour, where personal toughness comes from men 'who hadn't much beyond a sense of themselves and weren't inclined to have that sense diminished'. McIlvanney is respectful of that violence, seeing it not only as the result of a particularly oppressive social history, but also admiring it; in a pub full of such men, 'just by coming in you had shucked the protection of your social status. In this place your only credentials were yourself' (*Laidlaw*, p. 94). But he also sees this violence as self-defeating; this is a theme he explores most fully in *The Big Man*, but in the two crime novels also, working-class violence is most often turned against itself, or exploited by underworld hoodlums, or riven by contradictions (the most violent man in Laidlaw is also, in a twisted version of 'honour', the most righteous), or utterly destructive of personal and emotional life (the victim's father in the same novel contributes to his daughter's death by frightening her into secrecy).

The figure in whom those contradictions and ambivalences meet is Laidlaw himself. In one way he shares the characteristic of other sympathetic policemen in crime novels – he is distinguished from his colleagues by not being a machine policeman, as being somehow of the system yet not of it.[23] Often this is signified at the superficial level by the car that the policeman now drives – if it is a vintage car (or an English sports car in American thrillers) then the hero can be distinguished from the machine cops, his colleagues. Laidlaw takes this to such extremes that he travels around Glasgow by public transport. More seriously, the two novels – and especially *Laidlaw* – are almost overloaded with explanations of Laidlaw's motivations, and how they differ from conventional policing ones. The 'bottom-line moments' have almost overtaken the texts, though that in no way diminishes their status as *minimal* valuations, the least that can be maintained in the face of social breakdown. Here is one such moment of articulation in *The Papers of Tony Veitch*:

> If all I'm doing is holding the establishment's lid on for it then stuff it. I resign. But I think there can be more to it. One of the things I'm in this job to do is learn. Not just how to catch criminals but who they really are, and maybe why. I'm not some guard dog. Trained to answer whistles. Chase whoever I'm sent after. I'm not just suspicious of the people I'm chasing. I'm suspicious of the people I'm chasing them for. I mean to stay that way.   (p. 59)

Perhaps this passage takes us to the heart of the contractions which surround Laidlaw, for it is a very unusual defence of police work. It reminds me of another defence of policing offered by Laidlaw, which provides in fact the title of this essay – 'We're the shitty urban machine humanised. That's policemen' (*Laidlaw*, p. 72). McIlvanney goes to great lengths to substantiate this claim for Laidlaw, carefully distinguishing him from the ethos of the other policemen in the books, and providing an antitype in the crass and rather brutal 'professional' policeman Milligan. Yet a hard critic might say that this account by Laidlaw of what it means to be a policeman – the *donnée* of the two crime novels, in effect – makes the texts imaginary. Certainly we must applaud the attempt to drag the meanings of policing away from the ones offered by, say, *Juliet Bravo* or *Rockliffe's Babies*; but the knowledge that he is a fiction is never more evident than at these moments. Having said as much, however, we can still see in the figure of Laidlaw an attempt to carry forward the contradictions of contemporary working-class Scottish life towards some provisionally optimistic resolution. His moralism; his guilt; his tenderness; his potential for righteous violence – all are carried in a plausible individual characterisation.

Laidlaw is not the only guide to Glasgow, though he tends to be the most sympathetic. It is Laidlaw who provides the description of Glasgow as 'the biggest housing-scheme in Europe' – 'Glasgow folk have to be nice people. Otherwise they would have burned the place to the ground years ago' (*Laidlaw*, p. 32). And it is Laidlaw who, if not continually cast in the hard-boiled mould, is certainly continually streetwise, familiar with the rituals of those housing-schemes, and of the East End, and of the petty-bourgeois suburbs also. Altogether the books provide an impressive account of the social landscape of Glasgow, finding in the narrative of crime a thread to hold together the multifarious contradictions of a modern city without simplification but without simply accepting them either.

Finally, however, we need to ask not only whether the project to shift the form of the crime novel in democratic or socialist directions can be achieved – 'to humanise' it, in McIlvanney's terms – but also what has been achieved when you have done so. Perhaps those of us who are committed to those directions expect too much of a book, and certainly expect too much of those books which seem to be saying things we agree with. It is certainly possible just to enjoy these two novels as a 'good read' without troubling yourself about their social and cultural implications. This is as much a matter of rhetorical strategy as readerly expectations. Caught between two apparently exclusive choices – minority publication by small presses where you can be a 'left-wing thriller', or mass publication by commercial publishers where you risk being praised by the *Daily Mail*, McIlvanney has unhesitatingly chosen the latter. It is finally arguable whether he has always succeeded in wrestling round the meanings prevalent in mass publication to his own effect or not – the danger of homophobia in *Laidlaw* could be a case in point, despite McIlvanney's deliberate attempts to close this option down. But this is finally not McIlvanney's problem but that of his readership, for no writer can be in complete control of the meanings that his readers take from his texts. McIlvanney has used a form that others have been trying hard to push up the 'cultural escalator', to use Hall's striking metaphor; equally resolutely, he has tried to use it while still in the bargain basement of popular culture. I am confident that being praised in the élite cultural form of the academic essay will not spoil that for him.

Notes

1.   William McIlvanney, *Laidlaw* (1977; London: Coronet, 1979); *The Papers of Tony Veitch* (1983; London: Coronet, 1984). Subsequent references to these books are given in the text.

2. Fredric Jameson, *The Political Unconscious: Narrative as a Socially Symbolic Act* (London: Methuen, 1981) pp. 140–1.
3. Stuart Hall, 'Notes on Deconstructing the "The Popular"', in *People's History and Socialist Theory*, ed. Raphael Samuel (London: Routledge and Kegan Paul, 1981) p. 234. I recognise that 'genre' and 'form' are not interchangeable, but the differences do not affect the contrast here.
4. Peter Brooks, *Reading for the Plot: Design and Intention in Narrative* (Oxford: Clarendon Press, 1984). See especially the chapter entitled 'The Mark of the Beast: Prostitution, Serialisation and Narrative', pp. 143–70.
5. Ken Worpole, *Dockers and Detectives* (London: Verso, 1983) pp. 29–49.
6. Stephen Knight, *Form and Ideology in Crime Fiction* (London: Macmillan, 1980) pp. 135–67.
7. Peter Lovesey, *Rough Cider* (London: Bodley Head, 1986; Mysterious Press, 1987) p. 84.
8. Gordon Demarco, *October Heat* (San Francisco, 1979; London: Pluto Press, 1984) p. 1.
9. G. D. H. and Margaret Cole, *The Death of a Millionaire* (London, 1925; Harmondsworth, Middx.: Penguin, 1950).
10. Raymond Chandler, *The High Window*, in *The Chandler Collection*, vol. 2 (London: Picador, 1983) p. 25.
11. Jonathan Valin, *Final Notice* (1980; London: Futura, 1987) pp. 113–14.
12. Ibid., pp. 13–14.
13. See n. 6 above.
14. William McIlvanney, 'Where Greta Garbo Wouldn't Have Been Alone', in *Shades of Grey: Glasgow 1956–1987*, photographs by Oscar Marzaroli, words by William McIlvanney (Edinburgh and Glasgow, 1987) pp. 32–3.
15. Chandler, *The High Window*, pp. 60–1.
16. Roland Barthes, *S/Z*, trans. Richard Miller (London: Jonathan Cape, 1975) p. 20.
17. Derek Raymond, *He Died With His Eyes Open* (London: Abacus, 1984).
18. As an example, Peter Brooks writes that 'the clearest and purest example of the hermeneutic would no doubt be the detective story, in that everything in the story's structure, and its temporality, depends on the resolution of enigma' (*Reading for the Plot*, p. 18).
19. Valin, *Final Notice*, pp. 15–16. I see this is my third quotation from this novel. The Valin novels strike me as an especially intelligent attempt to continue the tradition of Chandler and Hammett into the late twentieth century.
20. Raymond, *He Died With His Eyes Open*, p. 11.
21. The details of the second and fourth books in this list are: Hannah Wakefield, *The Price You Pay* (London: The Women's Press, 1987); Ernest Larsen, *Not a Through Street* (1981; London: Pluto Press, 1985).
22. William McIlvanney, *The Big Man* (London: Hodder, 1985; Sceptre, 1986).
23. Jerry Palmer has written well about the anti-bureaucratic nature of the thriller hero in *Thrillers: Genesis and Structure of a Popular Genre* (London: Edward Arnold, 1976).

3

The Voices of George V. Higgins
GRAHAM DALDRY

It's like you're in a movie, and the other guy's in the movie with you, but he knows *you're both in a movie, and what comes next. And you don't.*
The Friends of Eddie Coyle

The Friends of Eddie Coyle is Higgins's first novel. Eddie 'Fingers' Coyle got his nickname when he sold a gun that was traced; the Mafia put his hand in a drawer and kicked it shut. Now, back in business, he has a problem. He is due to be sentenced for a burglary that went seriously wrong, and he urgently needs someone in a place of power to do him a favour. As a supplier of guns, he has access to a lot of information, but when the bank robbery gang he is supplying are caught, ironically through none of Eddie's doing, the Mafia decide that it is time something was done about him.

The novel traces Eddie's demise; but this is really only the continuous thread in a shadowy portrait of law and underworld that the novel paints. Eddie is the central figure in that most of the narrative is about him, but the most important characters in the novel are the two figures who are least fully portrayed, the detective, Foley, and Dillon, the mysterious bar owner who turns out to be the eyes, ears and killing tool of the people who matter. Although these two figures remain peripheral to most of the action of the novel, it is between them that it takes place. They represent the two kinds of authority that have a place in the novel: the authority of the law, and the rather shadowy but often, it appears, all-seeing power of the gangland bosses who lurk behind Dillon.

Of these two authorities it is certainly the second that makes the fiction and drives the action of the novel. While Foley and his side have their successes, he is shown to be merely a preventative force. He perceives this himself; the words quoted above are spoken by him half-way through the novel, and they reflect what becomes the central theme of Higgins's early novels. For in confronting crime and criminality, the forces of legality and order find themselves subject to a peculiar crisis of confidence. As here, Foley finds

himself acting in a movie that someone else directs, absorbed into it
involuntarily, and without any foreknowledge or control. Someone
else writes the script, and that someone is in a sense not Higgins
either, but the vaguer and more threatening voices who in *The
Friends* command Dillon.

There are some obvious parallels to be made here between Foley
and Higgins, and between the narrative as Foley perceives it and
the narrative as Higgins the novelist presents it. As sometime
Assistant DA for the District of Massachusetts, Higgins too is a
lawman (prompting Norman Mailer to remark of this novel, 'What I
can't get over is that so good a first novel was written by the fuzz').
Dillon, and the men behind him – and probably the men behind
them – are never quite reachable, to Foley, to Higgins, or to us, as
readers. Whoever you do successfully catch and identify, the
procedure only raises more questions about the people in the
background that elude you. You never reach the source of authority
in the world of crime, dealing unendingly with the controlled, and
never with the controller. So that the story that Foley cannot quite
grasp is never quite grasped by writer or reader either. What the
novel ultimately demonstrates is that Dillon and whoever is behind
him really do know more than any of us.

This pervading sense that 'someone else' is in control is felt both
fictionally, in the knowledge that there are more powerful people
behind Dillon, and in reality, since we know that the same forces act
upon Higgins's 'real' persona as Assistant DA. And it does some
odd things to our sense of fiction and reality in the novel. The classic
omniscient detective, solving crime and restoring order, is invented precisely in order to keep the fiction fictive, and to produce a
reassurance that the disorder of crime and criminality is only a story
told by an authority that remains capable of restoring order. It does
not matter how preposterous this authority is, for it is a demonstra-
tion of authorial control over fiction, as well as of law over disorder.
Remove this figure of authority, as Higgins does, and the status quo
of crime fiction is reversed. Authority, the power to tell the story,
seems to be invested elsewhere; and because the power to
fictionalise, to make things up, is rarely seen at work within the
novel, we are left necessarily with 'realism'. There is no authorial
control over the fiction, no one to keep it fictive, so that characters
and events appear disturbingly real.

This realism is then translated directly into speech, for Higgins's
first three novels, *The Friends of Eddie Coyle*, *The Digger's Game* and

Cogan's Trade, are dialogue novels above all else. Their medium is the vernacular of an underworld of bars, covert meetings and petty crime.

Higgins has repeatedly been praised for the realism of this dialogue, 'the actual sound of people talking', 'people so real it doesn't matter what they're doing or how they go about doing it'. But as we have seen, 'reality' is not quite such a simple matter in these novels. The speech of the characters that appear in Higgins's writing appears to be real because none of it is reproduced for the artificial purpose of making the story. Higgins's story-tellers never appear directly in the action; the story is predetermined, as it were, by people we never see. Consequently, everything that is said – or almost everything, as we shall see – is subject to conditions that are already imposed. The freedom to make or redirect the fiction is removed from even such traditionally powerful figures as police-men and lawyers. The act of story-telling, of fictionalising, is removed from the pages of the novel, and the speech we hear is given its ring of authenticity by its helplessness, its determination by other things, other people, other stories. The characteristic realism of a Higgins novel lies in the fact that we never see the invention that has dictated the course of the narrative, but that we continually see and hear its effect.

This realism, then, emerges in the territory that in *The Friends* is created between Foley and Dillon, and occupied by a whole spectrum of small men, people who matter little to anyone but themselves. But as the people who are subject to a fiction that is beyond control, they are the people who matter to Higgins. For both in fiction and in reality, both in his capacity as author and in his capacity as Assistant DA, they are the people for whom Higgins feels helplessly responsible. In the disordered world of gamblers, chancers and desperados, the story we understand marginally has its direct effect in action, for it is in this world that people rob, steal, win, lose, kill or are killed. If Dillon is the furthest that *The Friends of Eddie Coyle* ventures towards the story-teller – the source of control – the whole novel is nevertheless composed of the real effect of the story.

What we read is then the fiction as it is made real, and as it reveals its consequences in action; as it dictates reality. We are given the script, to continue Foley's metaphor, of a movie that nobody is ever quite in, a script that is only understood as it happens. The action becomes the evidence of a story we cannot read, and what is said is said to comfort the continual sense of exclusion, the feeling that somewhere, someone else is dictating reality, writing the story, making things happen.

In this 'real' world, then, speech and dialogue become an important, active element, but do so in a frightening and impersonal way. Speech is reduced to the level of action. It becomes the mere evidence of things done or not done, for in a world where the story is always told by someone else, language is either dangerously superfluous or functional. With the power to fictionalise, to tell stories, excluded from the action of the novel, what is said is inevitably immediate, and inevitably real, in the most reductive sense of that word.

The beginning of *The Digger's Game* demonstrates the peculiar power of speech in these novels. The novel opens with the Digger being briefed for a break-in and robbery. All the action occurs in the dialogue, as he is told in detail what is to be done. We never witness the actual doing of the crime. We do not need to. The words have been made 'real' because they belong to the story told off the page, the story that tacitly dictates what is to be done. The next chapter opens after the crime has been perpetrated and we assume that what was said is done. We do so because the speech we have heard is the effect of a more powerful fiction – which no doubt we could trace back as far as an enigmatic figure such as Dillon, but no further – that in turn gives language the force of fact. Straight away, then, the novel demonstrates the direct crossover from speech into action, and from fiction into fact.

We come closer to finding the source of this factualistion of speech in the figure of Cogan. While Cogan is controlled by Dillon, who by the end of *Cogan's Trade* has died (of natural causes – a sign in itself of his power), Cogan repeats much of Dillon's character and function; and in this novel we see more of the way that he works, and of the way that he is himself controlled.

Cogan's Trade has a plot of almost classical simplicity. A small-time gangster, Johnny 'The Squirrel' Amato, hires two young gunmen to hold up a Mafia card game; Cogan is brought in to identify and kill them by Dillon. Cogan, however, has one minor problem. Amato knows who he is, and the man he brings to help him out turns out to have gone hopelessly to seed. So in order to hit Amato, Cogan finds he must identify and get the help of one of the gunmen, Frankie. (The other finds himself arrested on a drugs charge.)

Cogan solves this problem by exerting a power of omniscience that is almost like that of the traditional detective, except that it works negatively, to trap his victim. Having found Frankie, who has no idea who he is, Cogan gains his end by telling Frankie about himself:

> 'Gotta car too, I understand.'
> 'Yeah,' Frankie said.
> 'Lemme give you some advice, alright?' Cogan said.
> Frankie did not answer.
> 'I had one of them things myself,' Cogan said, 'They first come out. You got the hood scoops, right?'
> Frankie did not answer.
> 'Ah, come on,' Cogan said, 'you got the green Geetoh with the scoops. Don't fuck around with me, right?'
> Frankie nodded.
> 'You're gonna have trouble with it,' Cogan said, 'couple months or so.' . . .
> 'Now, lemme tell you what you got to do,' Cogan said. 'You got to pack them scoops. Mine just had one, the split one in the middle. But, well, you got the two, I bet you're still gonna have the same trouble, the car just won't warm up.'   (p. 172)

Cogan has the power invested by the script of the movie, as it were, which allows him to do whatever he wants. He lets Frankie know that he has so much of his story in his power that the rest is already written. He may not be the man with the authority himself – we know that Dillon, at least, stands behind him, but he knows more, and is closer to its origin, than Frankie is. As he tells Frankie, if he does not wish to co-operate, it's just a matter of time before he catches up with him anyway. The fiction is already fact; just like the dialogue at the beginning of *The Digger's Game*, the speech is functional, claiming a direct crossover into action. What he says of Dillon is also true of himself, as he recognises at the end of the novel:

> 'he knew the way things oughta be done, right?'
> 'So I'm told,' the driver said.
> 'And when they weren't,' Cogan said, 'he knew what to do.'
> 'And so do you,' the driver said.
> 'And so do I,' Cogan said.   (p. 191)

This chilling ending is probably as far as Higgins can go down this path.

Cogan has effectively written the novel. Language, as the power of plotting and of compelling into plot, has never been more potent or more threatening than in this alliance with the world of crime. In Cogan's words, speech is action, and the authority here is not Higgins, not a power of right represented by a solving detective, not even a macho voice that lives on in spite of a world without values, but instead a speech allied to mere action. It is a language that is utterly compelling, driving the narrative, and forcing all other languages to conform to its plot, but it is a language without feeling, without humanity, and one that in factualising its own story leaves no room for any fiction but its own.

In this world, the failures begin to look more important than the successes. In the two novels so far discussed, the losers have a hard time. We see in Eddie Coyle and then again in Johnny Amato and Frankie that there is a high price to be paid for not doing things properly. But both of these novels are concerned with the nature of authority, with figures like Dillon and Cogan, and with the kind of power they represent. But *The Digger's Game* is a different kind of novel; it is concerned primarily with the small men, with the losers, and presents further and more subtle variations of the relation between saying and doing, and their consequences.

The plot of *The Digger's Game* is more elaborately conceived than that of *The Friends*. If the latter placed the small men between Foley and Dillon, *The Digger's Game* is dedicated almost exclusively to the investigation of the shades of grey between these two representatives of authority.

The novel centres upon a disastrous card game in Las Vegas at which the Digger, a small-time bar owner of Irish Catholic descent, loses $18,000 he has not got.

The story is then worked out between three distinct groups of people. The first consists of the Digger, his wife, his customers and his priest brother. The second consists of the three men who ran the gambling trip that gave the Digger the opportunity to lose his money – and to whom he now owes his debt – who are respectively the businesslike Schabb, Richard Torrey and the debt collector, 'The Greek'. The third group consists of the Mafia elders who in turn run the gambling operation: Maglia, Masseria and Barca.

The plot of the novel centres on the second of these groups. The Greek, who has been brought in as a stand-in after the imprisonment of his predecessor, begins to cause trouble, and Torrey seeks permission from his elders to remove him. He fails, and is shot dead himself. Schabb finds himself left with Barca and the gambling operation, while The Greek is put back into running petty crime.

The Digger, meanwhile, pulls off a successful fur robbery and pays off his $18,000, although not without some hints that by the end of the novel trouble is once again about to loom in the form of arrest for this burglary. The sense of irresolution at the end of the novel, and the untidiness of the narrative, is consistent with the way the story is told, for in this novel we remain a lot further from the story-teller than we do in *The Friends of Eddie Coyle*. Instead, the novel is a chaotic mess of smaller figures.

For the most part, language is seen to work in the same way as in the other novels; what is said is put more or less immediately into effect. But the effects of speaking and the relationship of speech and action are demonstrated more interestingly in this novel.

The fates of Schabb, Torrey and The Greek are almost predetermined by the way they speak to each other, and what they say. The Greek talks too much, while he and Torrey keep up an incessant, degenerate repartee that alternates between mutual agression and sex:

> 'I look good because I want to look good and I work at it' the Greek said. 'Not because I want to go around like a goddamned pervert. You want to go around in them yellow things, shirts, pants, the white shoes, its probably alright, you look like a nigger pimp. Don't matter to you. I got some self-respect.'
> 'You're afraid,' Torrey said. 'You work so hard taking showers there, you probably don't think, you're not sure you can get it up.'
>
> (p. 28)

This degenerate exchange goes on at some length, and is interspersed with Schabb's business phone call, as he does a deal to set up the next gambling trip.

Once again, the talk plots itself, conforming to the stories Dillon and Cogan tell; Schabb talks to act, and so narrates himself on, while Torrey and The Greek, absorbed in their own rivalry, lay the foundations of their own fates.

The representation of speech as action has other variations. Unlike the other two novels, we are shown the process of decision making, the people who are ostensibly behind the action. But in the figures of Maglia, Masseria and Barca, we realise that the Mafia are controlled by their own rules, just as others are, and are themselves subject to the same conditions of uncertainty and doubt. At the meeting called by Torrey in his attempt to seal The Greek's fate, the attempt to ritualise speech is shown to belong to a world that has been superseded. A meal is eaten in silence, and 'business' then talked in a formal way, as if dictated by procedural conventions. This attempt to impose a formal control upon talk itself fails as Barca and Torrey later talk behind the backs of the others. Barca emerges as the man with power in his hands – but as he does so he only demonstrates that the Mafia are as subject to what we might call the Dillon principle – that someone is always in control of the person who appears to be in control – as anyone else.

Higgins comically demonstrates the mutual paranoia upon which the narrative is founded at the end of this novel, when Schabb and The Greek are shown running away from each other, each convinced that the other is a bigger and more powerful figure than himself.

So far, it would seem, *The Digger's Game*, although more complicated than the other novels, works under exactly the same conditions. And in some ways, of course, it does. It operates in the same criminal underworld, and speaks a language that for the most part sounds exactly the same. But the comical twist of the narrative as it deals with Schabb and The Greek indicates one way in which *The Digger's Game* represents a slightly different direction. The criminal characters of the early novels always have a comic capacity, but in *The Friends of Eddie Coyle* and *Cogan's Trade* this is obliterated by the insistence of the narrative, by the power asserted by Cogan, Dillon and those who lurk unaccountably behind them. Survival in these novels is ultimately more urgent than comedy, and in the delicate balance of horror and exuberance upon which all crime fiction thrives, it is the element of threat that dominates the novels. In *The Digger's Game*, however, this is not the case. The grip of Dillon is loosened (although it is never lost), allowing this novel to become a comedy of the underworld.

The Digger's Game is a comedy of a rare type, however, for it must be re-emphasised that Higgins does not create a special comic world in which to replace his characters. In this novel we find the same urban America as in the other novels, but we also find a comedy that exists in spite of the world it is set in.

At the centre of this comedy, then, is the Digger, who is in some ways a version of Higgins's recurrent loser. The Digger, however, is subtly different, for, unlike Eddie Coyle, he has a classically comic capacity to be diplomatic, to keep everybody that matters more or less happy while doing exactly what he wants to do himself. This is no mean feat, for it involves remaining on good terms with a brother who wants to be a bishop, the Mafia, the small-time customers who frequent his bar and his wife. He achieves all this with variable success; but what he gains in the process is a measure of independence, something that no other character in the three novels I have considered can lay claim to.

This independence allows the Digger to avoid the direct link between speech and action that seems to dominate these novels, and to escape from the control of the movie that nobody seems to direct. Instead, the Digger writes his own scripts, and provides us with something none of the other characters possess: a purely personal commentary upon, and therefore a personal intelligence about, his own often awkward predicament. It is this that produces the comedy, for it provides us with a voice that is apparently resilient to events that in any other context would constitute disasters. The Digger tells a story that is distinctive; it is distinctive because it involves an enjoyment that seems irrepressible and befits his independence of the action, and illustrates the rule of mere effectiveness that becomes the dominant value of the other novels.

One of the most entertaining parts of the novel is the Digger's painful account of his gambling spree. Having already lost and then won back much more than he can afford, he decides to try to stay out of trouble by playing golf:

> 'I ask the hotel, can I rent clubs. I get out onna course. I played thirty-six holes. Its over a hundred. I'm all alone. I hate what I'm doing and I'm lousy at it and there's all these fat bastards zooming around inna carts and having a hell of a time, and I walk and I sweat and I walk and I sweat some more.' (p. 85)

What makes this funny is that the Digger himself knows it is funny, in spite of his own discomfort. The ability to laugh at himself gives the Digger the right to tell his own story. For the first time, we hear a voice that is not dictated by necessity, and is indeed divorced from necessity, for all the while we know that however the Digger lost the money, it will have to be repaid. Here, then, we hear a story that is truly a fiction, and is not made real by the law of effectiveness. The Digger's story departs from the realism that dictates the narrative, and writes a script of which he is temporarily in control.

The effect of this is, momentarily, a liberating one. Where Cogan and Dillon bring fact and fiction together, and make the narrative inescapably real, removing it from individual authorship and making it the collective script of a criminal world, the Digger restores the difference between reality and fiction. By making up his own story, he demonstrates that fiction has its own value as an assertion of individuality, and keeps his right to tell his own story apart from the hard fact that he owes the Mafia $18,000. He speaks, not to make facts and to complete actions, but for the sake of hearing his own voice – that is, his *own* voice.

This assertion of the right to speak is an important one, and it is essentially a comic one. But like all rights in comedy, it is also a precarious one. The novel closes with the Digger still at large, but with a question mark hanging over his freedom in the form of a betrayal that, within the narrative, remains unresolved. The comedy is thus sustained as all good comedies are in spite of the narrative, and is never confirmed or accepted within the direction of effective events.

If this is not a problem so far as the success of *The Digger's Game* is concerned – and it is not – it remains a problem for Higgins in his persona of lawman. The alternative to a script nobody writes, and to a narrative without values, is here a story that would write us out of narrative, authorship and control altogether, a comic alternative to the direction of real events. This presents a way around the problem of authority, and a comic voice to counter the voices of power, but it does not provide a place for Higgins the attorney, or a voice for the law, the 'right' and social mores.

This exclusion of the law is in some ways the achievement of these three books, and it distinguishes them from the vast body of crime fiction, which returns again and again to the imposition of the authority from without, and so allows the gory enjoyment of Gothic fictionality. While this is of course a legitimate, and highly bankable, pleasure, it is not one we find in Higgins's narrative. Higgins takes crime too seriously to allow a Gothic style to enter his fiction, and what he gains in doing so is a narrative that succeeds in conducting a serious investigation of the authority of crime, and of the kinds of claims the world of criminality makes upon living in modern America. And in the course of this investigation he gains access to the liberation from seriousness offered by a comedy that becomes a genuinely humane voice throughout the three early novels I have discussed.

But the lack of a voice of legal power is clearly something that concerns Higgins, as is evidenced by the way his later writing changes direction, and particularly by the autobiographical nature of the figure that he places at the centre of several later novels, the lawyer Jerry Kennedy.

The Digger remains representative of a way out of a trap that is unacceptable to the narrative voice of the lawman and the attorney. The following observation of this endless circularity, which to such voices constitutes an undefeatable difficulty, is made by Foster Clark, counsel for defence for Jackie Brown at the end of *The Friends of Eddie Coyle*. They could be Foley's words; later, they could be Kennedy's; and, of course, they are Higgins's:

> 'in another year or so,' Clark said, 'he'll be in again, here or someplace else, and I'll be talking to some other bastard, or maybe even you again, and we'll try another one and he'll go away again. Is there any end to this shit? Does anything ever change in this racket?'
>
> 'Hey Foss,' the prosecutor said, taking Clark by the arm, 'of course it changes. Don't take it so hard. Some of us die, the rest of us get older, new guys come along, old guys disappear. It changes every day.'
>
> 'It's hard to notice, though,' Clark said.
>
> 'It is,' the prosecutor said. 'It certainly is.'   (p. 183)

Note

Quotations from the works of George V. Higgins (and page references) are from the following editions: *The Friends of Eddie Coyle* (London: Robinson Publishing, 1986); *The Digger's Game* (London: Pan, 1974); *Cogan's Trade* (London: Coronet, 1975).

4

Investigating Women: The Female
Sleuth after Feminism

LYN PYKETT

There have also been a number of women detectives, but on the whole, they have not been very successful. In order to justify their choice of sex, they are obliged to be so irritatingly intuitive as to destroy that quiet enjoyment of the logical which we look for in our detective reading. Or else they are active and courageous, and insist on walking into physical danger and hampering the men engaged on the job. Marriage also looms too large in their view of life; which is not surprising since they are all young and beautiful.[1]

Since Dorothy L. Sayers, in 1929, noted the paucity and relative lack of success of women detectives in fiction, there have been several sea changes in both the number and nature of female sleuths. Just as the increasing independence of American women in the early decades of this century produced a spate of 'career girls against crime',[2] the post–1960s women's movement has produced a new breed of female detective and interesting modifications of the form of detective fiction on both sides of the Atlantic. In Britain, changing perceptions of society, and of women's place in it, have led to a questioning of the conventions employed by such 'Queens of Crime' as Agatha Christie, Patricia Wentworth and Josephine Tey. Inquisitive, genteel spinsters of a certain age, like Christie's Miss Marple and Wentworth's Miss Silver, have been replaced by self-assured, sexually experienced, independent women such as Antonia Fraser's Jemima Shore, P. D. James's Cordelia Gray and Jessica Mann's Tamara Hoyland. In addition, the pastoral settings and conservative social values of Christie and Wentworth have been updated, parodied and interrogated by these new 'Queens of Crime', and latterly abandoned by a radically new kind of British feminist crime novel the in 1980s. In America, since the 1960s,

Amanda Cross (the pen-name of feminist literary critic Carolyn Heilbrun) has been updating the 'formal detective novel'[3] in fictions that engage self-consciously with feminist issues. In the 1980s a number of American feminists have appropriated and revised the conventions of the hard-boiled detective novel, substituting young, lively and often lesbian women for the 'middle aged machismo'[4] of their male prototypes in the work of Chandler, Hammett and Macdonald.

While there can be no doubt that feminism, as Cora Kaplan has recently argued, 'has made space for a new breed of female protagonists in a traditional field of popular fiction', there remains the question of whether this intervention has significantly altered 'the politics, sexual or otherwise, of the genre itself'.[5] I want to explore this question further by examining the way in which a selection of post-1960s British and American novels, by and about women, intervene in particular traditions of detection fiction to explore, exploit and remodel their conventions.

Superficially, nothing could be further from Miss Marple than Antonia Fraser's Jemima Shore, a smart, sexy, Cambridge-educated media-person, investigative journalist and presenter of her own television programme. However, this modern career-girl is involved in preposterous plots that reproduce (often in a parodic or decadent form) the dominant concerns of the country-house murders of Christie and her contemporaries. In *Quiet as a Nun* (1977) Jemima is summoned to her former school, the Convent of the Blessed Eleanor, to investigate the death of Sister Miriam and other strange events, such as the apparition of the Black Nun (actually the disguise of the male villain who has attempted to gain possession of Sister Miriam's property, which includes the convent itself). Jemima's 'Eve-like' curiosity, which is persistently associated with her unconventionality and love of mischief, and is the driving force of her detective activities, leads her from crisis to crisis; her life is saved by a pistol-toting nun, and after further adventures the mystery is solved, the property is restored and the convent resumes its orderly life.

Jemima's second adventure, *The Wild Island* (1978), also concerns the disruption and restoration of the order of a closed community: a semi-feudal family in a remote region of Scotland. Fraser's tale of the Beauregards' pretensions to the throne of Scotland offers a highly caricatured version of the conservative royalism of her 'Golden Age' predecessors. She also parodies, and perhaps also

reproduces, these earlier novelists' implicit fears about the disruption of the family by, among other things, sexually predatory
females like Jemima herself. The murders uncovered in this novel
are committed in the name of the family, by the mother, the centre
of it all' (p. 178). Interestingly, while this bizarre family, with its
philandering patriarch and deranged, jealous mother, is represented ironically, even satirically, the ideology of the family as an
institution is reinforced by the *ex cathedra* pronouncements of
Mother Agnes, the Catholic nun who acts as the inner voice of the
Protestant Jemima: 'Passions so often run high in big families; such
feelings are of course intended by Almighty God for the preservation and protection of his ordained unit, the family, but in certain
cases, as with all human passions, the instincts, being perverted,
can go awry' (p. 142). Jemima's own subsequent judgement of the
events directly echoes her mentor's words, and the plot ensures the
continuation of God's ordained unit as the younger Beauregards
make suitably dynastic marriages in 'this man's valley' (p. 190), a
paradise from which the worldly female is expelled.

The preoccupation with the family and the nostalgia for a stable,
hierarchical village life that characterised much British detective
fiction between the wars, and beyond, is also taken up by Jessica
Mann in *A Kind of Healthy Grave* (1986). As well as adopting,
sometimes in parodic form, the conventions and themes of the
'Golden Age' detective novel, Mann also explores its ideology.
Mann's female investigator, Tamara Hoyland, a Cambridge-
educated archaeologist, is, strictly speaking, not a detective in the
Marple–Shore tradition, since in addition to her job with the Royal
Commission on Historical Monuments she is also employed by
Department E of the Secret Service. However, *A Kind of Healthy
Grave* is worth looking at here, since it is centrally concerned with a
particular investigation of a woman and the women's movement
she heads, as well as with a broader investigation of modern
women and *the* women's movement. Tamara is called in to monitor
the activities of Dame Violet Hutber, whose public persona is a
topical combination of Lady Olga Maitland and Mary Whitehouse,
and whose speeches appear to have been written by the Conservative ideologue Ferdinand Mount.[6] Dame Violet is the
founder-president of Watchwomen, a repressive, authoritarian
women's movement, dedicated to motherhood and the child,
formed in reaction to *the* women's movement, which has (in Dame
Violet's view) been hijacked by the lesbian left.

The central setting of the novel, Carmel (the name of a traditionalist boarding-school for boys and the small town in which it is situated) is a relic of the 'Golden Age', 'an island of the good old standards', dedicated to the preservation of 'honesty, probity, fidelity, family life, the rights of parents, the obedience of children, virtuous Victorian values' (p. 62; the speaker is Carmel's Mayor). In a series of nicely observed ironies, the plot exposes this community and the 'Golden Age' of the 1930s as a source of incest, illegitimacy and murder.

On one level the novel engages quite seriously with contemporary feminist issues, and offers a critique of the currently ascendant right-wing ideology of the family. It also plays interestingly with the dominant feminine stereotypes of the madonna and whore. Usually polarised as two conflicting images of womanhood, the madonna and whore are here combined in the characters of Violet Hutber and Zoe Meredith/Cory. Dame Violet's public and political life, dedicated to the defence of motherhood and the family, conceals a private past of incest, sexual depravity and the abandonment of her child. There is a similar (but reversed) contrast between the libidinous public image of Zoe Meredith, former teenage pin-up and current star of television soap-opera (in which she plays a glamorous female sleuth), and the emerging reality of her private life as Zoe Cory, headmaster's wife. The novel's treatment of Zoe is interesting and rather disturbing. As Tamara, the liberated woman of action, uncovers the dreadful secrets of Carmel and the founder of Watchwomen, her contemporary, Zoe, a product of post–1960s permissiveness, is progressively absorbed into the 'healthy grave' of Carmel life and the roles of headmaster's wife, mother-to-be and the new president of Watchwomen. In her joint role of archaeologist and secret investigator, Tamara uncovers the truth about the private origins of the public ideology of Watchwomen, and she defuses Violet Hutber as a potentially powerful national political figure. But she does not involve herself in the gender politics of Watchwomen: like the novel, she merely observes Zoe's incorporation with ironic detachment.

Jemima Shore and Tamara Hoyland are both modernised, post-feminist versions of the female detective. Jemima's detection (if it can be so called) derives from the enthusiastically pursued curiosity that also makes her a successful journalist, while Tamara, who is the author of a book and eleven articles in her disciplines, employs her academic mind more subtly in the deductive process. While neither heroine relies on 'feminine intuition' – the great resource of some earlier female detectives – each retains a feminine mystery: they are both private, self-contained and (mainly) self-controlled. They may give themselves up temporarily to sexual passion (Jemima), it is suggested that they have interesting sexual pasts, but they eschew emotional involvement because of previous painful experiences that the narrative hints at. In short, these female detectives resolve mysteries, but remain themselves essentially mysterious.

P. D. James's Cordelia Gray shares many of these qualities but combines them with some significantly revised aspects of the hard-boiled detective. Circumstances have prevented Cordelia from taking up the Cambridge education that beckoned, and she has become instead a professional private-eye, trained by a Chandleresque former policeman who, on his death, bequeaths her the standard-issue sleazy office of the private detective agency. The relationship between Cordelia's gender and her professional status becomes a central issue in the second Cordelia Gray story, *An Unsuitable Job for a Woman* (1972). All those in the narrative who comment on the matter regard the role of private eye as involving either a denial of Cordelia's gender, or an exploitation of those essential but negative aspects of femininity, 'infinite curiosity, infinite pains, and a penchant for interfering with other people' (p. 100). The narrative demonstrates that, irrespective of her gender, Cordelia is eminently suited to the role of investigator. She is cool, logical, detached, observant and possesses a quiet authority. Formed by 'a childhood of deprivation' (p. 19) and the contrasting pressures of a peripatetic childhood as the motherless daughter of a revolutionary father, and a six-year period of stability and order at a convent school, Cordelia has developed into a resilient, self-reliant and self-contained adult. Indeed, she seems to have that deep inner loneliness that many commentators have associated with male detectives of the hard-boiled genre. Like some of the cases of these detectives, Cordelia's case in *An Unsuitable Job* becomes a kind of quest. She is hired by the father of Mark Callender, a Cambridge drop-out, to investigate the circumstances of his son's apparent suicide. However, when she moves into the cottage where Mark died she begins to identify imaginatively with the victim, wearing his leather belt, for example, as a kind of talisman. The detection plot becomes a kind of romance in which the superfluous daughter (Cordelia) identifies with the misunderstood son (Mark) and works to exonerate the younger generation by exposing the murky secrets of their elders. Like romance, the plot of this novel is structured around concealed births and inheritances. It also turns significantly on questions of justice and morality, which involve bonds between individuals and the payment of moral debts, rather than on mere issues of legality.

In this novel the solution of the case does not provide narrative resolution, but rather develops an important thematic strand. Cordelia's emotional and imaginative involvement with the victim leads her to confront his murderer with less than her customary cool preparation. She temporarily loses control of the situation, and in the resulting confusion the murderer is killed by his secretary/ mistress, who is also Mark's natural mother. Cordelia's guilt about her bungled confrontation, and her sense that the cause of moral justice has been served by this second killing, lead her to ignore the legalities of the matter, and the detective becomes an accessory to the crime of concealing a murder.

The latter stages of the novel make explicit what has been implicit throughout, and the female investigator herself becomes the subject of investigation as the redoubtable Adam Dalgliesh steps in to attempt to discover what the narrative has thus far been unable or unwilling to reveal – the real meaning of Cordelia Gray. It is in this final stage of the narrative that the question of Cordelia's gender is most crucial, as the narrative sets her the task of withholding her inner knowledge from Dalgliesh, who is equipped with all the trappings of male authority and a powerful interrogation technique. Cordelia proves herself equal to the task, despite the added vulnerability that results from her sexual attraction to the powerful older man. The poet (and hence culturally feminised?) Dalgliesh, and the female investigator intuitively understand the extent of their knowledge of each other, and of the events that Cordelia is concealing, and they implicitly collude in acting as the agents of a morality that is authorised by their own privileged awareness, rather than conforming to strict matters of law. Cordelia withstands the temptation to make Dalgliesh her father-confessor, and thus betray her sense of loyalty to the wronged mother who has killed her son's murderer, and the narrative squares the circle of its morality by ensuring that this avenging angel also perishes. In the detective novel of the 1970s, as in the Victorian novel, it seems that the fate of the transgressive female is still death.

Although these novels by Fraser, Mann and James update the

spinster sleuths of the earlier 'Queens of Crime', and by turns parody and explore the conventions of the genre, or reproduce them in decadent form, they do not seriously challenge the conservative social values and gender politics of the earlier novels. The plots of these later writers, like those of their predecessors, require the cool, detached female sleuth to unravel the consequences of the disruptions of social order and familial stability that result from the transgressive behaviour of socially ambitious and sexually predatory women.

In America, Amanda Cross has updated the formal detective novel in a series of modern comedies of manners, tales of the times, which engage with feminist issues largely as they are experienced by middle-class professional women. For example, in *A Death in the Faculty* (American title, *Death in a Tenured Position*, 1981), Cross's detective, Kate Fansler, a New York English professor, is summoned to the closed, would-be pastoral world of the Harvard English Faculty, whose stable hierarchy has been disrupted by the advent of a tenured female professor. The form of this stylish novel, which is enlivened by Fansler's wit and her (and her author's) use of apt literary allusion, embodies the power of the educated female whose cause it argues.

Kate Fansler, the main source of the novel's considerable energy, is something of a 'rich bitch'; privileged, gutsy, and adversarial. She has rejected her family with its Ivy League connections, and the mores of Harvard itself. Nevertheless this formidable woman is empowered by her own Ivy League education, and ruthlessly exploits her politically powerful social connections in furtherance of her investigation of the death of Harvard's first woman professor of English. Indeed, Fansler seems to be an American, female version of that stock type of the comedy-of-manners detective novel – the English gentleman amateur who, as George Grella argues, 'can succeed where the official police cannot [because] the characters accept him socially', and who 'understands the social code of the world he investigates'.[7] Fansler's investigation also brings her into contact with an interesting range of female characters, and enables the novel to investigate the ways in which various women respond to the female predicament in modern society. However, despite her radical sympathies, Kate, like the novel, remains cocooned in a world of middle-aged, middle-class privilege.

While the writers discussed so far have been concerned with updating the genre, other women writers have attempted to appropriate it on behalf of a different perspective and a more radical politics. In particular, a number of feminist publishing houses have begun to publish and commission self-consciously feminist detection novels and radical thrillers. Sometimes this has resulted in little more than a kind of designer or life-style feminism and radicalism. Hannah Wakefield's *The Price You Pay* (1987) seems to fall into this category, as a fairly conventional romantic plot acted out against the background of Chilean politics and other radical causes. Wakefield's female investigator is Dee, an American solicitor in a women-only law practice in London, who turns to detection when one of her clients, a young Chilean, is found dead in bed with the wife of her current romantic interest, David Blake. David becomes chief suspect, and Dee, following a common pattern of the female sleuth, determines to save her man. As the novel proceeds, the main object of Dee's investigation, and that of the narrative, is a woman: David's wife, Amanda. The key to the novel's mysteries lies in Amanda's past, and in her involvement with the covert operations of the CIA. The attempt to unravel these mysteries takes the novel on a sentimental and satirical journey to the America of the 1960s and 1970s via the middle-aged radicals of that era who have survived (in one form or another) into the Reaganite 1980s. The plot creates a world of conspiracy politics in which no individual is safe from the machinations of secret state bureaucracies. But the form of the paranoid thriller sits uneasily with the novel's part-nostalgic, part-humorous treatment of 1960s radicalism, and with its love plot, which results in the kind of writing that ought to be parodic, but, I fear, is not: 'Hesitantly he [David] lifted his gaze and stared into my eyes. It was a brief look that in clock time I suppose lasted no more than half a second . . . the tacky coffee bar shimmered. All that existed was his face' (p. 31).

Each of the works in the last group I want to examine develops the genre of the female detection novel in a number of interesting ways by appropriating various of the conventions and stylistic devices of the masculine hard-boiled novel. In particular, Gillian Slovo's Kate Baeier mysteries, Barbara Wilson's Pam Nilsen stories and Rebecca O'Rourke's *Jumping the Cracks* (1987) all develop the theme of 'big city loneliness'[8] that Ross Macdonald discerned in the hard-boiled novels of the 1930s and 1940s. Indeed, all three writers develop, in a variety of interesting ways, the genre's capacity, first noted by G. K. Chesterton,[9] for creating the poetry of modern urban life.

The streets of Seattle, for example, are a central interest of Barbara

Wilson's novels, and they become the object of a sustained, but questioned, urban anthropology in *Sisters of the Road* (1986) as Pam, the narrator, eschews the hard-boiled mode of narration when she becomes aware that she is watching the street scenes, 'looking at this society from the outside, with an anthropologist's eye'. The reader too is jerked out of his or her voyeurism by the narrator's insistence that 'There were things here that I needed to feel as well as witness. The sexual energy, the danger, the excitement' (p. 53).

Similarly, the topography of London is an important element of the plots and the broader concerns of the novels by O'Rourke and Slovo. O'Rourke's third-person narrative in *Jumping the Cracks* occasionally makes a quite self-conscious attempt at expressing the mundane poetry of city life:

> Dawn broke over London as it breaks over any city. The first exodus of people to work happens by half-light, cold and frosty. They mingle, interchangeable with people going home from night shift. . . . Large parts of a city like London never sleep, they change their rhythms and patterns to fit the ebb and flow of activity around them. . . . Machines ticking and humming, lights flashing on and off in sequence, a rhythm overseen, intervened into, by people. So many, they become a mass. Undifferentiated, simply working. Whether they pour tea into a cafe's chipped mug . . . or pick up the mug, people meet across the simple facts of living, producing warmth, exchanges of conversation, the rub and bustle of a city moving into gear.   (p. 4)

Slovo's narrator, on the other hand, does not entirely avoid the anthropological gaze, but Kate is also a journalist, as is clear from her narrative register:

> Dalston had, for a long time been an area where families, black and white, lived quietly side by side. But rising house prices, a corresponding influx of the young white middle class . . . and a growth of militancy amongst the black community had changed the atmosphere. The events of the summer had only accelerated that trend.   (*Death by Analysis*, p. 40)

Each of Slovo's three Kate Baeier novels (*Morbid Symptoms*, 1984, *Death by Analysis*, 1986, and *Death Comes Staccato*, 1987) develops a journalistic feel for the pressures of inner-city life in the 1980s.

Slovo's terrain is Thatcher's Britain and she offers a grim, though not defeatist, picture of a society that is beginning to display 'morbid symptoms'.

Kate Baeier, like P. D. James's Cordelia Gray, is struggling to earn a living as a professional investigator, but she supplements this work with investigative journalism. She is a socialist feminist who makes her life amongst politically active people. Her first case, in *Morbid Symptoms*, begins as the investigation of the death of a member of a political research group for which she works, and, as it progresses, develops into an investigation of the group and a re-examination of her own socialism and feminism. In the latest novel, *Death Comes Staccato*, Kate is occupied full time as an investigator monitoring the implementation of new work practices, such as Contract Compliance, introduced by the recently abolished Greater London Council, and subsequently adopted by the London boroughs. Kate's job is to check 'that the enormous number of firms that supplied [the council] . . . were prepared to go along with its anti-racist, anti-sexist policies' (p. 11).

In each of the novels Kate's first-person narrative naturalises and takes for granted a radical, left-wing political perspective, but the novels also test and explore this radicalism in Kate's own experience. The narratives repeatedly force Kate to test, and sometimes to modify, the ideological baggage she has been carrying around since the 1960s, when

So many of us had thought we could change society; we hadn't succeeded but we still carried the ideas and hopes with us.

We also had to carry with us the mechanisms to deal with the changes the years, and the recession had wrought. (*Death by Analysis*, p. 34)

The narratives are also structured so as to force Kate, and hence the reader, to explore the legitimacy of Kate's investigations, and to question the limits of her authority. For example, as each of the mysteries approaches its resolution, and Kate thinks she has solved all the deductive problems, she is faced with a period of reflection and struggle about the morality and, more importantly, the political efficacy of making her knowledge public. This problematic is explored most minutely in *Morbid Symptoms*, where the death at the centre of the investigation is the consequence of discord within the 'African Economic Reports' collective resulting from its infiltration by South African security police.

'I think somebody we know killed Tim. Somebody who's fucked up, but somebody who's not the enemy in the sense that a member of the South African security police is.' . . .
'I don't know what to do about it. . . . Does justice have to be done?' . . .
'Scientific method: the truth will out. But that's talking in ultimates. This isn't the revolution; just one of those hiccups probably caused by the frustrations of all our lives. Gramsci called them morbid symptoms.' (p. 139)

Here, as in the other novels, Kate's dilemma is not merely a matter of private conscience, but is articulated within a specific group, and worked out within a particular community of values. In other words, unlike Cordelia Gray and Tamara Hoyland, neither Kate, nor the novels in which she is situated, unquestioningly accept or embody the authority of the privileged individual judgement of the investigator. As one of the characters in *Morbid Symptoms* puts it, 'you can't bear the burden. It's not for you to hold the power in your hands' (p. 139).

In each of the Kate Baeier novels, small events as well as large persistently confront the narrator with issues of race, class and gender. As, for example, in *Death Comes Staccato*, when Kate catches herself out in an inadvertent racism when she realises that she has asked her assistant, Carmen, to interview a particular young man simply because he, like Carmen, is black. While the novels repeatedly foreground specific issues of gender and class politics, sometimes (as in my last example) in a slightly moralising way, for the most part their politics is implicit.

Kate is self-reliant, resilient, independent, well organised and tough, without being a superwoman. She shares the isolation of the modern female sleuth; she is an exile, a naturalised Briton with an unspecified revolutionary past in Portugal. Kate, however, has constructed a full and committed personal and political life in London. She has no family, but inhabits a network of relationships that break down the barriers, implicit in the ideology of the family, between the private and the public, the personal and political. She divides her time between her own flat, the home of her American friends, Dan and Anna, and the flat of her lover, Sam, a gentle 'new man'. Sam is divorced and sharing the care of his young son, with whom Kate has a good-humoured, sparring, but definitely non-maternal relationship. Although no ascetic (she is a saxophone-playing foodie who pokes gentle fun at the radical life-style of health foods and Citroën Dyanes), Kate nevertheless leads a politically vigilant life, committing herself seriously to relation- ships with similarly committed individuals and groups, and engaging in the radical struggle as best she can. In other words, she is an archetypal member of what the popular press calls 'the loony left', although Slovo's handling of the first-person narrative is, of course, designed to encourage us to read Kate as an image of sanity.

Kate's prose is sometimes reminiscent of the style of the macho heroes of Chandler and Hammett. Like them, she inhabits an urban jungle, is occasionally sucked into the world of the filthy rich and engages with crimes that are the by-products of political and social corruption – political infighting, bureaucratic graft, police ter- rorism and so on. However, when Slovo appropriates the conven- tions of the hard-boiled novel and sends her heroine 'down those mean streets', she also revises the genre. Instead of the lonely hero, 'a man . . . who is neither tarnished nor afraid', who is 'the hero . . . everything . . . the best man in his world,'[10] she sends a tarnished, frightened woman equipped with a sound political analysis and supported by a network of personal and political commitments. The lonely quest for the Great Good Place is replaced by fragile and provisional settlements, and a life of purposeful struggle. Slovo refashions the genre into a form that makes tentative affirmations, and develops in the reader, as Kate and her assistant develop in a despondent young working-class widow, 'the beginning of an awareness that maybe she could do more than just survive in a hostile world' (*Death Comes Staccato*, p. 162).

In America, the hard-boiled detective novel has been appro- priated on behalf of a radical lesbian perspective. Mary Wings, for example, has wittily turned the macho, male-bonding world of Chandler and Hammett on its head in *She Came Too Late* (1986) where the girls, very definitely, 'want to be with the girls' (as the David Byrne lyric used as an epigraph reminds us). Emma Victor, Wings's narrator, is a fast-talking, streetwise investigator in the Marlowe mould: a tough, self-confident, self-mocking lesbian, who has no doubts about her sexual identity, and who handles her pick- ups and put-downs with enviable aplomb. Like the hard-boiled heroes, she is detached and isolated, but, unlike them, she is delighted to discover that she can still really desire someone (after a series of rather half-hearted affairs), and that she can develop an emotional commitment to Frances Cohen, a medical researcher who is secretly working to reproduce life from pairs of female frogs.

Emma is at work at the Woman's Hotline, guiding 'women down

probable paths to possible solutions' (p. 2) when she is called personally and asked for help. This call takes her on a Chandler-esque tour of odd-balls and grotesques: a high-society family with its powerful and ambitious patriarch and his lesbian wife; an appalling, silk-pyjama-clad, drug-addicted younger brother who inhabits a luxurious padded cell; and Stacy Weldemeer, the threatening beautiful woman of the hard-boiled novel. This is a funny and parodic novel, which glances at serious issues such as lesbian motherhood and the control of women's fertility, but which mainly does for women's fantasies of power and control what the hard-boiled writers did for men's. Wings also offers some sharp observations on the games people play, especially lesbian role-playing, and has some pert comments on sexuality and sexual mores.

Although Wings plays it mainly for laughs, in changing the gender roles and the sexual identities of the main protagonists she is participating in a significant revision of the hard-boiled novel. In place of the lonely hero, isolated from a corrupt society by his private integrity, the lesbian detective novel gives us female investigators who inhabit a society within a society, and engage with the corruptions of the wider society from a triply marginalised position: they are marginalised by their gender, by their sexual identity and, usually, by their oppositional politics.

Barbara Wilson puts this revision to more serious use in her two Pam Nilsen novels, which not only have a woman investigator, but which also investigate women, from a variety of perspectives. Indeed the central subject of investigation in these novels could be said to be Pam Nilsen herself. In *Murder in the Collective* (1984), a proposed merger between two print collectives, one left-wing and one radical lesbian, apparently results in the murder of one of the members of the left-wing group. By becoming involved in the investigation of this death, Pam is forced to reassess her politics, the nature of her responsibilities and her sexuality. Pam is a reluctant detective, 'are we detectives or what? We're not really qualified; we might really screw things up' (p. 74), but she is spurred on by her comrade's democratising definition of a detective as simply 'some-one who wants to find out what happened', and by her notion of detection as a form of personal responsibility:

> We have a stake in all this. And I want to find out how all of it links up, what it all means. We're certainly more qualified than

any old male detective they'll put on the case. Hell, Pam, we know
these people don't we?   (p. 74).

Like Slovo, Wilson explores and challenges the morality and
politics of detection, questioning the privileged perspective of the
conventional detective. Pam is forced to reassess her assumptions
about detection by the activities of June, another member of her
collective, who pursues her own path with a 'sense of direction
[which] had been as keen as or keener than ours, but she hadn't
pursued Zee like a detective, she'd confronted her like a woman and
stayed to comfort her like a friend' (p. 179).

Pam's attempts to discover the murderer in the collective run
parallel with her process of self-discovery as she becomes increasingly involved with co-worker Hadley and discovers her own
lesbianism. 'It's not just Hadley', she assures her twin sister, 'If I am
a lesbian, and I *am*, Penny, you know my life is going to be different.
It's got to be. I've got to find out what it all means' (p. 173). Thus the
investigation in *Murder in the Collective* is not simply the traditional
reconstruction of a completed retrospective narrative that leads
back to, and unlocks the mysteries of, the original murder; it is also
the investigation of a dynamic process within the novel's narrative
present, a process whose meaning and significance will be further
illuminated beyond that narrative present. In fact, Pam's self-
discovery and self-definition is continued in *Sisters of the Road*
(1987) as she tries to work out her feelings about Hadley (now
returned to Houston) and begins to learn about what Mary Wings
calls 'dyke reality' and about living alone, having moved out of the
communal household she had previously shared with her sister.
Indeed, Pam becomes involved in her second case – the search for
Trish, a missing teenage prostitute – largely out of her own need to
care for someone apart from herself.

Wilson uses Pam's journey through the Seattle streets in search of
Trish as a means of exploring the lives of a wide range of women,
and of investigating various images of women in Western culture:

History and novels gave you . . . the myth of the *grand horizontal*,
sensual, charming, clever, and the myth of the harlot, the scarlet
woman, the whore, the most pitiful and despicable creature on
earth. Men said you were one or the other; somehow you
suspected you might be both. All the same you chose. Good girl,
bad girl.   (p. 134)

This dualism is also figured in Wilson's doubling of her heroine by providing her with a twin sister. Penny, who is Pam's heterosexual *alter ego*, a good girl, an achiever and mother-to-be. The mystery plot itself focuses on attitudes to sexuality, on sexual violence and on women as victims and survivors. In this novel, the investigator also becomes a victim when Pam is raped, an incident that exposes a complex of social and psychological attitudes as horrifying as the physical violation:

> I didn't feel 'good' anymore. I felt 'bad'. In other people's eyes anyway. . . . They were there to help me . . . but I still felt I was the one who had transgressed. . . . Being a victim doesn't make you self-righteous; It makes you suspicious, defensive, ashamed.   (p. 196)

Here, as elsewhere in Wilson's novels, the investigator herself becomes the subject of the narrative's investigation, and, simultaneously, the gap between investigator and victim is closed.

The Pam Nilsen novels, like Wilson's earlier political thriller, *Ambitious Women* (1983), and like Gillian Slovo's Kate Baeier books, use the form of the entertaining detection fiction to create novels of ideas that investigate women's experience and explore the problems of women coming to terms with personal and political responsibilities. Both Wilson and Slovo look seriously at women at work. The activities of the print workshop and the problems and pleasures of collectives are carefully worked into the fabric of Wilson's books, while Slovo situates her heroine in a closely observed milieu of journalistic and investigative work. Indeed, of all the novelists examined so far, these two are most firmly committed to realism, and it is interesting to note that both writers represent a milieu that is very close to their own experience: Wilson is co-founder of the Seal Press in Seattle, and Slovo is a London-based journalist and film producer. Pam Nilsen and Kate Baeier would seem to be autobiographical projections of their media-professional authors.

In this last respect, at least, Wilson and Slovo might be linked with almost all the other writers looked at in this chapter. For, while they certainly produce heroines who are far removed from the fantasy super-sleuths like Jemima Shore, both novelists could, nevertheless, be said to adhere to the convention, which goes back to Sayers's Harriet Vane and beyond, that the investigator should be middle class and well educated. Working-class women, as Craig and Cadogan argue, have generally been considered to be 'too busy working, or suffering hardship, to get involved in the lives of others';[11] they lacked the 'authoritative manner' usually considered essential in the detective figure.

This last convention is abandoned in Rebecca O'Rourke's interesting first novel, *Jumping the Cracks*, whose central character, Rats, is a northern, working-class lesbian, precariously employed and housed in London. Apart from Cordelia Gray (one of nature's Cambridge graduates), Rats is the only one of these female detectives who has not received a college or university education. She reads the *Sunday Mirror*, and she certainly does not write for any newspaper. She is extremely unpoliticised, and her lack of interest in politics is a source of conflict with her estranged lover, Helen.

Rats becomes a sleuth when she discovers a body in a Rolls Royce parked in a derelict Hackney street, and when this apparently random instance of pervasive urban violence begins to link up with other mysteries she encounters in her workplace. Perhaps to an even greater degree than Slovo or Wilson, O'Rourke uses the detective plot as a paradigm for the experience of modern urban life. The fragmentary plot of this novel, its misleading appearances, false clues, loose ends and paths that lead nowhere are used to figure the marginal individual's experience of surviving in the city. The conventions of the detection genre demand that the fragments fit together, that the disparate signs add up to a text that is readable once the detective has broken the code and provided the key of interpretation. Thus, conventionally, the detective is a super-reader, who discovers the story and constructs the plot by revealing how the fragments fit together.

In O'Rourke's novel, although the isolated heroine reads the mystery, she is, in fact, a very slow reader and we see the pattern before she does. Rats's slowness derives partly from her lack of self-confidence and authoritative vision, and partly from the fact that she is deeply involved in solving the mysteries of her own story and the questions it raises about social and sexual identity, and about taking responsibility for one's own life. Once more the female investigator and the problems of her relationships with a particular individual and with society at large become the central subjects of the novel's investigations. Moreover, in this novel Rats's discovery of the meaning of the detective plot is not accompanied by its resolution. There is no confrontation scene in which the articulate heroine demonstrates her *mastery* of all the details of the case. (Slovo, incidentally, also disrupts this convention by allowing Kate to deduce the general drift of events but ensuring that she gets some important details wrong.) Instead, Rats sends the police an anonymous dossier on the crime in question, and leaves them to fit the pieces together and take action. Although Rats can flush out the villain, Cruse Pershing, she cannot take him on. He inhabits a male world of money, power and a highly bureaucratised form of organised crime that is deeply enmeshed with the bureaucracies of the welfare state. Rats, on the other hand, is an extremely vulnerable female, socially powerless, herself dependent on the welfare departments which Pershing is defrauding.

Jumping the Cracks, like each of the novels looked at in this chapter, has been produced within and by a culture in which women's roles have come under increasingly close scrutiny from a variety of political perspectives, a culture in which the definitions of women's lives and meanings have been fiercely contested. Has this cultural situation significantly changed the detective fiction genre within which these novelists are working? The female investigators at the centre of these fictions are undoubtedly modern 'liberated' women, inspired by the women's movement, but do they, and the narrative structures in which they occur, really challenge the conservatism of the earlier 'Queens of Crime' for whom crime is often a symptom of unwelcome social change, and a disruption of the supposed (and desired) fixities of class and gender? The novels by Fraser and Mann would tend to suggest that these new 'Queens of Crime' and their liberated heroines do disrupt some of the conventions and assumptions of their predecessors, through parody, play and satire; while P. D. James makes the link between genre and gender a central concern of *An Unsuitable Job for a Woman*. However, while these novels alternately parody or problematise the conventions of the earlier forms of the genre, ultimately, for the most part, they reproduce both its conventions and its conservative ideology.

On the other hand, there is a growing body of feminist detection fiction, usually published by the feminist presses, which demonstrates that detective fiction may not, after all, be an 'unsuitable genre for a feminist'.[12] While some of these post-feminist novels offer a kind of designer-feminism, simply by locating a wise-cracking, independent heroine in a self-consciously radical environment, others appropriate and revise the genre in order to engage seriously (and entertainingly) with issues of gender and class. Writers like Slovo, Wilson and O'Rourke use the 'narrative pleasures of the genre – the chase, the investigation, the mystery'[13] as a metaphor for the experience of urban life in the late twentieth century, with its potentially alienating fragmentariness and its pervasive violence, particularly violence against women. In these narratives women are the prey, the hunted, but the conventions of the detection genre also enable women, in the person of the female investigator, to become the hunter. This is not a simple role reversal in which the victim becomes aggressor, but it is a transformation, in which the potential victim, by becoming active and vigilant, avoids, and helps others to avoid, victimisation.

Several of these writers appropriate aspects of the hard-boiled detective novel, and in doing so revise the genre in the direction of more radical, feminist perspectives. They interrogate or parody the aggressive masculinity of the earlier hard-boiled novels, and replace its (often) individualist defeatism with a more optimistic vision of the possibilities of building transforming personal and social relationships. The first-person narratives of Slovo and Wilson, in particular, also develop the journalistic realism of the hard-boiled novel, and give it a specifically feminist inflection; the cynically authoritative observing eye of the hard-boiled male narrator becomes the closely observing female recorder, whose authority is that authority of individual experience which is a central tenet of many feminisms. In the feminist novels this individual experience, the experience of the investigator herself, becomes a central focus of the narrative's investigations. More generally, these novels are concerned with the varieties of female experience and with the varying definitions of the feminine in an uncertain and constantly changing world.

In all these respects detection fiction can be said to be an extremely powerful genre when appropriated by the feminist. By adapting a popular cultural form that is widely read by both men and women, the feminist novelists I have examined have found a medium in which to investigate changing meanings, values and attitudes. Of course, it remains to be seen whether these feminist interventions, the products of a very particular historical conjunction, make any lasting impact on the genre, and indeed how widely disseminated they will be among readers of crime fiction. It seems likely that these radical novels, which appear on the 'Women's Crime' lists of specifically feminist publishers, will attract a smaller and more self-selected readership than will the more conservative fictions of the new 'Queens of Crime', which appear on the general crime lists of mainstream publishers. However, at the very least, in their particular versions of the figure of the female investigator, the unexceptional but resourceful woman at the centre of most of the novels discussed here, the feminist writers have made a significant contribution to a development that the female detection novel will find difficult to ignore: the development of a 'unique figment of popular culture', a figure who 'stands out as the most economical, the most striking and the most agreeable embodiment of two qualities often disallowed for women in the past: the power of action and practical intelligence'.[14]

Notes

Unless otherwise stated all publication dates in the text refer to the first British edition.

1. Dorothy L. Sayers, 'Introduction', *The Omnibus of Crime*, reprinted by Robin W. Winks, *Detective Fiction: A Collection of Critical Essays* (Englewood Cliffs, N.J.: Prentice-Hall, 1980) pp. 58–9.
2. Patricia Craig and Mary Cadogan, *The Lady Investigates: Women Detectives and Spies in Fiction* (London: Oxford University Press, 1986) p. 130.
3. George Grella offers this useful anatomy of the formal detective novel in an essay, 'Murder, Manners and the Formal Detective Novel' in Winks (ed.), *Detective Fiction*: 'The formal detective novel, the so-called "pure-puzzle" or "whodunnit" ... subscribes to a rigidly uniform, virtually changeless combination of characters, setting, and events ... [typically it] presents a group of people assembled at an isolated place – usually an English country house – who discover that one of their number has been murdered. They summon the local constabulary, who are completely baffled. . . . To the rescue comes an eccentric, intelligent, unofficial investigator who reviews the evidence, questions the suspects, constructs a fabric of proof, and in a dramatic final scene, names the culprit' (pp. 84–5).
4. Cora Kaplan, 'An Unsuitable Genre for a Feminist?', *Women's Review*, 8 (July 1986) p. 18.
5. Ibid.
6. Lady Olga Maitland is the leader of the right-wing, pro-NATO, Families for Defence; Mary Whitehouse is a veteran campaigner against the portrayal of sex and violence in the broadcasting media; Ferdinand Mount is the author of a revisionist history of the family, *Subversive Family: An Alternative History of Love and Marriage* (London: Unwin, 1983).

7. Grella, 'Murder, Manners', p. 91.
8. Ross Macdonald, 'The Writer as Detective Hero', reprinted in Winks, *Detective Fiction*, p. 183.
9. G. K. Chesterton, 'A Defence of Detective Stories', in *The Defendant* (1901), quoted by John Cawelti in *Adventure, Mystery, and Romance: Formula Stories as Art and Popular Culture* (Chicago and London: University of Chicago Press, 1976) pp. 140–1.
10. Raymond Chandler, 'The Simple Art of Murder', quoted by Macdonald, 'The Writer as Detective Hero', p. 182.
11. Craig and Cadogan, *The Lady Investigates*, p. 232.
12. Kaplan, 'An Unsuitable Genre?', p. 18.
13. Ibid., p. 19.
14. Craig and Cadogan, *The Lady Investigates*, pp. 163, 245.

5

The Phantom at the Limits of Criminology

RICHARD W. IRELAND

I was carrying on for several months researches in the prisons and asylums of Pavia upon cadavers and living persons in order to determine upon substantial differences between the insane and criminals, without succeeding very well. At last I found in the skull of a brigand a very long series of atavistic anomalies. . . . At the sight . . . of these strange anomalies the problem of the nature and of the origin of the criminal seemed to me resolved. This was not merely an idea, but a flash of inspiration. At the sight of that skull I seemed to see, all of a sudden, lighted up as a vast plain under a flaming sky the problem of the nature of the criminal.[1]

He thrust the assistants away, and plunging his hands into the hay that was soaked with blood, he seized the severed head by the hair and stared at it . . . 'Oh, curse him! Fantômas has escaped! Fantômas has gotten away! He has had some innocent man executed in his stead! I tell you, Fantômas is alive!'[2]

These two Gothic revelations mark respectively a beginning and an ending. The beginning is that of what became known as the 'science of criminology', generally accepted as having its origin in this discovery in 1870 by the Italian physician Cesare Lombroso. It was to lead to an explosion in criminological theory that was felt throughout Europe and the United States. The criminal might be identified, categorised by science, and science was to be in the vanguard of the fight against crime. The ending is that of a crime novel, *Fantômas*, written by Marcel Allain and Pierre Souvestre and published in 1911. The book (published in translation most recently by Picador in 1987) was a sensation in its time – thirty-one sequels immediately followed it, and five films by the director Louis Feuillade were released. As the above quotation demonstrates, it is a work in which the criminal evades capture, thereby proving his superiority over the scientific theory and practice ranged against him.

The aim of this chapter is a simple one: it seeks to examine the vision of the criminal as presented by Allain and Souvestre against the background of the vision of the criminal that was being presented in the writings of the criminologists of their time. The limitations of this inquiry need to be admitted. Firstly, I shall not consider the literary antecedents of *Fantômas*, such as Rocambole (the hero of Ponson du Terrail), whose name is mentioned early in the text of *Fantômas*, Arsène Lupin or the others.[3] Nor will I concern myself with the subsequent history of Fantômas, but concern myself entirely with the first novel. Perhaps more importantly, I am not able to speak with great authority on the issue of how much direct knowledge of the science and discourse of criminology was possessed by either the authors of the novel or its readership as a whole. As to the former, however, I regard it as significant that both authors had studied law before becoming journalists, their occupation when they wrote the text. Souvestre had even been admitted to the legal profession. Evidence from within the text shows a practical familiarity with the workings of the penal process. It would seem to me implausible that the authors were unaware of significant developments in the growth of criminology that were taking place in the last quarter of the nineteenth century and the opening decade of the twentieth. At the very least, their time as law students can hardly have been spent in total ignorance of the events that were causing such excitement, uproar and outrage within European legal and academic circles. In addition, it is clear that fear of crime and discussion of methods of dealing with it were issues that had attained a high profile in journalistic and political discourse in the decade before the publication of *Fantômas*. Moreover, it will be argued here that the internal evidence of the text suggests that not only an appreciation of criminological theory but also a clearly defined attitude towards it form an important part of a proper understanding of the *Fantômas* phenomenon. For Fantômas is terrifying, not only because he perpetrates outrageous crimes, but also because he proves to be incapable of incorporation into, indeed may even stand in direct contradiction to, the theories of those who asserted comfortably that criminality could be located within precise scientific boundaries. He represents the popular fear of crime without the consolation of scientific intelligibility.

THE BIRTH AND GROWTH OF CRIMINOLOGY

Lombroso's moment of inspiration in 1870 marked, it was stated

above, the birth of the 'science of criminology'. Now clearly there
had been precursors in the field: the physionomists like Lavater,
the phrenologists Gall and Spurzheim, alienists such as Grohmann,
but Lombroso's work was to have a massive effect in the promotion
of knowledge of matters criminological. As one commentator puts
it:

> Within a remarkably brief period, perhaps no more than twenty
> years after the appearance of Lombroso's 'L'Uomo Delinquente' in
> 1876, this knowledge developed from the idiosyncratic concerns
> of a few individuals into a programme of investigation and social
> action which attracted support throughout the whole of Europe
> and North America.[4]

Yet among the precursors mention must be made in particular of
the French 'statistical' tradition, which went back as far as the 1830s
with the work of the 'moral statisticians', Quetelet (himself a
Belgian) and Guerry. For criminology both made use of statistics
and provided data, its captive subjects yielding ever more statistical
information in pursuit of scientific proofs.

The achievement of Lombroso and his fellow 'Positivists' Enrico
Ferri and Raffaelo Garofalo was to shift the attention from the study
of crime to the study of the criminal. Lombroso's own conclusion
was that criminality resided in a distinct anthropological type, an
atavistic species characterised by malformations of the skeleton and
skull, facial asymmetry and other physical stigmata – a receding
forehead, high cheek bones, bushy eyebrows, big ears, a projecting
or receding jaw, a hairy body and overdeveloped arms. Such a
theory, it should be pointed out to the reader (who may have just
returned from a desperate dash to the nearest mirror), may still have
its legacy. Many will be familiar with popular warnings not to trust
those whose eyes are too close together. There is also (although this
may be the origin rather than the consequence) the evidence of
psychologists that we tend in some circumstances to judge harshly
persons we find to be unattractive.[5]

Lombroso's major work, *L'Uomo Delinquente*, was published in
1876. His theories became very well known thoughout Europe and
were published as *L'Homme Criminel* in Paris in 1887 and as *Le Crime,
Causes et Remèdes* in 1899. The work of the Positivists fired
controversy and imagination and the 'science of criminology' grew
rapidly. In 1889 the International Association of Criminal Law was

established, three years after the launch of the periodical *Archives d'Anthropologie Criminelle*. The International Congresses for Criminal Anthropology (Biology and Sociology) had been founded as early as 1885 and by 1911, the year in which *Fantômas* first surfaced in Paris, had met seven times. The work of the Positivists had impressed at least one major French writer, Emile Zola, who was to work out his 'scientific' views on homicide in *La Bête Humaine*, written during 1889.[6]

But it would be wrong to think that all this intellectual activity was devoted to the support of Lombroso's theories. Criticism had come early and with vigour from France, so much so that Lombroso's views had little support in that country in the first decade of the twentieth century. In particular, mention must be made of the influential member of the French sociological school, Gabriel Tarde, who wrote notable texts, *La Criminalité Comparée* (1886) and *La Philosophie Penale* (1890). Tarde's work stressed the role of learned criminal careers, with crime a profession as any other. He considered the difference that social environment might have on the phenomenology of crime, drawing a distinction between urban crimes (greedy, crafty and voluptuous – burglary, fraud and swindling) and country crimes (vindictive and brutal – murder and assault).

If these were significant strands in criminological thought at the end of the nineteenth century, there were many others. Economic analysis of crime propounded by Marx and Engels, and the work of another newly institutionalised discipline, that of psychology, had a role to play. The arguments grew, and by the turn of the century criminology was in ferment. In 1889 the Congress of Criminal Anthropology in Paris marked in dramatic style the beginning of a dispute that was to continue at other conferences. The influential French degeneration theorist Valentin Magnan was displaying a group of delinquent children with no apparent physical abnormalities. Lombroso got up, took measurements and pointed out the physical stigmata that he claimed Magnan had overlooked.

Within France in the first decade of the twentieth century the prevalent theory linked crime to degeneracy, a flexible notion that combined sociological and environmental factors with inheritance and allowed all manner of social pathology to be brought into debate. Degeneracy theory, propounded by a number of different observers, was the most potent counter-argument to Lombroso's atavism. The controversy raged and doubting voices began to be heard. In England, Pearson stated in 1910: 'In reality nobody knows whether crime is associated with general degeneracy whether it is a manifestation of certain hereditary qualities, or whether it is a product of environment or tradition.'[7] Yet the prevailing mood was that, even though criminology might become less dogmatic and more eclectic, the social problem of crime was nevertheless open to subjection by scientific theory. Zeal for the task was almost missionary. Indeed, Garland has neatly encapsulated the mood of the origin of the discipline. 'Despite its claims to be a positive science', he argues, 'criminology in this early period more nearly resembles a new theology with its dogmas, glosses and evangelists.'[8] In the fictional character of Fantômas, it might be suggested, it would also have its heresy.

Yet not all the science in the drive against crime was directed towards understanding the nature of the malefactor. Considerable efforts went into applying science to catch the criminal. The sophistication of forensic science and of crime-detection techniques was increasing rapidly and becoming a very important practical technique. The Austrian Hans Gross had a profound effect on this science of 'criminalistics', publishing his *Manual for the Examining Justice* in 1893, whereafter it went into several editions and translations. In France, the most significant steps had been taken by Alphonse Bertillon, who had introduced in 1883 the 'anthropometric' technique of recording the identities of criminals, by measurement of certain physical features and also photography.

'FANTÔMAS', THE NOVEL

It may be thought that the discussion above, though it may speak much of imagination and fantasy, has little place in a consideration of crime fiction. Let us turn, then, to the text of *Fantômas*. The story opens with the grisly murder of the Marquise de Langrune at her château. Suspicion falls upon Charles Rambert, a young man staying at the château, and he is accused of the deed by his father, Etienne Rambert. The famous Inspector Juve, who spends much of the novel in a variety of disguises, is called to investigate. Juve is called back to Paris where he discovers the body of the missing English aristocrat, Lord Beltham, in a trunk in the rooms of a man named Gurn. A third body is discovered, which is thought to be that of Charles Rambert, and his father is acquitted in court of complicity in his disappearance. Some time later the beautiful Princess Sonia Danidoff is taking a bath in her hotel room when she is interrupted by an elegant man in a dinner-jacket who, after learning to his cost that cutting electric wires with a razor is not a wise idea, departs with Sonia's money and Baronne Van den Rosen's diamond necklace.

Juve, again in disguise, interviews the staff at the hotel. He attempts to seduce the alluring Mademoiselle Jeanne, who turns out to be Charles Rambert in a dress, a fact that the great detective only begins to suspect when the Mademoiselle renders him unconscious with a blow to the temple as a response to Juve's advances. After episodes in an insane asylum and the St Anthony's Pig, a low dive, we move to the house of the saintly Lady Beltham, where Gurn, her lover, is captured. Etienne Rambert is presumed lost in the liner *Lancaster*, destroyed in mysterious circumstances. Gurn works out how to escape from prison but apparently does so only long enough to hurl from a train a material witness against him. He returns to prison and faces trial.

At the trial Juve maintains, but cannot prove, the theory that has driven him on throughout. That is that all the crimes have been committed by one man, the genius of crime, Fantômas, who is also Gurn, who is also M. Etienne Rambert. Given the fact that none of these characters in any way physically resembles the others, Juve is not believed. Gurn is, however, convicted of the murder of Lord Beltham but ensures that his place at the guillotine is taken by the actor Valgrand, who has been drugged. As the quotation that appears at the opening of this paper demonstrates, Fantômas escapes to allow the many sequels to this first novel.

This summary of the plot, inadequate as it is in revealing all the complexities of the narrative, will give those readers unfamiliar with *Fantômas* (and there are, I suspect, many) a flavour of the text. As one unschooled in the arcana of literary criticism, surrounded in the present volume by the works of those who are, it may be rash of me to attempt to evaluate its literary merit. Yet I feel bound to say that *Fantômas* is, in many respects, a truly awful book. Its plot is, as will have become apparent, highly improbable and at times the text is very difficult to take seriously. The master of disguise Juve seeks to merge into the background in the Parisian backstreets by apparently painting his skin green, a circumstance noticed by one of the minor characters because she is a trained nurse. The characters remain, almost without exception, completely undeveloped.

But *Fantômas* was, it would seem, not intended as a joke and was certainly very popular. It does have a certain excitement, the action is frenetic and has a shocking *grand guignol* goriness. It is marked throughout by ambiguity, which proves to be both its unifying and sustaining feature but which also becomes at times a tiresome artifice. This ambiguity may conceivably explain its appeal to the artistic avante-garde who hailed it as a great work of literature. The budding surrealists, in particular, might, because of their familiarity with the work of Freud and the stress upon ambiguity which that contained, have found the book stimulating on that score, or it may have been regarded as appealing in its kitsch. Of these matters I can speak with no confidence, yet the *Fantômas* phenomenon was one which apparently cut across social and educational barriers in its appeal.

IMAGES OF CRIMINALITY IN '*FANTÔMAS*'

A technique well established in crime fiction was to present the villain as being wholly different in type from the readership. Such distancing is still a persistent characteristic in, for example, contemporary tabloid journalism. Hence offenders may be stigmatised as belonging to a different species – a sex offender is described as a 'beast', a violent football crowd as 'animals' – or at the very least as belonging to a different nation – street robbers in their long indigenous history in England have been characterised as 'garotters', 'hooligans' or 'muggers' at different times in that history, with the connotations of Latins, Irish and black Americans respectively. The tendency within the canon of nineteenth-century French crime fiction was remarked on by Michel Foucault. 'Above all', he argues, 'its function was to show that the delinquent belonged to an entirely different world, unrelated to familiar everyday life. This strangeness was first that of the lower depths of society (*Les Mystères de Paris, Rocambole*), then that of madness (especially in the latter half of the century) and lastly that of crime in high society (*Arsène Lupin*).'[9]

But such a scheme would necessarily be at risk from the emergent science of criminology. True, the criminologists had an essentially similar aim: to locate crime within a distinct community – either a criminal type or a criminal class – but it aimed also to explain, to demystify the criminal. A truly terrifying criminal must needs be, in an age of criminological investigation, a criminal who defied the laws and expectations of criminology itself. I will suggest here that this is indeed the case with the character of Fantômas. Not only does he break the criminologists' rules but this feature is drawn attention to by contrasting Fantômas with more comfortable and predictable images of criminality, such as old Bouzille, the thieving tramp. In this way, just as the football 'hooligan' is marked off from the 'real supporter' or the threatening vagrant from the 'real gypsy', here we find Fantômas forms a terrifying contrast with the 'real' criminal, which latter remains amenable to scientific inquiry and, ultimately, to control.

The France presented within the novel is one upon which the new concern with the phenomena of criminality and related social pathology is well marked. At the very outset of the story, President Bonnet, a retired magistrate, treats Mme de Langrune's dinner guests to a breakdown of homicide statistics (p. 13). Bouzille praises the comfortable new prison at Brives, a great improvement on the old lockup it had replaced (p. 50), whilst Dr Biron's sanatorium, in which is confined Charles Rambert's mother, was a tribute to, even if its builder was not, 'that theoretical knowledge of insanity that has made French psychiatrists famous throughout the world' (p. 169). At the asylum we meet Dr Swelding, a Danish professor who has written a tract on the 'ideontology of the hyperimaginative' and is visiting for research purposes (p. 168). As we shall see, 'Bertillon' measurement and photography is employed, as is scientific scene-of-crime examination (pp. 40, 72, 195 ff.). Indeed, in one respect the authors would seem to have shown foresight, explicable perhaps since both had worked as journalists on motoring magazines. President Bonnet observes:

> Criminals who operate in the grand manner have all sorts of things at their disposal nowadays. Science has done much for modern progress, but unfortunately it can be of invaluable assistance to criminals as well; the hosts of evil have the telegraph and the motorcar at their disposal just as authority has, and some day they will make use of the airplane. (p. 13)

Later in the same year as the publication of *Fantômas*, Paris experienced its first robbery in which the criminals made use of a motor car. The ensuing panic was considerable.

Yet over all this towers Fantômas, much as he did in the posters

marking the celebrated advertising campaign that launched the
novel. He is both a character and a symbol, a symbol of criminality
which does not conform to theory, and deficiencies of the drawing
of his character are explicable by his potency as a symbol. Emil
Faguet of the French Academy had urged 'It is not necessary
to consider criminals as responsibles, semi-responsibles, irrespon-
sibles – that concerns only the philosophers. It is necessary to
consider them as very dangerous, semi-dangerous, and not
dangerous. Only that and nothing else should be considered.' This
was a tenet of the theory of 'Social Defence', which underlay the
early twentieth-century French drive against criminality.[10] And in
effect this is all that the novel does consider about Fantômas, how
dangerous he is. A most telling comment on Fantômas's symbolic
quality comes from Bonnet, who describes Fantômas as a *cause* of
the steady increase in crime (p. 14). He concedes that Fantômas is a
living person but none the less the language of a statistically
measurable cause of crime is reminiscent of the search for the grail
of causal connection that was the focus of criminological research.

   Yet Fantômas is a cause of crime that could not be accommodated
by existing theory. Let us begin with a theory that went back to the
statistician Quetelet, for he had argued for a 'thermic law of
delinquency', and the theory was still considered important
enough for Lombroso to devote the first chapter of *Le Crime, Causes
et Remèdes* to it. The theory stated that in France and elsewhere
crimes against the person occur in the summer, crimes against
property were more common in the winter. This latter seems to be
confirmed by the tramp Bouzille: 'in the summer there isn't so
much crime; you can find all you want on the road'. But with his
first appearance Fantômas shows no respect for 'thermic' laws: the
murder of the Marquise de Langrune occurs in winter, as does that
of his next victim Lord Beltham. Fantômas's only simple property
crime, the theft of the Danidoff pocket-book and the Van den Rosen
diamonds, is committed at the end of June, although admittedly we
are told that it had been a late and cold spring.

   If seasonal constraints apparently do not circumscribe
Fantômas's criminality, what evidence is there for his correspond-
ence to alternative theories? As to the physical stigmata of
criminality, then it is evident that Fantômas's capacity to assume
very different and wholly dissimilar appearances must cast doubt
on Lombrosian anthropology. It is true that when he robs Princess
Sonia he is blessed with a startling physiognomy 'What struck the

princess most was the abnormal size of his head and the number of wrinkles that ran right across his temples, following the line of the eyebrows' (p. 125). But this is a feature not mentioned in respect of his other manifestations and it is clear that the plasticity of Fantômas's appearance is in stark contrast to Lombroso's invariant physiological rules.

Indeed, it is tempting to see some deliberate satire of Lombroso's theories within the text. It is remarkable that the only person who is regularly pointed out as having the appearance of a criminal is Inspector Juve himself. His appearance is commented on at different points by no fewer than four persons, and while it is true that he is in disguise on each occasion (he generally is), the irony remains (pp. 52, 64, 101, 183). Similarly, the only other person singled out as a potential criminal ('Thick lips, a narrow forehead and prominent cheekbones suggested a material nature that would stop at nothing to satisfy its carnal desires') is Nibet, the man employed as a prison guard, and the diagnosis is performed by that 'experienced reader of character in faces' Fantômas/Gurn (p. 248)! Even if no irony is intended here, for Fantômas is correct about the man's venal nature, then clearly the genius of crime is himself unable to have his character read this way. The only person who does seem to read anything into Gurn's face ('he has the head of the assassin of genius') is the vain actor Valgrand, who later admits to his own physical similarity to Gurn and, on the occasion when he makes the former observation, is laughed at (p. 278). Whilst it may be that Allain and Souvestre are simply placing their creation above Lombrosian categorisation, there remains a feeling that they, like many of their fellow countrymen, had scant respect for Lombroso's theories. One of the attendants in Dr Biron's establishment explains to another the status of the visiting Dr Swelding: 'Just one of those foreign scholars who haven't succeeded in becoming famous at home and so go abroad to bother other people under a pretext of research.' Although Dr Lombroso had fame enough, it was true that many Frenchmen had little time for his ideas.

Nor do Gabriel Tarde's sociological theories fare much better in explaining Fantômas's criminality. Juve is convinced that the first of the crimes we encounter is a 'professional' one, a notion upon which Tarde had laid great stress:

Let us first of all ask ourselves how the murder of the Marquise de Langrune ought to be 'classified' in the technical sense. The first

conclusion of any observant person who has visited the scene of
the crime and examined the corpse of the victim is that this
murder must be placed in the category of professional crimes.
The murderer seems to have left the implicit mark of his character
upon his victim; the very violence of the blows dealt shows that
he is a man of the lower orders, a typical criminal, a professional.
(p. 69)

Yet throughout the book Fantômas resolutely refuses to become
typical. Moreover, and incidentally defying an economic analysis of
his criminality, Fantômas does not seem to belong to any particular
social class but slides between them; as Gurn, as the bourgeois
businessman Etienne Rambert and, in the image used on the
posters, as the immaculately dressed, upper-class burglar who
frequents the same drawing-rooms as Princess Sonia. Fantômas
does not appear to have a settled *modus operandi* – certainly he does
not restrict himself to the brutal and repeated use of 'one of those
common knives with a catch lock that street thugs always carry', the
use of which Juve regards as 'a point of primary importance' (p. 70).
Lord Beltham is strangled in a moment of passion and to protect
Fantômas's lover. The steward Dollon is subtly rendered unconscious by chemicals before being hurled from the train.

Nor does Tarde's distinction between city and country crime
bother Fantômas. Bouzille, the 'typical country tramp' (p. 49) seems
to fit a comfortable pattern (albeit his crimes are not brutal, they are
predictably rural – the theft of rabbits and chickens). Fantômas, on
the other hand, commits crime with equal facility in Paris or in the
countryside, or, in the case of the murder of Dollon, on a train
between the two. Again the only person directly contrasted with
Bouzille's rural criminality is François Paul, who turns out to be none
other than Inspector Juve again (p. 49). Moreover, if Fantômas is and
has always been Gurn (a point that it is difficult to establish) then he
has not served the apprenticeship that would have been expected of
one of Tarde's criminals, nor does he seem to fit the pattern of
degeneracy so popular at the time of the novel. Juve, on finding
Gurn's notice of promotion to the rank of sergeant 'when fighting
under Lord Beltham in the South African War', is astonished:

'It is extraordinary', he muttered, 'that seems to be perfectly
authentic; it is authentic, and it proves that Gurn was a decent
fellow and a brave soldier once; that is a fine record of service.' He

drummed his fingers on the desk and spoke aloud, 'Is Gurn really Gurn then, and have I been mistaken from beginning to end in the little intrigue I have been weaving around him? How do I find the key to the mystery? How do I prove the truth I feel so very close to, but which slips away every time I'm about to grab hold of it?' (p. 230)

No wonder Juve is taken aback. It was the perceived poor performance of British troops in the Boer War that had led to a parellel fear of national degeneracy within Britain at this time. Again Fantômas runs counter to stereotype.

If no rational categorisation can contain Fantômas, could he simply be written off as irrational, as a madman? Much is said within the text on the subject of insanity, but at no time does it appear that Fantômas is a lunatic. It is strongly urged at one point that the Langrune murder has been committed by a lunatic, whose lunacy has been inherited. But it is Charles Lambert who is being accused of both the murder and the insanity. The rational person making the accusation is none other than Etienne Rambert – Fantômas himself (p. 56).

If science is incapable of explaining the Fantômas phenomenon, is it more successful in its attempts to trap him? Certainly the achievements of criminalistics are brought into play at various points. The detective as scientist has become an established figure in literature – did not Watson have a famous meeting with Holmes whilst the latter was slaving over a blood test?[11] But in *Fantômas* Juve is let down by science, he cannot prove his theories because of the very rules of science.

Again the point being made in the text is not that science is useless – far from it, in *ordinary* cases it performs wonderfully. We know that Charles Rambert cannot have committed the Langrune murder – he is not sufficiently strong, as is conclusively proven by Juve's clever use of 'M. Bertillon's dynanometer', which enables the detective 'not only to ascertain what kind of lever has been used to force a lock or a piece of furniture, but also to determine the exact strength of the individual who used the tools' (p. 72). Use of Bertillon's name here is of course important, although whether the 'effraction dynamometer' was a genuine or fictional invention of the great forensic scientist I do not know. It would certainly have been less improbable than some of the criminological inventions of the day – Mosso, for example had invented the plethysmograph, a device for testing variation in the circulation of the blood as a response to mental processes.[12]

Certainly authentic is Juve's use of the Bertillon technique upon Charles Rambert in the 'measuring room' at the Tour Pointue:

> Charles obeyed and stood under the measuring stick, and then, as the assistant ordered him, he submitted to having his fingers smeared with ink so that his fingerprints could be taken; to being photographed, full face and in profile; and finally to having the width of his head, from ear to ear, measured with a special pair of caliper compasses.   (p. 197)

Juve can establish by this means that Charles and Mademoiselle Jeanne are one and the same person, thereby vindicating Bertillon's guiding principle that a man, though he may differ from all others, remains always constant with himself.

But although Fantômas himself appears not to have been subjected to these procedures, the extreme plasticity of his form, which is stressed throughout the text, leads the reader to believe that even Bertillon's first principle is being challenged by this criminal whom Juve describes as a 'Proteus'. The dynanometer can show that the Langrune murderer also performed the Danidoff robbery. Both the robber and Gurn have a scar. But the physical dissimilarity between Gurn, Etienne Rambert and the Danidoff burglar suggests that a single identity of the three men is impossible. Men who have met them in different guises – Muller from the Royal Palace Hotel, even Juve himself – are unable to complete the identification.

This is an obstacle that Juve cannot surmount in his court-room battle with Fantômas. Indeed, Juve is forced throughout to rely on instinct rather than science in a heretical return to pre-criminological crime solving. When all the circumstances point to Charles Rambert as the Langrune murderer, Juve feels in his bones, rather than observes in anyone else's, that Rambert is innocent. Juve finds Lord Beltham's body by what one of the characters calls 'extraordinary instinct' but which Juve himself dismisses, more disturbingly, as 'pure luck' (p. 138). Fantômas is a remarkable criminal unfettered by scientific boundaries. It takes a remarkable detective – the two are even thought by Charles Rambert to the same man at one point – to unmask him, and even then he is not believed. Leave aside his penchant for painting himself green and his difficulty in distinguishing between the sexes: Juve is a worthy opponent of Fantômas.

It may be thought that the above analysis reads too much into the text of a bad book, whose authors were capable of producing a novel in a couple of days.[13] Certainly, even if accepted, the thesis may not explain the popularity of the *Fantômas* genre. This is more readily explicable in terms of the clear and well-documented fear of crime amongst the public as a whole within the first decade of the twentieth century in France. The fear was growing despite the best efforts of criminology to account for the aetiology of criminality. Popular models of the criminal were rather simpler than those of the criminologists. The name of the Apache (again the alien connotation), a term coined by the journalist Arthur Dupin to describe members of the Parisian street gangs about whom he was writing in 1902, became a potent symbol at this time; the focus of what later criminologists would describe as a 'moral panic'. The arbitrariness of Apache violence threatened all, as does the violence of Fantômas. But Fantômas is not simply an Apache – a member of a defined suburban street gang – nor is he the personification of the gang itself; he is a less easily definable, unstereotypical menace than that. Indeed, the young men with oiled hair who make their way to the scaffold at the end of the novel (p. 314), and whose description recalls that of the Apaches given by Paul Matter in 1907,[14] seem very different from the sophisticated criminality of Fantômas and his independence from the structures of class and geography. It has been suggested also that the real-life activities of the Bonnot gang may have helped in the novel's success, but John Ashberry points out that eleven Fantômas novels had already been written by the time the Bonnot gang hit the headlines.[15] France may have been troubled by anarchist violence from the 1890s but that is not an explanation of Fantômas. Fantômas's anarchy is of a different kind: he stands in opposition not only to the rules of society but also to the rules of science, for Fantômas could and should not exist, his presence is an affront to criminology. In *Fantômas*, crime fiction firmly re-establishes itself as an imaginative genre at a time when criminology threatened to restrict its role to that of the illustration of theory.

Criminology at the present day is a rather less dogmatic and confident discipline than it was in its infancy. Yet more recently the popular imagination has been captured by academic opinion about criminality. The abnormal chromosome theory, which for a while enjoyed some currency in academic circles, made its way into the popular consciousness – I dimly recall a television series entitled, I believe, *The XYY Man* that adopted the model as a basis for popular entertainment. More general conclusions must appear trite. It is clear that the author of crime fiction will present an image of the criminal, an image that may be influenced by the contemporary views on criminality – popular, journalistic or 'expert' – of others. It is interesting too that 'crime fiction' tends to concern itself still with only certain forms of criminal behaviour and those the most extreme ones with which the general public are statistically less likely to have direct contact. I know of no novel that centres around the motivation and detection of the motoring offender, or the man who takes home pencils from work. There may, however, be sound reasons for this!

Notes

1. C. Lombroso, *Crime: Its Causes and Remedies* (London: William Heinemann, 1911) p. xiv as quoted in D. Garland, 'The Criminal and his Science', *British Journal of Criminology*, 25 (1985) pp. 109–37, see esp. p. 111. For general accounts of the development of criminological thought, see also L. Radzinowicz and R. Hood, *A History of English Criminal Law*, vol. 5 (London: Stevens, 1986) pp. 3–88; H. Mannheim, *Comparative Criminology* (London: Routledge and Kegan Paul, 1965). On particular figures in the history of criminology, see H. Mannheim (ed.), *Pioneers in Criminology* (London: Stevens, 1960). The fullest and most incisive account of French thought on crime and criminology in the late nineteenth and early twentieth centuries is Robert A. Nye's *Crime, Madness and Politics in Modern France: The Medical Concept of National Decline* (Princeton, NJ: Princeton University Press, 1984). I would like to thank Philip Rawlings for his help in providing references.
2. M. Allain and P. Souvestre, *Fantômas*, with an introduction by J. Ashberry (London: Pan, 1987) p. 324. This edition and translation have been used throughout and page numbers within the text refer to this edition.
3. On which see Ashberry, introduction to *Fantômas*, pp. 4–5.
4. Garland, 'The Criminal and his Science', p. 109.
5. On which see, for example, S. S. Diamond and C. J. Herhold, 'Understanding Criminal Sentencing: Views from Law and Social Psychology', in G. M. Stephenson and J. M. Davies (eds), *Progress in Social Psychology*, vol. 1 (Chichester: Wiley, 1981) p. 71.
6. E. Zola, *La Bête Humaine*, trans. and with an introduction by L. W. Tancock (Harmondsworth, Middx.: Penguin, 1977) p. 9. For Zola's views on the novel and science, see his essay 'The Experimental Novel' as reproduced in G. J. Becker (ed.), *Documents of Modern*

Literary Realism (Princeton, NJ: Princeton University Press, 1963) p. 161.

7. Karl Pearson, *Nature and Nurture: The Problem of the Future*, Eugenics Laboratory Lecture Series VI (1910) p. 10 as quoted in Radzinowicz and Hood, *English Criminal Law*, p. 21.
8. Garland, 'The Criminal and his Science', p. 128.
9. M. Foucault, *Surveiller et Punir*, trans. as *Discipline and Punish: The Birth of the Prison* (Harmondsworth, Middx.: Penguin, 1977) p. 286.
10. Quoted in Garland, 'The Criminal and his Science', p. 118. On 'Social Defence', see Nye, *Crime, Madness and Politics*, chap. VI.
11. Arthur Conan Doyle, *A Study in Scarlet*, the passage is quoted in Humphrey Jennings, *Pandaemonium* (London: Pan, 1987) p. 353.
12. Garland, 'The Criminal and his Science', p. 134.
13. Ashberry, introduction to *Fantômas*, p. 3.
14. On the 'Apache' phenomenon, see Nye, *Crime, Madness and Politics*, pp. 196ff.
15. Ashberry, introduction to *Fantômas*, p. 6.

6

Real Detectives and *Fictional* Criminals

JOHN SIMONS

This essay is an account of a small subgroup of texts in the hugely varied crime-book market: biographies and memoirs of pathologists.[1] Though this would seem to be unpromising material for best-seller status in the competitive field of popular publishing, such books have, in fact, achieved considerable currency. Take the example of Professor Keith Simpson's *Forty Years of Murder*: this text was published in 1978, paperbacked in 1980 and went through no less than ten reprintings up to 1986. This history shows very clearly the appeal that such material can have to a broad reading public, as does the fact that the BBC have recently felt it worthwhile to repeat their series *Indelible Evidence* in which actors present dramatised reconstructions of crimes that were solved partly through the production of forensic evidence. I do not, however, intend to carry out a statistical survey of the currency of such books or to produce a sociological study of patterns of consumption and audience composition. Rather I intend to examine the appeal of these texts by showing how they place themselves squarely in the space, both economic and critical, usually occupied by crime fiction and how they consistently mimic the forms and ambience of *purely* fictional work. Indeed, there are direct links: Professor Simpson has published a number of crime stories under the pseudonym 'Guy Bailey', a name that, with its invocation of the court with which he is so familiar, drags his fictional work into the realm of 'fact'. My contention is that the pathologist's 'history' (a word which perhaps obscures the fact – fiction polarity) achieves its appeal precisely because it consistently conceals its own claims to the authoritative ground of documentary and thus can be read as offering the same pleasures as the most far-fetched romance of robbery and murder.

Anyone browsing in the large chain bookshops will immediately be struck by the enormous number of crime books on offer and the correspondingly large amount of shelf-space devoted to them. This is the first factor in my account of the pathologist's history: where does one find it? Practically speaking, major chains such as W. H. Smith, Menzies, Martin, Sherratt and Hughes, and Hatchard's are more or less equally divided as to whether they shelve such books with fiction or non-fiction. This confusion is perfectly justifiable: just as many flowers mimic the forms of the insects that will pollinate them and thus ensure their survival, so these books adopt the patterns of crime fiction and thus share in the same massive readership. Before me are four recently published paperbacks: Keith Simpson's *Forty Years of Murder*, Tom Tullett's *Clues to Murder*, Robert Jackson's *Francis Camps* and Sir Sydney Smith's *Mostly Murder*.[2] Two of these have covers that are almost or entirely taken up by photographs of a human skull, the other two are covered in bric-à-brac: in one case a rusty knife, bullets, broken spectacles, a decayed automatic pistol; in the other a passport, a photograph, a betting slip, a jaw bone, a dirty playing card and so on – all the paraphernalia that, taken together, signify sensation-alised crime and most of which have nothing to do with any of the cases described in the book.

Similarly, the 'blurb' that is to be found on the fronts and backs of these books leads the reader very clearly to expect the excitement of sensationalised crime and not the humdrum world of court and laboratory. The texts are 'gruesome', 'compulsive', 'macabre'; we will learn in them of murderers who 'haunt the mind', who will be 'sent to the gallows'. This is surely not the language of documentary account or social journalism, rather it is the language of fiction presenting itself as an entertaining narrative.

Much needs to be made of the packaging of these texts because it is here that the reality – fiction divide is bridged as the covers appeal explicitly to 'those fascinated by the macabre handiwork of fiends and the scientific detection that can bring them to justice'. This sentence sums up the attraction of these books to a public interested in crime fiction (which is surely the only other place where such fascinations can be catered for), and the issues it raises will be dealt with in more detail below; but, briefly, we find here the combination of lubricious fascination, moral indignation and worship of technology which is held in common between crime fiction and the pathologist's history. Of Professor Simpson it is said that: 'he spares his readers none of the chilling details, the whip-marks, the maggots, the skeletal remains'. Is this the language of objective reporting or that of sensationalised fiction?

In no case is the attempt to present documentary through the modes of fiction more marked than in the quotations from reviews cited on the back of Smith's *Mostly Murder*. These show that the newspaper reviewers took little interest in keeping Smith's work separate from the general run of crime fiction or, if they did, that the publishers were interested in maintaining a confusion: 'For the strong-stomached here is the authentic Sherlockian fascination. The embodiment of a greater-than-fiction Sherlock Holmes.' But more interesting than these remarks from the *Daily Telegraph* and the *Daily Express* is the response of the *Lancet*: 'Murders considered with a precision and elegance of style which give the author more in common with de Quincey than with most of those writers for whom murder is a stock-in-trade.' What is clear in all these remarks is the reviewer's impulse to find in the, admittedly extraordinary, accounts of Smith's cases a common ground with fictional or literary treatments of similar material. The *Lancet* in particular seems anxious totally to conflate Smith with writers of crime as literature.

Furthermore, these texts are invariably well stocked with photographs that combine dignified portraits and domestic snaps of the pathologist with gruesome images of decomposed or mutilated corpses. Smith's book actually carries on the cover a warning presented as a label or stamp informing us that 'SOME READERS MAY FIND THE ILLUSTRATIONS DISTURBING!' (note the exclamation mark). This is, of course, the strategy of pornographers and moral hypocrites, who enjoy titillating material under the guise of informing themselves. The reader is, in these texts, constantly led down the road of sadistic revelation only to be brought up short by the admonitory finger of moral stricture. True knowledge of good and evil is withheld in the pathologist's history, and so the reader, like the consumer of pornography, is led on in the constant hope of full exposure and the knowledge, born out of experience, that disappointment will inevitably ensue.

Thus, the pleasure of the pathologist's history may be seen as analogous to the pleasure of almost any *narrative* text: the pleasure of reading is, as David Lodge's Morris Zapp would have it, the voyeuristic pleasure of strip-tease. The gradual revelation of clues open up to the reader a world bounded by iniquity and intelligence as surely as the pathologist dissects the already mutilated corpse. It is fundamental to any understanding of these texts that they do enable the general reader (especially one educated in the conventions of crime fiction) to follow the technical deliberations of the pathologist through the language of the fictional detective fleshed out by copious personal information that establishes the pathologist as a presence in the text that will be more than pure authorial consciousness or fictive technician. The laboratory trace is the fictional clue. This tendency results very frequently in a highly artifical distortion of the role that forensic evidence often plays in the solution of crime, a distortion vital if the narrative function of the pathologist as hero is to be sustained. Thus, in Tullett's account of Professor J. M. Cameron's part in the investigation of the murder of Diana Davidson in 1969 it is stated that: 'The case was a triumph for forensic science, the first time that a blood spot led straight to a murderer' (*Clues to Murder*, p. 96). In fact, though the murderer was questioned by police on the basis of his having a blood group identical with that of a spot found on the murdered woman's dress, the murder was actually solved when he confessed to the crime after the police had found what seemed to be fragments of the victim's clothing in his house. Other forensic evidence was subsequently discovered to link the murderer with the crime but the actual role of the blood spot seems minimal, especially when one considers that the crime was committed in a relatively small town and that the murderer had been questioned by police before any forensic evidence was taken into account. Tullett adds:

[the murderer] had moved into the area only a few months previously and was considered something of a mystery. He had been orphaned at an early age and had been raised by the local authority and then trained at a farm school in animal husbandry. He had a passionate love for animals and country life and was extremely sensitive about cruelty to animals. He would talk freely on these subjects, but always went silent when women or sex were discussed. He lived near Eastlands Farm and had recently become friendly with a middle-aged bachelor who worked locally as a railway-crossing keeper. (*Clues to Murder*, p. 92)

Here the murderer, who was plainly an unfortunate and deprived character, is set up as a sinister newcomer of dubious sexual proclivities, a mystery man who will be unmasked by the intellect of the scientist. Tullett's account shows clearly the course of the investigation, but then deflects from this narrative to over-stress the forensic evidence and thus polarise the roles of pathologist and murderer into those of hero and villain. This is plainly essential for a satisfactory narrative and, as the *Spectator* review said 'Tullett . . . tells his stories lucidly.' In spite of the fact that the careful reader can see clearly how the murder was solved, the aesthetics of the pathologist's history demand that this be obscured in favour of a clear narrative line that establishes the pathologist as protagonist and hero and changes 'fact' into *story*.

Thus the text folds in upon itself and entices the reader into an essentially fictional world that belies the book's documentary status. The biographers strive for this effect and when it proves difficult to achieve they fall into an impasse. Robert Jackson was beset by problems in his work on Francis Camps, whose eccentric and, it seems, unreliable behaviour made it difficult to sustain any mythology of heroism. As Simpson pointed out:

> Edgar Lustgarten, himself an experienced counsel with an astute eye for detail, commented, some years later, in reviewing Robert Jackson's biography of Camps, that though setting out confidently enough, Jackson was 'first surprised, then halted, finally overwhelmed, by unfavourable evidence from sources unimpeachable' that the subject of his biography was not as sound as a Crown pathologist is expected to be. (*Forty Years of Murder*, p. 232)

These remarks apply specifically to the biographer, but it is noteworthy that Smith and Simpson, who wrote their own memoirs, share in the tendency to appropriate the ethos of fiction. This is particularly true of Smith, whose book was singled out above as one that attracted reviewers particularly keen to compare him with Sherlock Holmes. The comparison is not so far-fetched, for Smith was taught surgery by George Chiene who regaled him with a fund of anecdotes about the legendary Joseph Bell, the surgeon who employed Conan Doyle as a clerk and whose deductive powers supposedly established the Holmesian method:

> 'Why', said a fellow-guest at a dinner party, 'Dr Bell might almost be Sherlock Holmes.'
> 'Madam,' Dr Bell replied, 'I am Sherlock Holmes.'[3]

Holmesian deduction is, in fact, frequently dependent on the same sort of narrative sleight of hand that made the blood spot seem more

important than it was in Tullett's account of the Davidson murder
and Bell himself spoke of 'the cataract of drivel for which Conan
Doyle is responsible' (*Mostly Murder*, p. 29), but the analogy
between Holmes and the pathologist is so persuasive that to lose it
would break the strong bond between autobiography and fiction.
Smith uses his account of Bell's career as the occasion for a
mediation on Conan Doyle's fiction that makes some telling points
in the context of the present analysis:

> Therein lies the value of the Sherlock Holmes stories apart from
> their excellent entertainment. Today criminal investigation is a
> science, and the plodding policeman gaping admiringly at the
> gifted amateur is an anachronism. This was not always so and the
> change owes much to the influence of Sherlock Holmes. An
> author may feel satisfaction when his fiction is accepted as true to
> life: Conan Doyle had the rare, perhaps unique, distinction of
> seeing life become true to his fiction.   (*Mostly Murder*, pp. 30–1)

Smith clearly understood the complexities of the relationship that a
work of his kind enjoys with fiction, especially where the idea of
truth as a concept that might develop out of a misapprehended
fiction is concerned. It is, therefore, no surprise when we find that
Smith's book is in a series called 'True Crime', the back pages of
which carry advertisements for the same publisher's series 'Crime
Fiction'.

The prefatory material to Smith's book is also revealing. Smith
himself says that: 'The book consists mainly of the story of these
cases – a plain unvarnished tale without embellishment or emotion'
(*Mostly Murder*, p. 7). Simpson, however, who provided a foreword
to the reissue of 1973 (reprinted twice in 1984 and again in 1986)
goes much further:

> His sparkle and enthusiasm turned the most drab situation into a
> tale . . . he retained a remarkable 'nose' for a good story . . . he
> wove stories from murders . . . all told with an effervescence that
> compels reading . . . recounting his tales with sparkle and his
> own unquenchable enthusiasm   (*Mostly Murder*, pp. 5–6)

Clearly, Simpson sees Smith's autobiography as more than documentary and expects that it will be read mainly for the aesthetic
potential of its narratives. It will be seen that in spite of Smith's own

disclaimer (very much like that of the ironic novelist), the book as narrative predominates over the book as documentary. We should certainly take Simpson seriously and use his thoughts here as a guide for the reading of his own book, expecting to find in it the traces of an authorial activity designed to develop the aesthetics of narrative. This expectation is not disappointed in Simpson's report on the sadistic murderer Heath:

> 'Isn't your name Heath?' he interrupted.
> Heath denied it but found the suggestion so chilling that he said he was going back to his hotel for his jacket. The police obligingly fetched it for him. . . . Heath was still denying he had killed Margery Gardner when a swarm of flies behind some rhododendron bushes led to the discovery of Doreen Marshall's mutilated naked body in Branksome Chine. (*Forty Years of Murder*, pp. 128–9)

Here the ironies of the first three sentences establish the mood for a narrative that culminates in the attempt to set up a time-scheme strictly unnecessary for the straightforward recounting of a case study but highly effective in the context of a fictional narrative. Indeed, Simpson's own description of Heath, 'Few men look handsome and debonair in the dock of No. 1 court at the Old Bailey, but this sub-human Heath managed it' (*Forty Years of Murder*, p. 129), seems more consistent with the stance of the imaginative writer than of the scientist called to give technical evidence as an expert.

> 1876: The publication of Cesare Lombroso's *The Criminal Man*. Lombroso, an Italian physician performs an autopsy on the body of the dreaded brigand Vilella when struck by what he perceives as the apelike structure of the criminal's skull. Lombroso gazes upon this, the object of the first positive criminological investigation.[4]

Both Simpson's text and the above citation from a contemporary work on post-modernism demonstrate clearly the point at which the objectivity of the scientist exceeds the discursive limits that divide the scientific, the rational and the real from the notionally opposing domain of the ideological, the imaginative and the fictional. Both Simpson and Lombroso make sense of their own monstrous knowledge by exploding it out of the scientific, and therefore non-juridical, paradigm and into that of everyday moral platitudes, where it can be fixed and exorcised. This too is surely the pleasure of crime fiction. Here the cruel reality of everyday crime is defused by incorporation into a highly conventional and value-loaded realm of narrative. As Smith suggested:

> To Holmes's three qualities necessary for a successful detective he might have added a fourth – the power of constructive imagination, always strictly controlled by intellect, an essential quality when there are no more facts to be observed and no further inferences to be drawn. (*Mostly Murder*, p. 31)

So the role of the pathologist is not merely that of technician and analyst, it is also that of narrator: where science fails, aesthetic organisation is expected to take over and the task of forensic investigation is transformed into one of story-telling. The story must satisfy the desire for an unveiling, an identification and a naming. In the fictional crime story this unmasking is provided vicariously in the realm of the unreal, and it is surely the case that the pathological historian's appropriation of the fictional is directly related to an unwillingness, both public and individual, to face the ineffable facts of murder. *Truth* is only possible here through the mediation of a conventionalised poetics of narrative that allows space for appropriate *frissons*, titillations and judgements. All readers know that it is aesthetic pattern, not content, that really communicates.

This discussion has led into the question of form and it is proper to consider this in some more detail. Just as Michael Shepherd has recently connected Freud's psychoanalysis with Holmesian deduction, identifying the common ground as a form of scientific method combined with a mythopoeic imagination, so we find Jackson comparing the contrivances of Edgar Wallace with the science of Francis Camps:

> Before the celebrated Edgar Wallace became a household name, he kept the pot boiling by writing thrillers in serial form. A typical situation would arise when the hero had been trapped in a snake-pit twenty feet deep which men armed with rifles were guarding. . . . A journalist . . . asked how on earth Wallace would extricate his hero. Wallace advised his colleague to watch how

easy it would be the following week. The journalist opened the magazine to see the solution. 'With one bound our hero was free. . .'   (*Francis Camps*, pp. 126–7)

Jackson then recounts the case of Albert Kemp, whose wife had been found dead in a trunk with a stocking knotted around her neck. Camps saved Kemp from a conviction for murder by 'pointing out what may have happened' (*Francis Camps*, p. 127). In fact, if Jackson's account is accurate, what Camps pointed out was that the victim had been asphyxiated – a fact that seems to have been clear to everyone – and that the stocking may well have been added after death, as Kemp claimed. Kemp was acquitted after the following incident:

> The jury deliberated for two hours twenty-five minutes, and returned with a request for Camps' evidence to be read over to them again. This was not possible. Camps had left for another session of work and had taken with him the only transcript of his evidence. The judge said he would help the jury by reading over his own notes and after this had been done the verdict was 'not guilty'.   (*Francis Camps*, pp. 131–2)

It will be seen that one of two things is happening here: either in his desire to simplify matters and thus tell a good story Jackson is not doing Camps justice, or the reporting is accurate and Camps's part was relatively trivial but is being over-emphasised to stress his position as the book's hero. It is plainly significant that this rather weak tale needs to be prefaced by the example from Edgar Wallace: it was not Kemp who needed a Wallace-like contrivance but Jackson who has chosen some fairly drab material from which to construct an exciting and impressive tale.

What all this amounts to is that to reach the large reading public of crime fiction the pathologist's history must offer the same pleasures. Pfohl and Gordon offer the following as the pleasures of criminology and we may consider whether these are the same as the pleasures of the pathologist's history and the crime story: sadism, surveillance, the truth of the normal subject.[5] What is bounded by these three pleasures is essentially a discourse of mastery that penetrates and isolates through sadism, objectifies and imprisons through surveillance and orders through truth. I have already suggested that there is a strong sadistic urge in the pathologist's history and this is surely present in many crime fictions. The pathologist is a master of surveillance as he opens up the crime to public gaze, finding it in the dissected body of the victim and, ironically, in the post-mortem of the convicted killer; a symbolic cleansing that takes the place of quartering and is pounced on as a symbol by the watchful author as the occasion of a particularly nasty observation:

> Before the post mortem reports went into the archives, the final notes could be assembled concerning the last minutes in the lives of the condemned man. It was found that Godar had had some whisky with his breakfast, Cull had had neither whisky nor breakfast and Muldourney and Johnson had faced breakfast but had done without the last traditional glass of whisky. It is doubtful whether any of the many murderers on whom Camps performed post mortems ever drank their last drink as a toast.   (*Francis Camps*, p. 240)

In crime fiction, this presentation of the victim's and murderer's bodies as actors in a theatre of cruelty is replicated but now vicariously without the sustaining fantasy that beneath the levels of the aesthetic lurks a real crime. Both history and fiction act as a purgative anatomy in which the inspection of dissected crime deflects attention from the pleasures that impel both dissection and voyeurism. This leads us to the pleasure of truth and the way that this term, which occupies the dual ground of concept and value legitimates the power that separates the normal from the perverted; the reader from the criminal. The pleasure of truth operates in both history and fiction to privilege the reader to a point where he or she can claim normality as a self-defining quality beyond the reach of any authenticating power: outside lurks the imprisoned criminal. The reader is also impelled to an identification with a victim whose body has been broken in a perverse version of the due process of legal dissection and now, through an articulation of sadism, surveillance and truth, achieves a pleasure which would do credit to the court of the Mikado.

The history and the fiction come together through a shared set of conventions and a shared ethos. In particular, rivalry and fame and the worship of intellect and ingenuity seem almost inevitably to be held in common. It is not so much that every crime fiction and every pathologist's history works through these conventions as much as that they combine as the generic markers of a discourse on crime. That such markers enter conciousness can be seen in the coroner Bentley Purchase's foreword to Tullett and Browne's biography of Sir Bernard Spilsbury: 'The word Spilsbury is simply a name to the general public. It tends to connote violent or mysterious death. It would not be surprising if it also connoted a man of exceptional ability but without much humanity' (*Sir Bernard Spilsbury*, p. 5). It is clear that Spilsbury, a 'real' person, has been converted through the fictionalising glamour of fame into a pure signifier of murder, and it is interesting that Purchase has reversed the expected order of the terms 'word' and 'name' in his observation. The role of the biographer is to replace the meaning (that is, the truth) that has been drained out of the word as a result of this process. This is important because it discloses a gap between perception and aesthetic realisation that may be bridged through the mediation of the book.

The stuff of the pathologist's history, as of the crime story, is the progressive revelation of meaning out of seemingly meaningless clues and the confrontation of crime and criminal on the public stage of the court. The pathologist will stand opposed to the criminal, revealing what the criminal has attempted to conceal; but, at the same time, pathologists themselves may become rivals. Smith and Simpson, significantly the pathologists who wrote their own memoirs, are especially keen to chart the passage of professional rivalries: in the former case with Spilsbury, in the latter with Camps. In both cases the pathologists reveal their readiness to cast both themselves and their rival in moulds that are eminently suited to formulaic fiction and consistently imply that they use the legal process as a stage on which to practise rhetoric and to confirm their own function in the juridical ritual. At all times the need for a satisfying narrative appears to take precedence over other consider-ations, and anyone reading a number of pathologists' histories will be struck by the way in which the scientists take a more than objective interest in the outcome of cases. In Simpson's account of his rivalry of Camps, an account traced through his various humiliations of Camps in court-room confrontations, professional and scientific disagreements are ultimately presented as clashes of personality that are more the stuff of the fiction writer than the expert witness.

Throughout the pathologist's history, the cleverness of the protagonist, his doggedness in the unravelling of bewildering clues and his tenacity in the pursuit of truth are rewarded by the fame that also attends the detectives of fiction. Indeed, public recognition or other reward is fundamental to this highly conventional discourse. The reader may exit from the text with a reinforced knowledge of truth achieved through the sublimation of sadism and voyeurism. He or she may now appear as 'normal', for sadism and voyeurism, the 'perversions' of the criminal, have been legitimised through the narrative. In other words, a satisfyingly complete story of transgression, retribution and reward has been able to compensate not only for the disturbing images of mutilation and incompleteness that it has contained but also for the dangerous urges it has both provoked and fulfilled.

In conclusion then, the positioning of the pathologist's history in the crime fiction market may be seen to have been achieved by means of the history's appropriation of the pleasures and structures of the fiction. In particular, the history must be seen as highly selective, and therefore aesthetic, in so far as it does not contain an accurate portrait of the pathologist's career and concerns itself with only a minuscule proportion of his work: the sensational murder. In the memoirs especially there is a strong authorial presence that operates a policy of selection and arrangement where concerns of ideology and aesthetics predominate over the need for objective documentation. This is almost inevitably the case with memoirs, but when the memoir falls into a field already generously provided with conventional markers it appears that fiction and history will always become co-extensive. This is reinforced when we encounter the writer's glee in his own cleverness at convicting or acquitting criminals even though it is judgement not evidence that brings this about. The 'blurb' of Simpson's book puts the body count very much in favour of the prosecution: 'his celebrated investigations . . . which proved the innocence of so many men and women . . . and sent so many more to the gallows'. This sort of thing does not inspire confidence in any righteous espousal of the virtues of truth and scientific objectivity, but it makes an excellent story, which, it is to be hoped, is kept on the pages of the memoir and not brought into court. One is forcibly struck by the difficulty of maintaining a meaningful distinction between fact and fiction when confronted with these cases. The texts are fully explicit in their connections with the fiction that shadows them; and in their display of the mastery that the full force of an engagement with law gives them, they enter directly that mastery of experience which the mediation of fiction gives to both writer and reader.

Notes

1. The texts on which this chapter is based are as follows: K. Simpson, *Forty Years of Murder* (London: Harrap, 1986); T. Tullett, *Clues to Murder* (London: Grafton, 1987); R. Jackson, *Francis Camps* (London: Granada, 1983); S. Smith, *Mostly Murder* (London: Granada, 1986); D. Browne and E. V. Tullett, *Sir Bernard Spilsbury* (London: Harrap, 1951). Subsequent references to these books are given in the text.

2. The recent paperback reissue of Browne and Tullett's book on Spilsbury also has a cover taken up entirely with a photograph of a skull.

3. Quoted in M. Shepherd, *Sherlock Holmes and the Case of Dr Freud* (London: Tavistock, 1985) p. 20. Shepherd points out that the Holmesian method is really only logical in the context of the Holmesian myth and that his solutions are by no means so evident as is often claimed, relying more on illogic and intuition than any more rational skills. I have already mentioned Tullett's treatment of Cameron's part in the Douglas case as an example of the tendency for pathologists to be presented as decisive in the solution of crimes, but for a further illustration of the way in which forensic evidence is presented as far more important than it actually appears to have been, readers should consult Simpson's account of 'the wigwam murder' (*Forty Years of Murder*, pp. 71–82) where again forensic evidence, which was plainly viewed with grave suspicion by the judge, is cited in great detail when, again, it has really been a corroborative aspect instrumental in pressurising the accused into making an inconsistent statement and not a factor that clinched an otherwise uncertain conviction.

4. S. Pfohl and A. Gordon, 'Criminological Displacements: a Sociological Deconstruction', in A. and M. Kroker, *Body Invaders* (London: Macmillan, 1988) p. 236.

5. Pfohl and Gordon, 'Criminological Displacements', pp. 230–1.

7

Unravelling a Web: Writer versus Reader in Edgar Allan Poe's Tales of Detection

FFRANGCON C. LEWIS

I

On 9 August 1846, Edgar Allan Poe wrote a grateful letter to his friend Philip Pendleton Cooke, in which he made a significant assessment of his own 'ratiocinative', or detective, tales:

> Thank you for the compliments. Were I in a serious humor just now, I would tell you[,] frankly, how your words of appreciation make my nerves thrill – not because you praise me (for others have praised me more lavishly) but because I feel that you comprehend and discriminate. You are right about the hair-splitting of my French friend: – that is all done for effect. These tales of ratiocination owe their popularity to being something in a new key. I do not mean to say that they are not ingenious – but people think them more ingenious than they are – on account of their method and *air* of method. In 'The Murders in the Rue Morgue', for instance, where is the ingenuity of unravelling a web which you yourself (the author) have woven for the express purpose of unravelling? The reader is made to confound the ingenuity of the supposititious Dupin with that of the writer of the story.[1]

Poe's words indicate, indeed, that the reader is expected to admire the 'ingenuity' of C. Auguste Dupin, and to employ powers of comprehension and discrimination, but his statement also functions as a warning against any simplistic identification of Poe with his 'French friend'. What appears, in Dupin's operations, to be logic, will at least sometimes be mere 'hair-splitting', and 'method' may turn out to be counterfeit rather than genuine intellectual

97

currency. The extract also makes it plain that Poe is by no means always to be found 'in a serious humor', and that he is ready to manipulate the reader's responses in a playful or mischievous manner. Poe points out the circularity and confidence-trickery of his weaving a web of obfuscatory spider's silk solely that his detective-hero may unravel it, thus suggesting that his tales of detection may best be approached as a ritual contest between the author, as spider, and the unwary reader, as increasingly entrapped fly. The reader who is most content to trust Poe's 'air of method' will remain least aware of the satirical or metaphysical implications of the tales. In 'The Murders in the Rue Morgue' (1841), 'The Mystery of Marie Roget' (1843) and 'The Purloined Letter' (1844), Poe is as much concerned with what is *not* resolved as he is to invest Dupin with a seemingly preternatural combination of 'the reasoning [and the] imaginative faculties'.[2] Dupin, the French aristocrat fallen on hard times, hiding behind his dark glasses, may be a truth-seeker, but his apparently conclusive success impresses itself on the Prefect of Police and on the narrator far more than it does on Poe himself, who seems to feel that the search for truth is necessarily *inconclusive*. Poe remains subtly aloof from Dupin's procedures, even as he encourages the reader to endorse the ratiocinative Frenchman's triumphs, and this equivocal stance is also characteristic of Poe's treatment of William Legrand and his narrator in 'The Gold-Bug' (1843). Poe's tone in these tales of detection is often sardonic, suggesting a sarcastic or satirical face behind the earnest narrator's mask. Two later stories, 'Thou Art the Man' and 'The Oblong Box', are also in their way stories of detection, although in them the comic or satirical voice is more clearly dominant.[3]

Poe declared, in one version of his review of Hawthorne's *Twice-Told Tales*, that 'Truth is often . . . the aim of the tale. Some of the finest tales are tales of ratiocination', and that the prose tale was 'more appreciable by the mass of mankind' than poetry. However, Poe also hints at his impatience with such an audience, and at the shifting nature of his own approach, when he argues that the writer of tales 'may bring to his theme a vast variety of modes or inflections of thought and expression'. Still more relevantly to a consideration of Poe's own tales, he isolates three such modes: 'the ratiocinative, . . . the sarcastic or the humorous'. Close examination of the stories of detection suggests that he often employed all three of these conflicting 'inflections'. Later in the same review, Poe voices an anxiety about Hawthorne's story 'The Minister's Black Veil': 'to the rabble its exquisite skill will be *caviare*. The *obvious* meaning . . . will be found to smother its insinuated one.' Poe's patrician tone suggests why he selected an 'illustrious' background for his detective, but it is his insistence on the conflict between overt and covert meanings that is so instructive. In a different version of the same review, Poe objected to allegory, but suggested one way in which it might be legitimately employed: 'Where the suggested meaning runs through the obvious one in a *very* profound under-current so as never to interfere with the upper one without our own volition, so as never to show itself unless *called* to the surface'.[4]

Dupin, whom one critic has ventured to call 'an allegorical figure',[5] develops the sense in which the reader may experience the interplay of these submerged and superficial currents:

> The material world . . . abounds with very strict analogies to the immaterial; and thus some color of truth has been given to the rhetorical dogma that metaphor or simile, may be made to strengthen an argument, as well as to embellish a description. ('The Purloined Letter', iii, p. 989)[6]

Just as Dupin feels that close observation of the 'material world' may reveal the laws of the 'immaterial world', so Poe's fiction 'leaves in the mind of him who contemplates it with a kindred art'[7] a sense of the insinuated or symbolic undercurrents that play powerfully below the superficial movement of Dupin's detective denouements.

'The Murders in the Rue Morgue' and 'The Purloined Letter' are the two most famous examples of Poe's 'ratiocinative' genre, and, partly because of the different appearance of the crimes with which they deal, they offer a complementary study of Poe's techniques.

II

It has often been suggested that the narrator of 'The Murders in the Rue Morgue' is a precursor of Conan Doyle's Watson, particularly in the reverential attitude he adopts towards his detective-mentor. Certainly, Poe intended that the narrator should comprehend Dupin's ratiocination slowly enough for most readers to feel that they could keep pace, but this function should not obscure what the narrator actually *shares* with Dupin.

They first met at 'an obscure library' where they were both 'in search of the same very rare and very remarkable volume': this coincidence, claims the narrator, brought them into 'closer communion'. The name of the work is never disclosed, and the reader is left to infer that Dupin and the narrator share a desire to attain an unspecified wisdom or truth. The spiritual connotations of their friendship, or 'communion', are heavily underscored, as the narrator seems to experience an almost numinous shock of recognition: 'above all, I felt my soul enkindled within me by the wild fervor, and the vivid freshness of his imagination' (ii, p. 532). Even though the narrator expresses an adulation of Monsieur Dupin when he describes 'the society of such a man' as 'a treasure beyond price', he nevertheless refers, on more equal terms, to 'the rather fantastic gloom of their common temper'. The narrator fancies further that the world would have regarded them *both* as 'madmen' and confesses that he has deliberately arranged their 'perfect' seclusion: 'We existed within ourselves alone.' It is the prospect of this communion of souls that attracts the narrator (and also Dupin), rather than the social or economic status of the fallen aristocrat and the anonymous gentleman-narrator.

The narrator experiences an odd combination of mutuality and submission in his friendship with Dupin: giving himself up to the detective 'with a perfect abandon', he notes that they 'busied' themselves 'in dreams' and sought in the 'true Darkness' of the Parisian night 'that infinity of mental excitement which quiet observation can afford'. This paradoxical condition resembles the interior exploration that the narrator of 'The Fall of the House of Usher' undergoes when summoned by his childhood friend, Roderick Usher.[8] Early in the tale, Dupin displays his imaginative intelligence by 'reading' the narrator's mind, and the reader is allowed to read a paragraph of the narrator's inconsequential flow of consciousness. By this means, however, Poe hints that the story itself is a further exploration of the interior-self or soul of the narrator, and that the identity of the 'very rare and very remarkable volume' is not, after all, so inscrutable.[9]

Dupin has a most ambivalent relation to the economic and social world: 'by a variety of untoward events', he has become so poor 'that the energy of his character succumbed beneath it, and he ceased to bestir himself in the world, or to care for the retrieval of his fortunes'. Yet he still retains 'a small remnant of his patrimony' and, despite the ostensible failure of his moral energy, is able to practise 'a rigorous economy' in order 'to procure the necessaries of life,

without troubling himself about its superfluities'. Dupin's circumstances thus result from – and represent – a society in a turmoil of
change, while at the same time he becomes separated from any
single identifiable stratum of it. The narrator is perhaps less
patrician in his origins than Dupin, and less impoverished, though
he writes evasively of his 'worldly circumstances' as being only
somewhat 'less embarrassed' than Dupin's. At all events, it is the
narrator who preserves their economic link with Paris by paying
the rent for their 'time-eaten and grotesque mansion', a building
that is 'tottering to its fall in a retired and desolate portion of the
Faubourg St Germain'.

In his ability to 'solve' the murders in the Rue Morgue, Dupin
might be seen as a 'remnant' of the values of the aristocratic order,
which even in decay, is the only instrument that can reimpose a
moral order on a materialistic world now belonging to the bourgeoisie. Thus, Poe might be interpreted as wishing to resist the
social, political and economic changes taking place in the world
around him. Such a view, however, assumes that Poe feels, as his
narrator does, that Dupin *has* 'solved' the murders and that social
stability and moral order *have* been restored.[10] A careful examination of the tale suggests instead that nothing of real significance has
been resolved, and that beyond his ravelling and unravelling web,
Poe is insisting upon the metaphysical intractability of the problems rather than on the social splendour of Dupin's solutions.

Into the men's seclusion comes the sensational news of the brutal
murders of Madame and Mademoiselle L'Espanaye, and Dupin's
initial reaction is revealingly equivocal: he suggests that an
investigation will afford them 'amusement', while he is also
impelled by the arrest of the innocent bank-clerk Le Bon. Le Bon
('The Good') has apparently done Dupin a favour, for which Dupin
is 'not ungrateful'. The spirit of his enquiry is therefore analogous
to the likely disposition of the reader of this magazine-story: a
desire to be amused, sitting uneasily with a lip-service allegiance to
the forces of an undefined 'Good'. Poe was obviously aware of the
American public's appetite for – and fear of – sensational and lurid
acts of violence, as his later fictionalising of the notorious Mary
Rogers case indicates, and he was equally clearly willing to cater for
that appetite. The important point is that his fiction explores the
significance of that violence, and of the public's desire to be 'amused'
by it, and to experience it vicariously. 'The Murders in the Rue
Morgue' is flawed, according to Thomas Mabbott, because of the

nature of the murders: 'The piece has a fault, shared by too many later detective stories, of one too gory passage' (ii, p. 521). However, it is precisely the 'outré' nature of the crime (as Dupin defines it) that determines the meaning of the entire story.

The victims are both female, and they have resided in an apartment similar to that occupied by Dupin and the narrator: the wholly cerebral nature of the activity in the male apartment contrasts starkly with the corporeal mutilation and dismember-ment of the women, which is the signal feature of this crime. This dichotomy of head and body is gruesomely enacted by the razor-stroke that ultimately causes the mother's decapitation. The nubile daughter has swooned at the first sight of the primitive beast, which, having dispatched the protecting mother, then discloses its essential nature:

> The sight of blood inflamed its anger into phrenzy. Gnashing its teeth, and flashing fire from its eyes, it flew upon the body of the girl, and imbedded its fearful talons in her throat, retaining its grasp until she expired. (ii, p. 567)

It has been observed that Poe's 'imagery of death often bears an obvious sexual connotation which does not require the extremes of Freudian theory for understanding', and that, in much American fiction of the period, 'sexual sin *meant* death, and, to a certain extent, killing *meant* sexual possession'. Both comments shed light on Mlle L'Espanaye's death, but the same critic provides an even better clue when he claims of the literary symbolism of the period in general: 'Social disorganization could be represented in its ultimate form in the union of sex and death.'[11]

In this connection, the history of the house in the Rue Morgue becomes relevant. Madame L'Espanaye owned the property, but had formerly let it to a 'jeweller', whom she accused of 'abuse of the premises' (ii, p. 539). Symbolically, the women themselves, and especially the daughter, are jewels, or 'treasure beyond price', to recall the phrase that the narrator applied to Dupin's companion-ship. Nothing is disclosed about the occupations of the mother and daughter, although one Pauline Dubourg claimed that the mother 'told fortunes for a living' (ii, p. 539), a gift that suggests an interesting counterpoint to Dupin's apparent ability to read men's minds. What is certain is that this subtle symbolism of the jewel or treasure unites the realms of money, sexuality and perception in the story: the bank clerk Le Bon has been incarcerated because the police have assumed a financial motive for the murder; the women live in a house formerly occupied by a jeweller; and the narrator is in pursuit of a 'treasure beyond price'. Even the orang-utan itself is attracted to the house by a symbolic 'jewel':

> The streets were profoundly quiet, as it was nearly three o'clock in the morning. In passing down an alley in the rear of the Rue Morgue, the fugitive's attention was arrested by a light gleaming from the open window of Madam L'Espanaye's chamber, in the fourth storey of her house.   (ii, p. 565)

The narrator's desire for Dupin's company, and Dupin's desire for 'amusement' in his investigation, represent two forms of *quest* in the story, and the orang-utan's seemingly fortuitous attraction to the gleaming light indicates another. The sailor's procurement of the orang-utan in the first place suggests still another: as one of a party of men in Borneo, the sailor had 'passed into the interior on an excursion of pleasure'. Poe guides the narrator and the reader on just such an interior excursion. The beast has become the sailor's 'exclusive possession', and one that he keeps 'carefully secluded', a seclusion mirroring that of Dupin with the narrator, and that of the ladies L'Espanaye. The sailor's journey into the 'interior' has immediate financial implications, however: he is a poor man, and, in contrast to the genteel impoverishment of Dupin, seeks riches. Thus, although he initially hides the orang-utan from the Parisian public, 'his ultimate design was to sell it' to them (ii, p. 564).

Poe's precise choice of the beast's species is crucial, in that he has determined that the murderer shall be non-human, but as closely related to *Homo sapiens* as possible. As Mabbott shows, interest in orang-utans, or 'men of the forest', ran high during this period, both in France (Poe's fictional setting), and in America itself:

> Georges Cuvier (1769–1832), the great French natural historian, . . . placed the Orang immediately after Man.
> . . . Poe himself read the following from Thomas Wyatt's compilation *A Synopsis of Natural History* . . . (Philadelphia. 1839) . . . 'Of all animals, the ourang is considered as approaching most nearly to man in the form of his head, height of forehead and volume of brain.   (ii, p. 573–4)

Indeed, Poe later exploited his readers' awareness of the confusing similarity of men and orang-utans in the comic tales 'The System of

Doctor Tarr and Professor Fether' (1845) and 'Hop-Frog' (1849), and, as Mabbott notes, 'Orangs were popular in America, having been occasionally exhibited as early as 1831' (ii, p. 524). The sailor's plan of selling the ape is well founded in fact, but in symbolic terms it suggests Man's desire to make a pact between the inner, un-governed and vigorous nature, and the external, organised and controlled social world. Dupin's investigation into the crime, and the 'method' by which he arrives at his solution, appear to be a celebration of a synthesis between intuition and rationality, and a reconciliation of 'head' and 'heart'. Yet there is a 'profound undercurrent' in the story that persistently questions this appearance.

It is above all the contradictory evidence of the witnesses – or audience – that gives Dupin a vital clue to the identity of the killer. The same babel of evidence that bewilders the Prefect of Police enables Dupin to discover the truth. Each of the witnesses repre-sents one of 'the five great divisions of Europe', and each is convinced that the 'high-pitched' voice he or she has heard at the scene of the crime does not belong to their own nation, but has spoken in the language of one of the *other* European nations, and this conflict prompts Dupin to speculate that the perpetrator is not European at all. His discovery of the severed nail and the hidden spring in the window of the locked room provides him with the killer's mode of entry and exit, and stresses Dupin's allegiance to rational solutions: he discovers the truth partly *because* he is unprepared to believe that the murders have been committed by a supernatural agent. Inspection of the mutilation of the corpses convinces him of the superhuman strength of their assailant, and the difficulty of reaching the fourth-storey window attests to the criminal's prodigious agility. A piece of forensic evidence clinches the matter even for the slow-witted narrator: the discovery of a tuft of hair that is demonstrably *not* human.[12] The finding of a sailor's knot in a piece of ribbon proves likewise that the inhuman criminal has a human companion. Dupin's procedure thus far seems entirely rational (although one might wonder why the fourth-floor window were fitted with hidden springs!) and he goes on to test his hypothesis and ensnare the sailor by placing an advertisement in the press to the effect that an orang-utan has been found, and will be returned to its rightful owner upon demand. It is, of course, a gamble, but one that Dupin takes on the basis of identifying himself with the sailor, and of reading his mind. Thus, Dupin calculates that the sailor was agile enough to reach the window by climbing the lightning-rod, but that only the orang-utan was physically able to climb into the room. Since the witnesses had heard *two* voices, it followed that the sailor had witnessed the murders but had been unable to prevent them: the sailor had thus fled the scene, too horrified to pursue the beast further. Dupin also calculates, correctly and cynically, that the sailor will reclaim his property in order to profit from its subsequent sale.

Despite this apparent triumph of observation and intuition, Dupin's procedure, the sailor's confession and the consequences of the resolution of the case all suggest darker meanings than the narrator acknowledges. The witnesses are unanimous that the words 'sacré', 'diable' and 'mon Dieu' were uttered by the second voice, evidence that convinces Dupin that the sailor has been only a horrified witness of the appalling outrage, and Poe ensures that Dupin declares of the interjection 'mon Dieu!': 'Upon these two words . . . I have mainly built my hopes of a full solution of the riddle' (II, p. 560).

Despite the rationality of Dupin's inquiry, these expressions imply a metaphysical or spiritual framework within which human beings seek to understand and control evil. It is important to remember that each witness has attributed the murderous orang-utan's cries to an alien, but none the less human, language. What the conflicting testimony reveals, of course, is that each witness is unwilling to acknowledge that evil could have been perpetrated by one like him or herself, but is eager to believe that it *could* have been committed by an outsider. Thus, as Dupin says of the sailor, each of the witnesses is, symbolically, 'cognizant' of the evil, but each wishes to feel 'innocent' of it, and this knowing innocence or naïve complicity is, in turn, the position that readers of detective fiction wish to occupy. In acquiescing to the solution that Poe magically produces from Dupin's ratiocination, the readers are offered the relief of externalising their sense of evil – they are not responsible for their terrifying world, and the terror can be exorcised by rational means. Yet Poe goes out of his way to imply that such reaching for relief is dishonest, that the responsibility for the evil lies *within*, and that it is active precisely to the extent that its existence is denied and repressed.

The narrator and sailor have both discovered repressed and more powerful versions of themselves – the narrator in Dupin and the sailor in his beast from 'the interior'. The sailor, peering helplessly through the lady's bedroom window, exchanges glances with the beast as it leaps upon the prostrate body of the young girl: 'Its wandering and wild glances fell at this moment upon the head of the bed over which the face of its master, rigid with horror, was just discernible' (II, p. 567). The sailor's dream-like loss of control over the beast was initially caused by the orang-utan's propensity for imitating, or impersonating, its human keeper: 'Razor in hand, fully lathered, it was sitting before a looking-glass, attempting the operation of shaving, in which it had no doubt previously watched its master through the keyhole of the closet' (II, p. 565). Thus, the prelude to the murders is the orang-utan's comical yet appalling attempt to shave the face of Madame L'Espanaye. The symbolism of social disorganisation reaches its climax at this point, as the beast blunders across all boundaries, confounding male and female genders, and providing, in his savage mimicry of a 'civilising' ritual, an ironic mirror for the sailor (and the reader) to stare into.

At this point, the narrator's description of Dupin's manner of speaking when inspired becomes relevant:

> Dupin went on, very much as if in a soliloquy. I have already spoken of his abstract manner at such times. His discourse was addressed to myself; but his voice, although by no means loud, had that intonation which is commonly employed in speaking to someone at a great distance. His eyes, vacant in expression, regarded only the wall.   (II, p. 548)

Dupin crosses all boundaries here, just as the sailor has done geographically and as the hapless orang-utan has done in all senses. The detective speaks to himself, yet also to the narrator, and beyond him to an audience 'at a great distance' (the reader, of course!). The narrator, staring into Dupin's vacant eyes, has an experience as unnerving (if not as appalling) as the sailor's looking into the eyes of his maddened and terrified beast. To resolve the case, Dupin advertises, in the significantly named *Le Monde*, that he has captured the orang-utan. Thus, Dupin informs the world (falsely) that the wild beast is in his possession, and the symbolic truth of this ruse is suggested when he confronts the sailor: 'Upon my word, I almost envy you the possession of him; a remarkably fine, and no doubt, a very valuable animal' (II, p. 562).

The sailor has possessed, but lost control of, a beast that has committed murder; Dupin pretends to possess and control a beast that in fact he has never seen! Both men are armed: the sailor with an appropriately phallic 'huge oaken cudgel', and Dupin with the more 'civilised' and lethal pistol. Dupin locks the door and confronts the sailor with the fact of the crime: this room is now sealed, and the murders, committed in another locked room, in the street of death, now confront Dupin and the narrator in the shape of the sailor's deathly expression. The detective has already chosen to believe in the sailor's innocence:

> Of the worst portion of the crimes committed, it is probable that he is innocent. I hope that I am right in this supposition, for upon it I build my expectation of reading the entire riddle. I look for the man here – in this room – every moment. (II, p. 548)

Psychologically, the cerebral seclusion of Dupin and the narrator must indeed search for the physical man at 'every moment', and the intellect of man needs to be able to find a means of justifying the desires that it regards as evil and outrageous. Once the sailor can be established as 'cognizant' but 'innocent' of the crime, the mind can contemplate itself with an assumed tranquillity once more. Thus, unlike the crowd who stare up at the house in the Rue Morgue with an 'objectless curiosity', as if transfixed by evil, Dupin scrutinises it wilfully, seeking the means to project the source of the evil beyond himself, and beyond his society: so he pledges the sailor 'the honour of a gentleman, and of a Frenchman' that he will exonerate him.

The murder story concludes, therefore, with Le Bon being freed, and the orang-utan being confined. In one sense, there *is* no murderer at all, and the figure of 'the good' is liberated to resume his task of ferrying money across Paris. To be sure, the orang-utan ends up behind bars, but they are the bars not of a prison but of the Jardins des Plantes, to which he has been sold by the sailor for 'a very large sum'. The sailor thus profits from the beast which he has discovered, and which has committed an outrage. It is not entirely clear just how sardonic Poe's grim joke is: it might even be insinuated that the creature fetches such a *very* large sum from the zoo because of the notoriety that he has attracted through his 'crime'. No doubt, people will seek to satisfy their 'objectless curiosity' at his cage, and it is surely Poe's implication that in staring through the bars at him, they will be staring into a moral and psychological mirror.

If the sailor profits from these events, so does Dupin, at least in the enhancement of his reputation with the Prefect of Police: as Dupin himself puts it, he has 'defeated him in his own castle'. The Prefect's jealousy is apparent in his sarcastic remark to Dupin 'about the propriety of every person minding his own business'. The 'profound undercurrent' in the story suggests a greater significance in this comment than the Prefect intends: the Prefect stands for the bourgeois predilection for keeping clear boundaries between private and public spheres of 'business' in society. Dupin has defeated the Prefect by transgressing these boundaries in a way that mirrors the boundary- and frontier-crossing of both the sailor and his orang-utan. Poe implies that such inevitable crossings of moral frontiers raise spiritual and psychological problems that remain unresolved by *any* of the figures in the story.

There is surely a good deal of irony in Dupin's final patronising assessment of the Prefect:

> in truth, our friend the Prefect is somewhat too cunning to be profound. . . . [H]is wisdom . . . is all head and no body, like the pictures of the Goddess Laverna, . . . I like him especially for one master-stroke of cant, by which he has attained his reputation for ingenuity. I mean the way he has 'de nier ce qui est, et d'expliquer ce qui n'est pas.' (ii, p. 568)

Poe and Dupin share a final joke at the expense of bumbling urban officialdom, since in Rome the goddess Laverna was the patron of thieves and impostors. However, Poe is still concerned with larger issues, and particularly with depicting the divided realm of mind and body, as illustrated in the dismembered corpse of Mme L'Espanaye and the contrary figures of Dupin and the orang-utan. As Poe's letter to Cooke hints, the tale's popularity may also depend on Dupin's ability 'to deny what is, and explain what is not': he explains the monkey-business of the implausible story, but glides smoothly over its 'profound under-current'. For the story challenges the reader to confront problems deeper than even Dupin can manage: what is Man's nature? What is Man's place relative to that which might be considered 'sacré' to 'Mon Dieu'? Where may readers find that 'rare volume' that both narrator and Dupin seek? Where is that 'jewel', that 'treasure beyond price', the truth? Under what circumstances can a man become transformed into a beast 'flashing fire from its eyes'? These are the questions Poe insinuates into a narrative that he knows will be read primarily for amusement and the reassurance of conventional expectations. Hence the relevance of the story's motto from Sir Thomas Browne's *Urn-Burial*, referring to questions with which the emperor Tiberius enjoyed tormenting his literary scholars: 'What song the Syrens sang, or what name Achilles assumed when he hid himself among women, although puzzling questions, are not beyond *all* conjecture' (ii, p. 527).

Clearly, Poe delighted in ravelling and unravelling his fictional web and valued both the 'method' and the '*air* of method' that Dupin deploys and represents; just as clearly, however, Poe was concerned with confronting those areas of conjecture that baffle both Dupin and his narrator in their darkened abode.

III

Poe wrote to J. R. Lowell (2 July 1844) that his new Dupin story, 'The Purloined Letter' (published in September), was 'perhaps the best' of his 'tales of ratiocination',[13] and later commentators as diverse as Thomas Mabbott and Ernest Mandel have agreed, praising 'the fascination of the purely intellectual plot and . . . the absence of the sensational'.[14]

The tale is concerned with theft and blackmail rather than the murders of the earlier tales, although its epigraph warning that 'nothing is more hateful to wisdom than too much cunning' (iii, p. 974) recalls Dupin's criticism of the Prefect at the end of 'The Murders in the Rue Morgue'. As the story begins, the narrator is mulling over the events in the Rue Morgue and the proposed solution of the Marie Roget mystery, a convenient 'mental discussion' that allows Poe to connect his new composition with the assured popularity of Dupin's earlier exploits. Indeed, it is as if the narrator invokes the Prefect, who this time brings Dupin a more refined enigma: no foul murder or sexually motivated outrage,[15] merely a 'purloined' letter. The brazen theft has been committed by government minister D——, who is using the Queen's knowledge that he possesses compromising information about her to exert influence on the very centre of state power, since the mere threat of showing the letter to the King is evidently sufficient to keep the Queen in his thrall. The Prefect of Police has been charged with the delicate task of recovering the letter without arousing the King's suspicion.

In this situation, the conventional, plodding rationalism of the Prefect is clearly inadequate: Minister D—— is an experienced courtier with a 'lynx eye'. Yet the Prefect's power and reputation are at stake, and, in desperation, he has appealed to Dupin, who torments the policeman while surrounding him with 'a perfect whirlwind' of sardonic pipe-smoke. The Prefect is enveloped in Dupin's smoke-rings, just as the unwary reader is trapped by the spider's web of the story as a whole. For the Prefect, in his conventional rationality, believes that all poets are fools, but Dupin, himself a poet, knows that D——'s mind exemplifies authentic reason by combining the poetic and mathematical faculties: it is what permits Dupin and D—— to be both 'creative' and 'resolvent'. The Prefect recounts the means the police have employed to detect and retrieve the letter: every millimetre of D——'s abode has been examined with a powerful microscope. The method epitomises the power-system of a bourgeois, materialistic society: authority knows and sees everything, but understands and creates nothing.[16] Poe's contempt for the Prefect's approach is succinctly expressed in the Prefect's fatuous boast that his agents 'not only opened every book, but ... turned over every leaf in each volume'. Such mechanical cunning, Poe satirically implies, will never aspire to the wisdom obtainable through actually *reading* the books! The whole story is in fact *about* the process of reading and writing, seeing and perceiving: Poe, the writer-spider, weaves his symbolic web around the reader-fly, so that the latter is forced to meditate on, and confront the literary process at the very moment of attempted escape into the fantasy of triumphant understanding that is the story's surface meaning. Poe makes the reader experience the tantalising nature of the quest for truth, wisdom and enlightenment: and that is why the contents of the purloined letter are never in fact revealed.

Despite Dupin's contempt for the Prefect's methodology, he relies absolutely on the Prefect having carried out these limited mental manoeuvres, before superimposing his own inspired and unorthodox ratiocinations. The same technique was applied in 'The Murders in the Rue Morgue', where Dupin based his solution on the reliable but uncomprehending evidence of the witnesses, and in 'The Mystery of Marie Roget', where Dupin (and Poe!) despise the lack of acumen in the newspaper accounts, and then proceed to discern a possible solution from a synthesis of those very accounts.[17] In 'The Purloined Letter', Dupin does intervene directly, meanwhile creating a diversion by advising the wretched Prefect to repeat his microscopic scrutiny of D——'s abode.

A month later, the Prefect begs Dupin to perform a miracle that he can claim as his own, ready even to sacrifice 50,000 francs of the reward to maintain his reputation. The policeman's motive is mercenary and his means dishonest: morally, therefore, he is as questionable as D——, and far less prescient. As Dupin instantaneously produces the missing letter, and requires the Prefect to pay up, the latent and actual power of the written word to create 'reality' is doubly emphasised in their exchange of documents: the letter *might* have destroyed a monarch, but has actually done nothing, while the Prefect writes the cheque that safeguards his own position. There is an uncanny symmetry in this exchange, and in the movement of the story between the three chambers (the Queen's, Dupin's, and D——'s), which, together with the tale's almost complete absence of overt action, suggests that the narrator is presenting a dream of the human will to power.

Dupin's explanation of his success stresses the importance of achieving a '*thorough* identification' with the mind of his adversary, and he quotes a child's version of it:

When I wish to find out how wise, or how stupid, or how good, or how wicked is any one, or what are his thoughts at the moment, I fashion the expression of my face, as accurately as possible, in accordance with the expression of his, and then wait to see what thoughts or sentiments arise in my mind or heart, as if to match or correspond with the expression.   (III, p. 984)

Poe is preoccupied throughout the story by such efforts of imitation, from acts of identification and occurrences of coincidence to instances of mockery, impersonation or imposture, and the purloined letter is the focus of this preoccupation. The Minister D—— has stolen the letter by placing another on the Queen's table to counterfeit the presence of the original. He then leaves the stolen missive in full view in his letter-rack, having transformed it into an inverted image of itself: 'It was clear to me that the letter had been turned as a glove, inside out, re-directed and re-sealed' (III, p. 992).

Dupin, in turn, recovers the letter by replacing it with 'a *fac-simile*, imitating the D—— cipher, very readily, by means of a seal formed of bread' (III, p. 992). Thus, D—— conceals the letter by revealing it: rather than hiding what he has stolen from the centre of power, he exerts influence over it by transforming it into a mockery of itself; Dupin steals power back through an imitation of the crime and a 'thorough identification' with the criminal.

However, the act of retrieval requires a diversionary tactic as well as fraud and forgery, and Dupin adopts a significant strategy. He knows just how to divert D——'s attention, because he understands what D—— fears most: the spectre of public disorder. D——, in stealing the letter, pretends that he will destroy the Queen; Dupin, in creating a mock street-riot, pretends to destroy the Minister. Dupin, himself, has experienced diminution of worldly power, having been reduced in circumstances from his aristocratic origins, but his response has been to wield power obliquely while remaining apart from the formal structures of power. Since Dupin fears that D—— may kill him, the story flirts at this point with violence that characterises the other Dupin stories, but it remains latent, a charade of disorder rather than the thing itself. As Dupin reveals: 'The disturbance in the street had been occasioned by the frantic behavior of a man with a musket. . . . The pretended lunatic was a man in my own pay (III, p. 992).

Money, the currency of power, is important in all the stories of detection, and it should be noted that Dupin's motive, like the Prefect's, is at least partially pecuniary. Money may play a more covert role, too: the purloined letter may refer to a sexual impropriety on the Queen's part, but financial considerations may also be involved, and the street-disturbance, had it been authentic, might well have been occasioned by the poverty of the citizens. Dupin, however, insists that his motives are not wholly pecuniary: 'You know' [he tells the narrator] 'my political prepossessions' (III, p. 993). Dupin sees himself as 'the partisan of the lady', gallantly retrieving the letter to preserve the Queen's honour and safety. Yet the reader does *not* know Dupin's 'political prepossessions', or not explicitly, anyway. The general political stance of this aristocratic scion may be inferred, alas, from his quotation from Chamfort: 'It is safe to wager that every idea that is public property, every accepted convention, is a bit of stupidity, for it has suited the majority' (III, pp. 986–7).[18] It is tempting to interpret Dupin as Poe's heroic intellectual who manages, wholly peacefully, to use his intuitive ratiocination to restore a threatened social order, and to turn evil neatly back upon itself, with a fine (and mathematically symmetrical) sense of poetic justice. The social ferment of the 1840s, especially evident in Paris, but latent in the cities of the United States, seems stilled by the exercise of this great mental agility. Undoubtedly, such a fictive exorcism of social anxiety partly accounts for the (continuing) popularity of the Dupin tales, but this story ultimately resists such an interpretation. Poe is more interested in the intractability of metaphysical and spiritual problems than in the solving, or containing, of social or political ones.

Harry Levin has pointed out some of the loose threads that Dupin's intellectual wizardry leaves hanging: 'Questions remain, which M. Dupin is much too discreet to raise: what was written in that letter? by whom to whom? and how did its temporary disappearance affect the writer and the recipient?'[19] Levin is in fact less worried by these unanswered questions than he should be, for they crucially affect the reader's sense both of D—— and of Dupin. Upon what moral principles is Dupin's allegiance to the Queen based? What experiences have formed his 'political prepossessions'? How can he justify his complicity in the Queen's hiding of the truth from the King? The reader who is not lost in the smoke-rings of Dupin's 'air of method' should surely ask these questions, and feel cheated by the ensuing silence.

To be sure, Dupin's *coup de théâtre* seems entirely delightful:

> For eighteen months the Minister has had her in his power. She has him now in hers; since, being unaware that the letter is not in his possession, he will proceed with his exactions as if it was. Thus will he inevitably commit himself, at once, to his political destruction. (III, p. 993)

Yet Dupin has earlier described D——'s ingenuity as 'daring, dashing, and discriminating': everything about him (including the alliterative adjectives) suggests a mind symmetrical with Dupin's own, and superior to all others. In defeating his 'desperate' counterpart, it is not clear whether Dupin acts from high-minded ethical considerations or from a more primitive desire for revenge: 'D——, at Vienna once, did me an evil turn, which I told him quite good-humoredly, that I should remember' (III, p. 993).

Above all, it is never clear just who has written the embarrassing letter to the Queen. The Minister has 'fathomed' the Queen's guilty 'secret' with a single glance of his 'lynx eye', and Dupin, behind his 'green spectacles', perceives the Minister's secret strategy equally swiftly. Their actions are based upon inferences and assumptions about the covert and guilty behaviour of others: the real knowledge remains undisclosed to the reader, who is allowed to glimpse the inner workings of power only through Dupin's revelation of his ratiocinative procedure. Ultimately, the reader is allowed to read a letter, but only the counterfeit letter that Dupin has left for D—— to read, and it deepens the ambivalence of Dupin's behaviour rather than clarifying it.

Dupin's note reads thus, in translation: 'So baleful a plan, if unworthy of Atreus, is worthy of Thyestes' (III, p. 993).[20] It refers the Minister, via Crébillon, to the classical legend of Atreus and Thyestes, and thus (despite Dupin's earlier stricture against making inferences from 'Pagan fables' as if they were 'existing realities') reminds the reader of the struggle for power in the very dawn of civilisation. The cryptic allusion implies that Dupin has driven D—— out, as Atreus drove out Thyestes; a consideration of the allusion in its mythic context, however, makes Dupin seem morally equivocal indeed, a figure who dissolves only too readily into his apparent mirror-image, his intellectual twin. The struggle between Atreus and Thyestes drew down the curse of the gods, and its violence makes the blundering orang-utan in the Rue Morgue seem a mere novice in the perpetration of outrages:

> pretending to be reconciled, Atreus recalled Thyestes, killed the latter's two sons and served up their flesh to him at a banquet. The sun turned back in horror, Thyestes fled, and the gods cursed the house of Atreus.
> . . . later variants . . . and elaborations of the story [involve] further incest, murder, and intrigue.[21]

Symbolically, this is the vision of disorder to which the silent letter and its purloining both relate, and which Dupin's cool ratiocination serves to conceal. Poe, however, encourages the reader who is capable of recognising the spider's web of his fiction for the contrivance that it is, to become aware of his more sombre theme: the futility of the human desire for a master-sleuth who will locate crime outside the self. To such a reader, Poe permits the horrified recognition that the twin-figure of the detective-criminal is a permanent fixture in the battleground of human experience, so that 'the essence of all crime' remains 'undivulged', and its burden 'can be thrown down only into the grave'.[22] Despite the apparently radical difference between the sensational corporeality of 'The Murders in the Rue Morgue' and the refined intellectuality of 'The Purloined Letter', the stories should be considered as mutually illuminating: both purport to allay anxiety and restore a violated order, while simultaneously insinuating the insolubility of the human predicament.[23]

Notes

1. John Ward Ostrom (ed.), *The Letters of Edgar Allan Poe* (Cambridge, Mass.: Harvard University Press, 1948) vol. II, p. 328.

2. Edgar Allan Poe, *The Narrative of Arthur Gordon Pym of Nantucket* (1837), ed. Harold Beaver (Harmondsworth, Middx.: Penguin, 1975) p. 73.

3. J. Gerald Kennedy, 'The Limits of Reason: Poe's Deluded Detectives', *American Literature*, 47 (1975–6) no. 2, pp. 184–96. Kennedy reads 'The Oblong Box' as an ironic farewell to the tales of ratiocination, but his sense of Poe's steady development from 'a rage for order' in the Dupin stories to a satire on that impulse seems too neat to be true.

4. Poe, 'Hawthorne, *Twice-Told Tales*', and 'Tale-Writing: Nathaniel Hawthorne', both in Eric W. Carlson (ed.), *Introduction to Poe: A Thematic Reader* (Glenview, Ill.: Scott, Foresman and Co., 1967) pp. 487. 488 and 495.

5. J. Lasley Dameron, 'Poe's C. Auguste Dupin', *Tennessee Philological Bulletin*, 17 (1980) p. 6.

6. *Collected Works of Edgar Allan Poe*, ed. T. O. Mabbott (Cambridge, Mass.: Belknap Press, 1978). All further quotations from the tales and from Mabbott's notes are from this edition (vol. II for 'The Murders in the Rue Morgue', and vol. III for 'The Purloined Letter').

7. Poe, 'Tale-Writing: Nathaniel Hawthorne', in Carlson, *Introduction to Poe*, p. 498.

8. As Richard Wilbur puts it: 'We must understand "The Fall of the House of Usher" as a dream of the narrator's, in which he leaves behind him the waking, physical world and journeys inward toward his *moi intérieur*, toward his inner and spiritual self. That inner and spiritual self is Roderick Usher.' Quoted in Daniel Hoffman, *Poe, Poe, Poe, Poe, Poe, Poe, Poe* (London: Robson Books, 1973) p. 299.

9. My understanding of the narrator's role has been influenced by James M. Cox, 'Edgar Poe: Style as Pose', in Dennis W. Eddings (ed.), *The Naiad Voice: Essays on Poe's Satiric Hoaxing* (New York: Associated Faculty Press, 1983) pp. 53–6, and, to some extent, also, by Robert Giddings, 'Was the Chevalier Left-handed? Poe's Dupin Stories', in A. Robert Lee (ed.), *Edgar Allan Poe: The Design of Order* (London and Totowa, NJ: Vision Press, 1987) pp. 88–111.

10. Julia A. Kushigian sees Dupin this way. Writing of 'The Purloined

Letter', she claims: 'Poe allows his detective to win and survive as a heroic figure.' See 'The Detective Story Genre in Poe and Borges', *Latin American Literary Review*, vol. 11 (1983) p. 33; Susan F. Beegel, however, argues that Dupin's 'ratiocinative heroics are enfeebled by the overpowering presence of the irrational'. See 'The Literary *Histrio* as Detective', *Massachusetts Studies in English*, vol. 8 (1982) p. 7.

11.   All three quotations are taken from David Brion Davis's fascinating study, *Homicide in American Fiction, 1798–1860* (Ithaca, NY: Cornell University Press, 1957) pp. 173, 175, 209. Davis does not examine 'The Murders in the Rue Morgue' specifically.

12.   Here, and in the matter of the high-pitched voice, I am indebted to Dennis W. Eddings's reading of the story in his 'Poe, Dupin and the Reader', *University of Mississippi Studies in English*, n.s. 3 (1982) pp. 128–35. Eddings is correct in perceiving the satirical tone of both stories, though I do not agree with his view that, 'by playing Dupin to Poe', the reader is enabled to 'see into the very unity of all things' (p. 135).

13.   Ostrom, *Letters*, p. 258.

14.   Mabbott, III, p. 972; Ernest Mandel, *Delightful Murder: A Social History of the Crime Story* (London: Pluto Press, 1984) p. 19. But see also James M. Cox's view, 'Edgar Poe: Style as Pose', p. 52.

15.   Poe drew his material for 'The Mystery of Marie Roget' from contemporary newspaper accounts of the scandalous death of Mary Cecilia Rogers, a New York cigar-store girl.

16.   This statement is my modification of Leonard W. Engel's neat insight: 'They have seen everything and have found nothing.' See 'Poe's Tales of Ratiocination and his Use of the Enclosure', *Clues: A Journal of Detection*, vol. 3 (1982) p. 84.

17.   Stefano Tani noted this technique in his book *The Doomed Detective: The Contribution of the Detective Novel to Post-Modern American and Italian Fiction* (Carbondale, Ill.: Southern Illinois University Press, 1984) p. 9.

18.   Dupin quotes in French, of course. The translation is taken from Mabbott, III, p. 995, n. 16.

19.   Harry Levin, *The Power of Blackness: Hawthorne, Poe, Melville* (New York: Alfred A. Knopf, 1970) pp. 141–2.

20.   For Mabbott's translation of Dupin's quotation, see III, p. 997, n. 27.

21.   John Warrington, *Everyman's Classical Dictionary* (London: J. M. Dent, 1961) pp. 86–7.

22.   These quotations are from the opening paragraph of Poe's tale, 'The Man of the Crowd' (1840; II, p. 507).

23.   See, for instance, Dupin's comment on radical differences (III, p. 991).

8

Chandler's Cannibalism
MALDWYN MILLS

I thought of nasty old women beaten to death against the posts of their dirty beds. I thought of a man with bright blond hair who was afraid and didn't quite know what he was afraid of. . . . I thought of beautiful rich women who could be had. I thought of nice slim curious girls who lived alone and could be had too, in a different way. I thought of cops, tough cops that could be greased and yet were not by any means all bad, like Hemingway. Fat prosperous cops with Chamber of Commerce voices, like Chief Wax. Slim, smart and deadly cops like Randall, who for all their smartness and deadliness were not free to do a clean job in a clean way. I thought of sour old goats like Nulty who had given up trying. I thought of Indians and psychics and dope doctors.[1]

Thus contemplates Marlowe, on p. 206 of *Farewell My Lovely* (*FML*), during the moment of repose when he is lying in the dark, in a waterfront hotel, waiting for the right time to make his trip to the gambling ships just outside the three-mile limit, and there, with luck, to find the pieces missing from his puzzle. This characteristic soliloquy is in fact a roll-call of nearly every character of importance in the novel, and here, as so often elsewhere, the mental processes of Marlowe seem very close to those of his creator. For Chandler, too, had 'thought of' all these characters, and not simply once, but twice in the course of his literary career. First, when he had created them to carry on the action in stories written for *Black Mask* and *Dime Detective Magazine* in the mid–1930s and second when, only a few years later, he re-created them and the events with which they were associated, to provide the bulk of *Farewell My Lovely*.[2]

Appropriately perhaps, the only ones who appear in the novel under their original names are members of the police: the noble ex-cop Red Norgaard and the less noble practising one, Galbraith, and even here there are minor differences. The first slightly alters the spelling of his surname; the second becomes more familiar to the reader as 'Hemingway', the alias foisted upon him by the bookish

117

Marlowe. But besides these and other superficial alterations are others so wholesale as to suggest the laboratory of Frankenstein in a Universal picture rather than the dimly lit hotel, proper to weak private eyes, in a Warner Brothers one. Personal attributes are changed or shifted around, and in one startling instance three distinct characters from the short stories are first dismembered and then reassembled into a new, composite monster. This is Mrs Lewin Lockridge Grayle, the lovely to whom farewell has finally to be said. But this, the most remarkable single piece of re-creation in *Farewell My Lovely*, was less one that was deliberately willed by the author, than the end-product of a whole complex of changes made to the structure and content of the material taken over, to prevent the seams from appearing too obvious, and the novel as a whole from bulging at them. The scale of the task facing Chandler can most quickly be gauged by passing in review the content of the three stories involved.

Private Investigator Carmady is retained to find the high-spirited Isobel Snare, who had left her aunt's home in company with a dog. This dog is traced to Dr Sharp, with whom it had been left by the bank-robbers Farmer Saint and his sister Diana. These appear on the scene after the dog has killed Sharp, so do Galbraith and Duncan, two policemen of very dubious honesty. They knock out Carmady; when he comes to it is to find himself hallucinating in a private nursing home run by Dr Sundstrand. He escapes from this, and, after confronting Galbraith and Duncan in the office of chief Fulwider, returns with Galbraith to the home. There, Galbraith kills Sundstrand with Carmady's gun; Saint and his sister turn up, and by the end of the scene, Galbraith, Duncan and Diana are also dead. Following a clue provided by Diana before she dies, Carmady makes for the gambling ship *Montecito*, which he finally manages to board with the help of Red Norgard, an ex-policeman dismissed the force for honesty. There Carmady finds the dog, as well as Saint and Isobel Snare (who have just married). The police arrive, and another massacre follows in which Saint, Fulwider and the dog are all killed. Isobel is returned to her aunt, and there follows a general clean-up of the police force in which Norgard is reinstated. ('The Man Who Liked Dogs' [MLD], March 1936)

Carmady meets with Steve Skalla, a gigantic ex-convict, outside Shamey's, the bar in which Skalla's girl-friend Beulah had once worked. In trying to find her there, Skalla kills the proprietor. Carmady traces Mrs Shamey who admits to turning Skalla in to the police, and getting regular payments for keeping quiet about the past of Beulah, now a rising star on a radio network. Marineau, the manager of the radio studio, confirms that Beulah is now Vivian Baring and gives Carmady her address. This proves to be Marineau's own house; there Carmady meets with the embittered Mrs Marineau, who gives him the girl's real address. After getting away from a crooked ex-policeman set on his track by Marineau, and learning that Mrs Shamey has been found dead, he finds Mrs Marineau at Vivian Baring's house, together with the corpse of Marineau, for which his wife takes the credit. Skalla then appears, and does the same; Mrs Marineau shoots Skalla, but he does not die immediately. Later, Carmady returns to the house waiting for Vivian to appear; when she does, she reveals that she had really killed Marineau, though in self-defence. She plans to make a break for it, but Carmady, after beating her up to give colour to her story, instead takes her in to make a statement. Skalla dies in hospital, with her holding his hand.   ('Try the Girl' [TG], January 1937)

Private Investigator Dalmas is retained by Lindley Paul to go with him to a deserted spot to buy back a jade necklace from the gang that stole it. Once there, Paul is killed and Dalmas knocked out; when he comes to he is confronted by Carol Pride, a journalist and policeman's daughter. Cigarettes found on Paul's body contain cards inscribed 'Soukesian the Psychic'; after tracking him down, Dalmas is taken to him by an overpowering Indian, chloroformed, and wakes up out of doors with the Indian's corpse beside him. Back in his office, he is visited by Carol Pride and the hard-drinking Mrs Prendergast, earlier identified as the owner of the jade necklace. Following up details that she gives of the actual robbery, Dalmas visits the beer parlour run by Moose Magoon, where he is very nearly shot to pieces, but is saved at the last moment by Carol Pride and the police. The criminal association of Magoon, Soukesian and Paul is established; in a final confrontation Dalmas accuses Mrs Prendergast of having engineered the killing of Paul by Magoon. She shoots at Dalmas but misses; he leaves her to her complaisant husband and goes off, affectionately, with Carol Pride.

('Mandarin's Jade' [MJ], November 1937)

Neither the selection of these particular stories as the basis of a single novel, nor the choice of *Farewell My Lovely* as its title, was arrived at at once, but came after what seems to have been an extended period of trial and error following Chandler's first success in combining two of his earlier stories to produce *The Big Sleep*. During the same period, *The Lady in the Lake*, the third of the omnivorous novels, was also being planned, and in the process took over some of the raw material and (perhaps) one of the working titles that had earlier been meant for *Farewell My Lovely*. The first title recorded for the latter seems to have been *Law is Where You Buy It*;[3] like *Farewell My Lovely*, this was to have been an amalgam of 'Mandarin's Jade', 'The Man Who Liked Dogs' and a third story, but this last was not 'Try the Girl', but 'Bay City Blues'; this would certainly have contributed effectively to what Chandler at this point claimed as the novel's real theme: 'the corrupt alliance of police and racketeers in a small California town, outwardly as fair as the dawn'.[4] According to Chandler's notebook, this was the state of play on 16 March 1939, but by the following month 'Try the Girl' must have replaced 'Bay City Blues' as the third contributory work, since 'The Girl from Brunette's' and 'The Girl from Florian's' are recorded, in rapid succession (on 12 and 18 April) as possible titles for the novel.[5]

By 23 August, however, *Farewell My Lovely* had acquired yet another title: *The Second Murderer*,[6] and this had the effect of shifting the emphasis to 'Mandarin's Jade', since it must refer to Lindsay Marriott (Lindley Paul in 'Mandarin's Jade'). From one point of view this could seem an odd choice, as Marriott, dead after less than twenty pages of activity in the story, has much less narrative staying power than the ex-convict's girl-friend (Beulah in 'Try the Girl'/Velma in *Farewell My Lovely*), evoked by the discarded *The Girl from Florian's*. But it was the literary overtones that counted here; in the letter in which the title is suggested, Chandler quotes to Blanche Knopf an exchange between the First and Second Murderers in *Richard III*, Act II, Scene iv, which concludes with the Second confessing that 'certain dregs of conscience' still stir within him. All this is picked up in a characteristic piece of Marlovian rhetoric in the first of the two pay-off scenes from the end of the novel:

I think he went to that canyon to be murdered, although he thought he went there to help commit a murder. But Marriott was a very bad murderer. . . . A very bad murderer. . . . Like

Shakespeare's Second Murderer in that scene in *King Richard III*.
The fellow that had certain dregs of conscience, but still wanted
the money, and in the end didn't do the job at all because he
couldn't make up his mind. Such murderers are very dangerous.
They have to be removed – sometimes with blackjacks.   (*FML*,
p. 242)

Adequate or not, the title seems to have survived until the first draft
of the novel was complete, and the first announcements for it had
gone out. But Chandler had grown to dislike it, and by the time
the manuscript was actually submitted, it was as *Farewell My Lovely*.
This time it was the publishers' turn to be uneasy ('not at all a
mystery title'[7]), but it was not changed again until Dmytryk's
screen version appeared in New York in 1944.[8]

Some of Chandler's remarks about the genesis of *Farewell My
Lovely* may be less than wholly trustworthy; it is noteworthy that in
his 1939 'Plan of Work' he claims not only that 'The Man Who Liked
Dogs' had provided a 'fairly long sequence' in *The Big Sleep*, but that
only 'Try the Girl' and 'Mandarin's Jade' had been used to produce
Farewell My Lovely. But as a whole his comments fit well enough
with what the internal evidence suggests had been the relative importance of the three stories, and the order in which they were
drawn into the making of *Farewell My Lovely*. What is immediately
obvious is the predominant importance of 'Mandarin's Jade'; the
longest in itself (fifty-four pages against forty in 'The Man Who
Liked Dogs' and forty-two in 'Try the Girl'), it is also the one that
loses least of its original content in the process of reworking (about
six pages of material against roughly twenty in each of the others).
What is more, this material is for the most part concentrated in a
section ('I Cross the Bar') that is in its tone incompatible with
Farewell My Lovely as a whole. It tells of Marlowe's escape from a trap
set for him in the sleaziest of beer-parlours, and the telling is dense
with the idiom of pulp-writing. ('Two more shots roared. . . . The
bar was old and solid but not solid enough to stop .45 slugs. . . .
Something hot and wet fell on my face', MJ, p. 594.)

Even more of the omissions of 'The Man Who Liked Dogs' are of
this kind, since here there are two scenes of massacre, at the middle
and end of the story. In 'Try the Girl', on the other hand, virtually
nothing of this sort is to be found; here the (quite sizeable)
omissions are motivated exclusively by content; in particular,
details concerning the radio station for which the elusive heroine

was working, its studio manager, Marineau, his unbalanced wife and the corrupt ex-cop who works for him. 'Try the Girl' as has been noted, was almost certainly the late arrival, and by the time it was brought in the complex of material already assembled from 'The Man Who Liked Dogs' and 'Mandarin's Jade' would have made it impossible to include the greater part of the Marineau story. At the same time, however, it was perfectly possible for 'Try the Girl' to supplant broadly cognate material in the other two stories, if its own version of it was clearly superior, or more malleable. This is what seems to have happened at the beginning and end of the new story; as a result, the vital frame of *Farewell My Lovely* is very much that of 'Try the Girl'.

In the broadest sense, of course, all three stories have the same outer structure. The hero is commissioned, or decides himself, to undertake a specific search at or near the beginning; this he achieves at the end. But in the actual form assumed by this search, 'The Man Who Liked Dogs' and 'Try the Girl' are very much closer to each other than either of them is to 'Mandarin's Jade'. In them, the quest is for a woman who is keeping – or had once kept – very dubious company; in 'Mandarin's Jade', it is for a jade necklace. This last is in fact so distinctive that it can co-exist with the game of Find the Lady within an extended tract of narrative, as long as it is introduced at a different point from the latter, and in fact Marriott does not hire Marlowe to find the jade until Chapter 7 of *Farewell My Lovely*, by which time the search for both Velma and Malloy (=Beulah and Skalla in 'Try the Girl') has to differing degrees run into the sand. But the opening sections of 'The Man Who Liked Dogs' and 'Try the Girl' are altogether too alike in their underlying narrative functions for both of them to be kept, even if 'stepped', and it is not surprising that it is the story of Isobel and Saint that gave way to that of Beulah and Steve Skalla. Not only is it less rich and arresting in itself, but the pseudo-Bonnie and Clyde duo of Diana and Farmer Saint (they 'dress up like country folks and smack down small town banks, state banks', MLD, p. 445), would not have been easy to work into the locations and events of 'Mandarin's Jade'. Like Skalla/Malloy on Central Avenue, they would have stood out like tarantulas on angel food.

All the same, one small part of Saint's role was taken over by Malloy; near the end of the story he too, a wanted man, is hiding out on the gambling ship *Montecito*, even if he is not actually encountered there by Marlowe. Still fewer traces are found in the novel of Saint's sister, Diana, or (finally) wife, Isobel. The first, while undeniably dangerous in a professional kind of way ('neat and dark, with a rakish black hat, and two gloved hands holding guns', p. 452) is no Poison Woman, like Mrs Pendergast or Mrs Marineau. Nor is Isobel, for all that her maiden name is Snare: 'She was not much to look at, like most of the people that make most of the trouble. . . . Her knees were bare and bony under the hem of the dress. She looked like a schoolgirl' (p. 463). But, by way of compensation, the other two stories ('Try the Girl' in particular) contain a multiplicity of female characters who have been partly or wholly absorbed into Mrs Grayle, and have made her responsible for a very large proportion of the disasters that befall the men of the story. Like Mrs Shamey in 'Try the Girl' (though not Mrs Florian in *Farewell My Lovely*), she proves to be the one who had turned in the hulking bank-robber before the story begins; like Mrs Marineau in the same story, it is she who finally shoots him; like Mrs Pendergast in 'Mandarin's Jade' (but more directly), she is responsible for the death of the weak escort. Nor is this all. Still other aspects of her role in *Farewell My Lovely* have been suggested or contributed by the Beulah/Vivian Baring of 'Mandarin's Jade'. She carries into effect what Vivian Baring had only planned to do: run for it, after committing murder; and she too, at an earlier stage in her career, had once been a singer in a dive. Initially, she even seems to be credited with the same appearance as this singer, since like Carmady at Mrs Shamey's, though after the expenditure of rather more effort, Marlowe finds at Mrs Florian's a photograph of her as Velma (Beulah in 'Try the Girl'), in earlier and more innocent days. Here the differences are as significant as the similarities:

> She wore a Pierrot costume, at least from the waist up. Under the high conical white hat her fluffed-out hair might have been red. Her eyes had laughter in them. I won't say her face was unspoiled. I'm not that good at faces. But it wasn't like the others. It hadn't been kicked around. Somebody had been nice to that face. Perhaps just a tough mug like Steve Skalla. But he had been nice. In the laughing eyes there was still hope.   (TG, p. 520)

> The girl wore a Pierrot costume from the waist up. Under the white conical hat with a black pompon on the top, her fluffed-out hair had a dark tinge that might have been red. The face was in profile but the visible eye seemed to have gaiety in it. I wouldn't

say the face was lovely and unspoiled, I'm not that good at faces.
But it was pretty. People had been nice to that face, or nice
enough for their circle. Yet it was a very ordinary face and its
prettiness was strictly assembly line. You would see a dozen faces
like it on a city block in the noon hour.   (*FML*, p. 33)

The grudging quality (and relative awkwardness) of the revision
suggests that at the moment of writing it Chandler really had meant
it to stand for the younger Mrs Grayle, but was well aware that she
was going to be much less unspoiled at the end of her story than
Beulah/Vivian Baring had been.[9] From one point of view the
passage foreshadows the way in which Mrs Grayle appears to
Marlowe in their last scene together, just before Malloy walks in:

She leaned forward a little and her smile became just a little
glassy. Suddenly, without any real change in her, she ceased to be
beautiful. She looked merely like a woman who would have been
dangerous a hundred years ago, and twenty years ago daring, but
who today was just Grade B Hollywood.   (*FML*, p. 242)

But by this stage in the book Chandler seems to have made up his
mind that Velma could not have grown into Mrs Grayle (as Beulah
had grown into Vivian Baring), and in a slightly later, retrospective
conversation, Anne Riordan remarks to Marlowe that the Pierrot-
photograph and the photograph of Mrs Grayle that she had given
him much earlier in the story were not of the same woman. Marlowe
agrees, and certainly, when we look back, we find that his reactions
to the second likeness were altogether more dynamic than those to
the first: 'It was a blonde. A blonde to make a bishop kick a hole in a
stained glass window' (*FML*, p. 84). (Which is, almost verbatim, the
reaction of Dalmas to meeting Mrs Prendergast in the flesh – MJ,
p. 585.) This is the ultimate twist; aspects of two characters,
originally quite separate, appear to have been combined in one, but
have not really.

Nevertheless, while Chandler finally discarded this particular
contribution to Mrs Grayle, he has still toned down some of the
material bestowed upon her by other, less engaging prototypes.
Unlike Mrs Prendergast in 'Mandarin's Jade', she is perfectly able to
carry her drink (MJ, pp. 586–9; *FML*, pp. 110–15), although this has
its unfortunate side-effects by keeping her sufficiently desirable to
draw Marlowe into an embrace that causes Mr Grayle, its accidental

and rather apologetic observer, to withdraw with 'an infinite sadness in his eyes' (*FML*, p. 119). Unlike Mrs Marineau in 'Try the Girl', she does not laugh as she shoots Malloy, nor spit in his face after she has done so (TG, p. 544; *FML*, p. 245). After this killing, the character takes off in all senses, in a coda in two stages, in neither of which is any of the detail from the short stories (although, as mentioned, the impetus to the beginning of it seems to have been suggested by the end of 'Try the Girl'). She takes to flight, then resumes her career as a singer, moves from drink to marijuana, and is finally recognised (this time from her looks, not her voice) by a Baltimore detective. When he refuses to do a deal with her, she shoots first him and then herself. True to type to the end, it would seem, but in the second stage of this coda, Marlowe, after a passage (discussed a little further on) in which he suggests that the suicide, at least, was not a selfish action, provides a valediction that seems meant to imply both a final escape and a reversion to an earlier, fresher personality: 'I rode down to the street floor and went out on the steps of the City Hall. It was a cool day and very clear. You could see a long way – but not as far as Velma had gone' (*FML*, p. 253).

A second character in *Farewell My Lovely* who has taken over features that were before attached to several figures is Laird Brunette. In contrast to Mrs Grayle, he does not appear in the story in his own person until very nearly the end, and, at first glance at least, a much greater part of what we are told about him seems wholly new. On closer inspection, however, he proves to have taken over narrative functions that were in 'Mandarin's Jade' and 'The Man Who Liked Dogs' attached to much less presentable-seeming characters. Like the two young hoodlums briefly mentioned in 'Mandarin's Jade' (p. 569), it is he who is responsible for the death of the Chief-of-Police father of the nice girl of the story (Carol Pride in 'Mandarin's Jade'/Anne Riordan in *Farewell My Lovely*), though now by removing him from office, through the agency of a venal mayor, and so breaking his heart (*FML*, p. 81). After this, all that we have is a carefully spaced series of allusions to his power over the town (pp. 176, 203, 218); like Moriarty or Macavity, he is everywhere and nowhere. That is, until Chapter 38.

There Brunette is at last confronted by Marlowe, on the gambling ship, after the detective has made two trips there, the second much more clandestine and dangerous than the first. In 'The Man Who Liked Dogs' (pp. 457–62), Carmady had made the same two trips, with the double purpose of making contact with the holed-up

Farmer Saint, and – after making sure that he too will come there – confronting Saint with Chief-of-Police Fulwider, the source of so much that is corrupt in Bay City. In *Farewell My Lovely* Marlowe too wishes to make contact with two gangsters, Malloy and Brunette, but now the second is to be primarily the means of getting a message to the first, to ensure that he, Marlowe, and Velma can meet. Nor is there any question of terminating the career of Brunette, like that of Fulwider, who in his principal reincarnation as Chief Wax also remains alive if gaoled at the end of the novel (p. 249). In any case, Brunette is given a good deal of quite sympathetic attention in his one big scene.

This is not entirely surprising; Marlowe has taken so much trouble in getting to see Brunette, that he must at least be made to seem worth it. 'Seem' is the word, since he neither really does nor discloses very much. The complex of real violence and retrospective explanation that is found at the same point in 'The Man Who Liked Dogs' is replaced by only the threat of violence from his henchmen (*FML*, p. 231), and no precise explanation at all; Marlowe tells him much more than he tells Marlowe. Least of all does he throw any light upon Mrs Grayle, which might, perhaps, have been expected given her own admission that she is a very good friend of his, and frequents his Belvedere club (p. 120), and Chandler's claim that *The Girl from Brunette's* preceded *The Girl from Florian's* as a provisional title for the novel. But then, Brunette is undeniably a gentleman.

This quality, like the Olympian lack of concern with practical details ('I don't know why I bother') impresses Marlowe, who here, as elsewhere, is a pushover for criminals who are on the grand scale, physically attractive and hard, and well mannered.[10] Compare the most assertive of Marlowe's speeches to Brunette with that of Carmady to Fulwider, Laird's low-grade counterpart in 'The Man Who Liked Dogs':

'You own a piece of Bay City,' I said. 'I don't know how big a piece, but enough for what you want. A man named Sonderborg has been running a hideout there. He has been running reefers and stick-ups and hiding hot boys. Naturally he couldn't do that without connections. I don't think he could do it without you.' (*FML*, p. 231)

I said disgustedly: 'Just what kind of a sap did you and your gang take me for? Your clean little town stinks. . . . A crook sanctuary where the hot rods can lie low – if they pay off nice and don't pull any local capers – and where they can jump off for Mexico in a fast boat, if the finger waves towards them.' (*MLD*, p. 466)

Even Red Norgaard, who claims to hate Brunette and his kind, commends him for his 'guts and brains', and stresses that he would only have a rival or nuisance eliminated after giving considerable thought to the matter (*FML*, p. 220).

Different again as the end-product of cannibalizing the stories is Lindsay Marriott, since he represents, not the fusion of detail and functions drawn from more than one character, but the extension of a single character (Lindley Paul in 'Mandarin's Jade') – that is preserved without significant alteration – into spheres of activity that are drawn from another story ('Try the Girl'). This extension is retrospective, with the facts relating to it coming out only after Marriott has been killed. The stitching across the seams is very deft, and Chandler must have been justifiably proud of it. At one point he certainly achieves one of his ideals of detective story writing:

> It is not enough that the facts be stated. They must be fairly stated, and they must be the sort of facts that can be reasoned from. Not only must important or any clues not be concealed from the reader, but they must not be distorted by false emphasis.[11]

Chandler leaves on Marriott's corpse one of Marlowe's cards, this in a distinctly tacky condition ('There was a round smear across one corner' – *FML*, p. 71). Given Marriott's general neatness, this should at once arouse the reader's suspicions, and perhaps recall the moment in the earlier scene between Marlowe and Mrs Florian in which that far-from-neat lady had set her empty glass on the card, as soon as Marlowe had given it to her (p. 29). When Marlowe himself makes the connection (pp. 94–5), he at once begins investigating the title to Mrs Florian's Tobacco Road property, and finds that it is held by Marriott. Another link between Marriott and his new friend, which may or may not be true, is provided by Mrs Florian herself (p. 103) and a fresh one within the 'Mandarin's Jade' material by Mrs Grayle (p. 118). And at the very end of the novel, Marlowe goes over the connections that have already been directly or indirectly made, and makes plain the degree to which the story of the jade has finally been subordinated to the story of Velma: 'when

Marriott called me up and gave me a song and dance about a jewel
ransom pay-off it had to be because I had been to see Mrs Florian
asking about Velma' (p. 247).

Chandler's own comments on his writing support what has been
inferred from the evidence of the stories and of *Farewell My Lovely*.
In particular, the composite/complex characterisation of Mrs Grayle
and Laird Brunette agrees, superficially at least, with his insistence
on the primacy of character over plot, as well as with his acknow-
ledgement that he was not very good at putting plots together
anyway.[12] The first finds clear expression as early as 1939:

> I was more intrigued by a situation where the mystery is solved
> by the exposition and understanding of a single character, always
> well in evidence, rather•than by the slow and sometimes long-
> winded concatenation of circumstances.[13]

as well as in a much later comment on *The Long Goodbye*:

> I didn't care whether the mystery was fairly obvious, but I cared
> about the people, about this strange corrupt world we live in, and
> how any man who tried to be honest looks in the end either
> sentimental or plain foolish.[14]

Written in 1953, this novel, like *The High Window* (1942) and *The Little
Sister* (1949) before it, was put together without any sustained
ransacking of his earlier work to provide the backbone of the
narrative,[15] and as a result is much more likely to achieve these aims
than was *Farewell My Lovely*, the greatest of the 'tied' novels. Up to a
point, indeed, we can stand these statements on their head and say
that in *Farewell My Lovely*, where the plotting is often neat as well as
complex,[16] the mystery of certain characters and their behaviour
can only be solved by the understanding of a 'concatenation of
circumstances', involving both derivative and newly contrived
material. Which brings us to the two crucial scenes of explanation
near the very end.

   For Chandler in 1940 the classic example of such a scene – and it
would have served as a warning as well as a model – must have been
that found at the very end of Hammett's *The Thin Man* (1932),[17] in

which Nick Charles sorts everything out for his wife Nora in an outpouring that fills over eight pages of the Penguin text. Like Miranda in *The Tempest*, Act ɪ, Scene ii, but with more scepticism, Nora serves to break up this monstrous slab of exposition into rather more manageable components ('How did you find that out? Don't skip details', 'But this is just a theory, isn't it?'; 'But that seems so loose'; 'Yes, but . . .'), but it remains indigestible, and Chandler must have been convinced he could do better. He certainly makes things easier for the reader by splitting the explanatory material into two scenes, the first with Mrs Grayle (pp. 241–4), the second with Anne Riordan (pp. 246–50). In doing this, as in his actual conduct of the first scene, at least, he anticipates what nine years later he was to lay down as desirable practice in such scenes:

> I hate explanation scenes and I learned in Hollywood that there are two rules about them. (1) You can give only a little at a time, if there is much to give. (2) You can only have an explanation scene when there is some other element, such as danger, or love-making or a character reversal suspected.[18]

Danger is certainly present in the first of the two expositions, with Mrs Grayle's hand moving ever closer to the gun in her handbag; in the second, Anne Riordan provides only a very mild degree of disbelief, and occasional comments, barbed and sentimental respectively, on Mrs Grayle and Moose Malloy.

Of the three characters we have considered, Laird Brunette is (unsurprisingly) the one least enhanced or complicated by anything Marlowe has to say. He seems as beyond Marlowe's reach as he is beyond that of the law ('He doesn't have to bother about his reputation'). Both Marriott and Mrs Grayle, on the other hand are further fleshed out by what he says. Part of the material relating to the first has been set out in connection with the *Second Murderer* title; it is essentially bound up with the consequences of involving Marriott in events (from 'Try the Girl') that he had not had to cope with in 'Mandarin's Jade'. There, as Lindley Paul, he was simply a blackmailer and a now-expendable lover who had to be put out of the way; here, in *Farewell My Lovely*, he must be killed because he knows too much about the lady's past, itself now more elaborate than before, and may, under pressure, reveal what he knows. But the new threat to Mrs Grayle's concealment of her past also (according to Marlowe) gave rise to the fiction that sent Marriott to his death; the detective was getting too close to the truth and must be silenced at a convenient location to which Marriott would take him:

> There was a rather weak motive for murdering me – merely that I was trying to trace a former Central Avenue dive singer at the same time that a convict named Moose Malloy got out of jail and started to look for her too. . . . But there was a much stronger motive for murdering Marriott, which he, out of vanity or love or greed or a mixture of all three, didn't evaluate. (*FML*, p 243)

On the level of plot, this is another neat piece of stitching, even if the psychological probability of it all may seem dubious. At all events, Mrs Grayle describes it as interesting but incomprehensible, not as fantastic.

Marlowe encounters a little more sales resistance when he explains the matter of the Pierrot-photograph to Anne Riordan, and indeed he does not sound too sure of his explanation himself:

> I doubt if even old Lady Florian knew they had been switched on her. She looked kind of surprised when I shoved the photo of Velma – the one that had Velma Valento written on it – in front of her nose. But she may have known. She may have just hid it with the idea of selling it to me later on. Knowing it was harmless, a photo of some other girl Marriott substituted. (*FML*, p. 247)

'That's just guessing' Anne retorts, very Nora Charles; to which Marlowe, very Nick Charles, verbally slaps her down ('It had to be that way': compare Nick's favourite 'It doesn't click any other way' in the final scene of *The Thin Man*). This, of course has to do with the diminution of Mrs Grayle rather than her enhancement, but this last is quite strikingly attempted in Marlowe's interpretation of her shooting of herself after killing the detective from Baltimore. He claims that this was done to spare her husband further suffering:

> I'm not saying she was a saint or even a half-way nice girl. Not ever. She wouldn't kill herself until she was cornered. But what she did and the way she did it, kept her from coming back here for trial. . . . And who would that trial hurt most? Who would be least able to bear it? . . . An old man who had loved not wisely but too well. (*FML*, p. 253)

But this time he is playing to a tougher audience, Randall of Central Homicide, who immediately snaps back, 'That's just sentimental'. And Marlowe half agrees with him.

Even within their own limits, such passages of character elaboration go off in too many different directions to be satisfactory. To some degree, at least, they reflect the multiplicity of literary impulses that drove Chandler on to produce this remarkable novel. It was certainly not just a matter of doing more with theme and character than had ever been possible within the limits of the magazine stories;[19] there was also the wish to produce something more real and less contrived than the detective stories of the 'Golden Age', with their crippling exaltation of the puzzle element (though, as noted, Chandler respected their concern with fair dealing by the reader). More specifically there was his strongly publicised abhorrence of James M. Cain's type of violent sexuality (to which he had come fairly close at the end of 'Try the Girl', in two passages not taken over into *Farewell My Lovely*[20]), and his feeling that even the great Dashiell Hammett had failed to provide certain overtones to character and action in his own novels.[21] The intermittent response to all these resulted in some uncertain shifts of tone, and tendencies to idealise and pontificate that can be a little wearing. However briefly, one misses the stylised, laconic force of the pulps that is perhaps best summed up in the very last lines of 'Try the Girl' where the heroine does not go into orbit, evoking images 'beyond a distant hill', but stays earth-bound, at the deathbed of the man whom someone else had killed.

> He died at two-thirty the same afternoon. She was holding one of his huge, limp fingers, but he didn't know her from the Queen of Siam. (TG, p. 550)

Notes

1.   Quotations from *Farewell My Lovely* are from the latest Penguin reprint (Harmondsworth, Middx., 1986); those from 'The Man Who Liked Dogs' (MLD), 'Try the Girl' (TG), and 'Mandarin's Jade' (MJ), from *The Chandler Collection*, vol. III (London: Picador, 1984). In the initial quotation the characters alluded to are, in order of mention: Mrs Florian (Mrs Shamey, TG), Lindsay Marriott (Lindley Paul, MJ), Mrs Grayle (Mrs Prendergast, MJ; Mrs Marineau, TG; and others), Anne Riordan (Carol Pride, MJ); Galbraith/Hemingway (Galbraith,

MLD) and Blane (Duncan, MLD), Chief Wax (Chief Fulwider, MLD), Randall (Reavis, MJ), Nulty (Hiney, TG); Second Planting (Second Harvest, MJ), Jules Amthor (Soukesian, MJ), Dr Sonderborg (Dr Sundstrand, MLD). The major exclusion is Moose Malloy (Steve Skalla, TG; Moose Magoon, MJ); Red Norgaard (Norgard, MLD) and Laird Brunette (Farmer Saint, MLD) have not yet appeared on the scene.

2. For a general view of this process of 'cannibalising' (Chandler's own word) see Frank McShane, *The Life of Raymond Chandler* (London: Jonathan Cape, 1976) pp. 67–8, 84–5; the second passage has particular relevance to *Farewell My Lovely*, though some of the detailed interpretations seem contestable. In the Introduction to the Hamish Hamilton/Penguin *Killer in the Rain*, which contains the stories relevant to the cannibalised novels, Philip Durham had already provided a succinct account of the making of *The Big Sleep* (Harmondsworth, Middx.: Penguin, 1966, pp. 9–11); some of the same or cognate material was gone over again by Julian Symons in 'An Aesthete Discovers the Pulps' in *The World of Raymond Chandler*, ed. Miriam Gross (London: Weidenfeld and Nicolson, 1977) pp. 19–29, see esp. pp. 26–9.

3. Chandler himself remarked that an allusion to this title in a 1939 diary would have been prompted by 'Bay City Blues', since 'That is a story which happens in a town so corrupt from the law enforcement point of view that the law is where you buy it and what you pay for it', in *Selected Letters of Raymond Chandler*, ed. Frank McShane (London: Jonathan Cape, 1981) p. 282. As McShane notes, the phrase also turns up within *Farewell My Lovely* in connection with Mrs Grayle's power over the police (*FML*, p. 122; *The Life of Raymond Chandler*, p. 90).

4. '1939 Plan of Work Taken from Chandler's Notebook', in *Raymond Chandler Speaking*, ed. Dorothy Gardiner and Kathrine Sorley Walker (London: Hamish Hamilton, 1962) p. 207.

5. *Raymond Chandler Speaking*, pp. 243–4; *Selected Letters*, p. 281.

6. *Selected Letters*, pp. 9–10, also *Raymond Chandler Speaking*, p. 245.

7. *Selected Letters*, p. 17.

8. RKO released this under Chandler's title in Minneapolis at the end of 1944, but it was retitled *Murder My Sweet* when it opened in New York three months later: see *Film Noir*, ed. Alain Silver and Elizabeth Ward (London: Secker and Warburg, 1980) p. 192. The first title, together with the casting of Dick Powell in the lead, seems to have made preview audiences apprehensive that it would be a musical (Philip French, 'Media Marlowes', in *The World of Raymond Chandler*, pp. 67–79, see esp. p. 70).

9. For all that she turns out later to have a police record, Vivian is still recognisably the girl of the photograph: 'Her hair even by the light of the one lamp was like a brush fire at night. Her face had laughter wrinkles at the corner of the eyes. Her mouth could laugh' (TG, p. 547).

10. See Michael Mason, 'Marlowe, Men and Women', in *The World of Raymond Chandler*, pp. 89–101, see esp. p. 96.

Chandler's Cannibalism

Chandler's Cannibalism 133

11. *Raymond Chandler Speaking*, p. 66. See also Chandler's comment on *The High Window* as a title: 'It is simple, suggestive and points to the ultimate essential clue' (ibid., p. 212).
12. For his limitations as a 'constructionist', see his own disparaging comments on this aspect of *The Little Sister* (*Selected Letters*, pp. 122, 175).
13. Ibid., p. 4
14. Ibid., p. 315.
15. Though the opening of *The Long Goodbye* makes considerable use of that of 'The Curtain', and the novel as a whole reproduces the *Farewell My Lovely* pattern of appearing to wind up the first main action before proceeding to another that seems wholly unconnected with it (in *The Chandler Collection*, vol. ii (London: Picador, 1983) pp. 199 ff. and 249–61).
16. In 1949 Chandler noted that in *Farewell My Lovely* 'The bony structure was much more solid' than in the other novels (*Selected Letters*, p. 192).
17. Dashiel Hammett, *The Thin Man* (Reading: Penguin, 1987) pp. 181–9.
18. *Raymond Chandler Speaking*, p. 221. The same ideas find expression in his 'Casual Notes on the Mystery Novel' written in the same year, with the modification that it is only on the screen that explanations 'need' to be short, though they should always be interesting (ibid., pp. 64–5).
19. In a letter of 1948 Chandler quotes an example of the kind of material that got taken out of his writing for the magazines: 'Their readers didn't appreciate this sort of thing: just held up the action. And I set out to prove them wrong' (*Selected Letters*, p. 115).
20. In the first, Carmady beats up Vivian Baring: 'Her eyes flamed at first and then turned to black stone. I . . . tore her up plenty, put hard fingers into her arms and neck and used my knuckles on her mouth.' After waiting a little, she looks in a suitable state to be taken downtown: 'Her face looked like a catcher's mitt after a tough season. She had a lower lip the size of a banana, and you could have cooked steaks on . . . her arms and neck, they were so hot' (TG, p. 550).
21. See 'The Simple Art of Murder', in *The Chandler Collection*, vol. iii, pp. 175–92, see esp. pp. 188–92.

9

Home is Where the Hearth Is: The Englishness of Agatha Christie's Marple Novels

ANNA-MARIE TAYLOR

I

Agatha Christie's popularity seems obvious to everybody except literary critics. In this chapter I shall explore this persistent popularity, and try to articulate it by drawing on German literary terms; in particular the notion of *Heimatdichtung*.

Although Agatha Christie is the world's best-selling English-language novelist, she has received remarkably little sustained critical attention. As a writer of 'middle-brow' detective fiction, and as the creator of a discretely charming world of the bourgeoisie, she has not appealed to most literary critics. Above all, the writer, whose works are a considerable presence in bookshops, libraries and homes, is quite noticeable by her absence in most surveys of female novelists and in recent studies of women's writing. Her books' popularity has, however, been tentatively investigated by writers on crime fiction.[1] What these studies overlook, though, is the way that the 'mechanical reproduction' of Christie's fiction by film and television has contributed to her continuing popularity. Therefore, I shall consider why the Christie texts in both their printed and reproduced forms have continued to satisfy their audiences. In doing this, I shall concentrate on those works that feature Christie's spinster sleuth, Miss Marple, and discuss their sustained cultural resonance.

The ability of Christie's novels to enthral has been attributed, in appropriately pharmacological terms, to her craft in distilling the formula for the 'Classic' detective story. All twelve Jane Marple novels and the various short stories follow a clue-puzzle scheme. Christie's satisfaction with the potency of the formula is demonstrated by her prolific output, with most of her novels adhering to the pattern of narrative established in very early texts, such as *The*

Mysterious Affair at Styles (1920) and *Murder on the Links* (1923).[2] The repeated ordering of her novels with a constant movement towards 'closure' through 'disclosure',[3] involving recurrent characters and types, offers predictability and reassurance. Her books' popularity depends on a certain propriety and familiarity of structure, and, moreover, on the decorum of her moral universe. Although peopled by murderers and petty criminals, the realm of the Christie novel is both materially and morally comfortable. Violence takes place in the wings. Unresolved needs and messy emotions remain unexplored and are eventually closed off for good by the solving of the puzzle and the expulsion of the wrongdoer. Crimes are individual, and it is rare for the Christie book to show the mass or group as culpable. *Murder on the Orient Express* (1934) may present more than one murderer, but it is made clear that each murderer has an individual grudge against the victim. Any explanations that move away from the individual and place the responsibility for crimes on wider groupings appear as improbable possibilities within Christie's conventionalised positioning of the individual inside a bourgeois value system. Disclosures such as civic corruption, poverty, the breakdown of established institutions and internecine struggles between interest groups are only hinted at. It is the comforting *bienséance* of the probable impossibility – the elaborate murder of a marriage partner, an ingenious way of revenging a past wrong, the cunning concealment of a desire for material gain – that contributes to her success. Moral, social and legal complexities are palliated in her novels, and we are left with a seemingly complex, but fundamentally simple, tale concerning the quest of individual detective. More complex aspects of the narrative lie hidden in the text, as we are directed to the detective's search for 'what has not been told and its reconstruction'.[4]

As a literary producer, Christie was able to complete three such works in a year. Christie moved to Collins from John Lane in 1926, and she stayed with these publishers until her death in 1976. A curious portrait of their productive 'Queen of Crime' is on the cover of some Fontana/Collins paperback editions.[5] A very old Christie, dressed in black, stares out at the prospective buyer. There are pearls at her neck, and on her wrist is a large, functional-looking watch. Her hands are crossed on her chest in a death pose. The photograph conveys many meanings: sagacity and experience, practicality and longevity, wry humour, the posture of a *grande dame* (of the British Empire) and possibly a *Doppelgängerin* for Jane Marple. There is also some suggestion, as in other equally deliberate portraits prominent on book covers, that she should be instantly recognised; that this once most private of literary figures is in the public domain. Such a publicising of Christie can also be seen in Janet Morgan's biography, where its subject is 'Agatha Christie, the world's best-selling author . . . a public institution'. Christie's part in the received heritage of Britain is scarcely elaborated upon by her publishers, and it is necessary to ask how this could be true. As 'The Queen of Crime', she occupies a paramount position in English-language literature, being its most translated and best-selling writer.[6] For instance, the Penguin 'Christie Million' 1950 imprint alone sold over two and a half million copies. Although any statements about readership, and how and where her texts are read, must be hypothetical, the high public profile of Christie novels is clearly evident. The manufacturing of Christie and her works as part of British tradition and national heritage is seen most clearly, though, in her recent veneration as part of the 'traditional' family Christmas on national television.

Christie's crime narratives had been presented in other media than print during her lifetime. Theatre and wireless were preferred to film and television. In particular, she wrote a body of plays for the stage, one of which, *The Mousetrap* (1952), stands as a semi-permanent memorial to its author as the world's longest-running commercial play. Despite well-crafted adaptations, such as *And Then There Were None* (1945), directed by René Clair, and Billy Wilder's *Witness for the Prosecution* (1957), Christie, who maintained considerable control over her work, became reluctant to sell the film and television rights to her novels.

Part of her reluctance may have stemmed from the Marple adaptations, *Murder She Said* (1961), *Murder at the Gallop* (1963), *Murder Most Foul* (1964) and *Murder Ahoy!* (1964). In these films the plot structure of the originals is tampered with, and Margaret Rutherford's forcefully eccentric, almost androgynous, performance disrupts the idea of Jane Marple as genteel upholder of social convention. Rutherford's Marple belongs more to the crime fiction tradition of the outsider sleuth, a type seen in Christie's Poirot. Few films and no television adaptations were made between those Marple films and Christie's death. The only film production of note was the lavish and highly profitable 'all-star vehicle' of *Murder on the Orient Express* (1974). Appropriate to Christie's regal status, it is reported that Lord Mountbatten was involved in persuading her to release the rights to EMI.

With Christie's death, 'Agatha Christie Ltd.' has released the rights to more novels to film and television companies. 'Agatha Christie Ltd.' was founded in the author's lifetime, and now consists of the Booker Company and Christie's closest relatives.[8] Adaptations made since her death fall into two broad categories: those versions sponsored from the United States for an international market, and British productions aimed primarily at the home audience, but which, with foreign investment and marketing, can be sold elsewhere. A product in the latter category was London Weekend Television's *The Seven Dials Mystery* (1981), which was made in collaboration with Mobil Showcase. Christie reproductions were well displayed in the programming for British domestic entertainment over the Christmas period 1987, when no less than six filmed versions of Christie texts and a radio play of *The Murder of Roger Ackroyd* were presented.

Not only the quantity of these reproductions is remarkable, but so too the recurrent notion that they are somehow 'true-to-the-original'. Her texts, which off screen offer brief pleasures, must be preserved intact on screen. The conservation of the Christie original is seen in three obvious ways: the choice of location, the casting of actors and a strict adherence to the plot formula. Fully 'authentic' settings are re-created, including crossovers between the real and fictional worlds of Christie such as the use of Greenway House, Christie's old home in Devon, for the location for LWT's *The Seven Dials Mystery*. An entry in the *Radio Times* for Christmas 1987 illustrates this craving after consistent realism. The chief engineer of the Severn Valley Railway apologises for the possible inaccuracy of the trains in the BBC's *4.50 from Paddington* by stating:

> As it is the 50's . . . strictly speaking, the carriages should have been red and cream – but we hadn't got enough of those. . . . But it's not wildly out, because the colours changed after the Great Western Railway was nationalised in 1948, it didn't all happen overnight.

A railway enthusiast's response, perhaps, for Christie's novel is not placed in such a definite historical context. Similarly, the actors for the Christie period pieces are fashioned with great care, and it is not regarded as a contravention of reality when Joan Hickson, 'TV's Miss Marple', takes on the guise of Christie's character to appeal for charity on the radio. After all, as Hickson says, 'She is a fiction, but is real to me.'[9]

The search for the 'authentic' has in part been set up by the demands and conventions of costume drama, and, more generally, by the aesthetic of consistent realism sustained by the medium of television. But the updating of some well-known works on film and television is in contrast to the deliberate 'dating' of the Christie books. For example, the BBC Shakespeare productions, and the James Bond novels, are repeatedly modernised – presumably as a response to a perceived need for 'actuality' in their audiences. The 'dating' of the Christie novels is particularly apparent in the BBC's Marple re-creations. The reason for this appears to be a conjunction between Christie as 'public institution' and a particular construction of Englishness in the Marple books.

II

The Marple novels can be seen as late pastorals, Arcadian versions of both the detective form and village life in the Home Counties, 'a dream of bourgeois rural living without the heights, depths or conflicts of real social activity'.[10] Pastoral may seem an attractive term alongside 'Golden Age', that other much-used description for Christie's fiction. However, at the risk of adding yet another label to be attached to Christie's 'Classic', 'Golden Age' crime writing, I should like to suggest that the German term, *Heimatdichtung*, allows a more successful discussion of the Marple novels. 'Pastoral' has too diffuse and complicated a historical development to be applied with any precision of meaning to Christie's novels.

Heimatdichtung (regional writing) flourished in Germany in the latter part of the nineteenth century and the early part of this century as part of a wider *Heimatkunst* (regional art) movement. *Heimat* writing included ballad poetry, autobiographical sketches and novels. Drawing on nineteenth-century antecedents such as Gotthelf, Stifter and Storm, the *Heimat* novelists favoured the small town or village as the setting for their books, with the inhabitants of the province as their heroes. Such a setting is used as the location for Gustav Frenssen's *Jörn Uhl* (1901), which enjoyed a remarkable commercial success, and can be regarded as Germany's first best-seller, selling over 130,000 copies in its first year of publication. *Jörn Uhl* charts the life of a decent, hard-working farmer's son, who tries to preserve the family farm, despite the shiftlessness of his own family and a succession of natural catastrophes. Eventually, Jörn is forced to give up the farm, and he founds a cement works. In this new occupation he can aid the community by maintaining dikes and canals. At the end of his career he is able to review his life's work with satisfaction. Sometimes the *Heimat* novelist locates the text in the city, but then moves its location to the country to emphasise the regenerative value of rural life. This change of setting occurs in Clara Viebig's *Eine Handvoll Erde* (*A Handful of Earth*) (1915), where a country woman by birth, Mine, who now lives in Berlin, rents a small weekend plot in the country. The novel is resolved by a benefactor buying the freehold of the plot for Mine and her family, thus ensuring them of further contact with the countryside. Unlike Britain, where crime fiction has dominated the best-seller lists, many best-selling novels in the earlier part of this century in Germany were not examples of 'Classic' detective fiction, but were *Heimat* texts of some kind.[11] These *Heimat* bestsellers include Paul Keller's *Waldwinter* (1902) and Felicitas Rose's *Heide-schulmeister Uwe Karsten* (1909), both of which had sold over half a million copies by the middle of the century.

The main ideological thrust of the *Heimat* narrative is a con-sciously anti-urban and anti-cosmopolitan stance, expressed at times in the portrayal of a 'reactionary Utopia'[12] rooted in German soil. Outside pressures threaten this Teutonic haven, and, in the novels with a contemporary setting, this threat very often takes the form of the 'asphalt world' of the city. In many of the works, there is a sense of cultural pessimism. The new urban world puts the traditional farmstead and village at risk. They are presented as the right and natural bases of economic production, and, as such, must be fought for in the face of human and natural dangers. In this backward-looking Arcadia, the organic and native are emphasised. This organicism was stressed even further in the National Socialist appropriation of the *Heimat* forms in *Blut und Boden* (blood and soil) writing and the *Heimat* film, when questions of racial determinism, duty to the fatherland and *völkisch* biological arguments became increasingly prominent.

The concerns of *Heimatkunst* were perpetuated after World War Two in the Federal Republic, in the *Heimatfilm*, for example, the cinematic equivalent of printed literature. Indeed, it is this form of the *Heimatfilm* that was reshaped and problematised by Edgar Reitz in his epic family saga, *Heimat* (1984), filmed in his native Hunsrück. A late example of *Heimatkunst* is perhaps West German television's popular soap opera, *Schwarzwaldklinik* (*Black Forest Clinic*), which combines *Heimat* elements with the doctor-and-nurse tale of best-selling romantic fiction. *Schwarzwaldklinik's* debt to *Heimat* preoccupations can be seen in the idealised portrayal of both the landscape and the clinic. The extended happy family of Professor Brinkmann's chalet-like clinic is positioned against a German forest Utopia (a composite created from thirty-two different location shots and not a drop of acid rain in sight). The stability of his medical haven is continually under pressure from events and visitors from the less idyllic world outside this cosy corner of the Black Forest.

Heimat texts are 'realistic', with dialect forms frequently used to accentuate the regional location, such as Hermann Löns's works set on the Lüneburg Heath. In common with other popular and folk forms, the *Heimat* text is generally resolved by a happy ending. Class, economic and gender antogonisms are placated by the affirmation of belonging to a particular region, village or family. Continuity is stressed, not change. Above all, the importance of *Heimat* is made prominent; a word that conveys many meanings – hearth, country, region, place of origin, home. *Heimatliteratur* can be seen as a response to rapid changes in the socio-political life of Germany from unification onwards. It reveals a crisis in what constituted 'Germany' and being 'German', and in many, but not all, quarters, represented an arch-conservative reaction to a newly industrialised and urbanised world. This is shown to some extent by the great number of texts endorsing the small-scale, indigenous and domestic that are published at times of expansion, modernisation and urbanisation.[13]

The 'Golden Age' crime writers created an idealised version of bourgeois life at a time of great social and political changes, when they perhaps perceived a threat to their own class position. The *Heimatdichter* created an agrarian Utopia as their answer to historical change. I do not wish to make any parallels between the historical positions of the *Heimat* writers and that of Christie, or impose a critical terminology crudely on the Marple books. But, with due caution, these novels may be read as English *Heimatdichtung*, and their recent film and television enactments as *Heimatfilme*.

Although Christie's texts do not promote the pronounced regional identity of German *Heimatdichtung*, and the ideal state in her novels has little to do with the agricultural world of the German peasant-farmer, or any agricultural world for that matter, the Marple novels share many of the ideological concerns of *Heimat* writing. *Heimat*, as used to describe literary and cinematic texts, has acquired a much broader application since it was used to categorise the work of members of the *Heimatkunst* movement. Nowadays it is widely used to describe works that enshrine or come to terms with a quintessentially 'German' rural experience. I should also like to argue that the Marple books in their printed and more obviously in their filmed forms encapsulate a similarly cherished and narrowly circumscribed picture of England and Englishness. Christie's 'regional writing', which I shall refer to as *Home* writing, is similarly concerned with national and parochial identities, with a desire to site Englishness. And the recent reception of the Marple texts has been coloured to a large extent by a widespread nostalgia for the old values and setting of a traditional England.

III

So how do the Marple texts function as English *Home* writing? Certainly all the books are located in a sheltered provincial England, apart from the occasional visit to London as in *At Bertram's Hotel* (1965), and the transplanting of Jane Marple to an exotic terrain in *A Caribbean Mystery* (1964). Furthermore, questions dealing with both national and regional identities occur throughout the novels, becoming more frequent in the books written after World War Two. A preoccupation with the nature of English self-identity is intensified throughout the works. The distant authority of Jane Marple in *The Murder at the Vicarage* (1930), *The Moving Finger* (1942) and *Sleeping Murder* (written in the 1940s, but published in 1976) gives way to a much more obviously *author*itative voice in the later works. Indeed, in writing the later texts, Christie adjusted Marple's age, which by that time must have reached treble figures, to her own, and many aspects of modern Britain that Christie bemoaned when she made herself public in her autobiography (completed 1965, published 1977) are reiterated by Jane Marple. Christie's increasing cultural pessimism about the state of *post bellum*, Welfare State Britain becomes prominent in the Marple books.

In *The Mirror Crack'd from Side to Side* (1962), the physical decline of Marple's health is paralleled by a deterioration in the environment of her native St Mary Mead. She laments the passing of the old, and is saddened by the 'intemperate' modernisation, which, to her mind, finds its worst expression in the sinisterly named 'Development' on the outskirts of the village. The Development is an 'estate' of new houses, and clearly violates Christie/Marple ideas of *Home*. It stands outside the collective value system of the village proper. Order, tradition, rank and a sense of place have been replaced by atomisation, stratification, impersonality and *anomie*.

The pre-war organisation of St Mary Mead is presented as the natural and preferred economic and social system. When subjected to change, this arrangement can have grave consequences for the well-being of the individuals. This is shown by the way some of the motives for murder in the later novels stem directly from post-war realities, such as the perceived excessive burden of taxation in *4.50 from Paddington* (1957), and a zealous devotion to the rehabilitation of juvenile delinquents in *They Do it with Mirrors* (1952). In that novel, the point is put that money spent on treating young offenders would be better used to give poor, but not delinquent, children the chance of work. The care lavished on young offenders is seen as modish and ill-advised, as the boys are outside any accepted value system. Integration into this system for the boy of humble means comes in the form of appropriate employment.

In German *Heimat* texts, the work process is often made prominent to illustrate both the stability and closeness to the soil of the old agrarian order, or the upheavals created by the new city world, as seen in the difficulties rural newcomers have in adjusting to urban employment. Similarly, Christie calls attention to the organisation and distribution of occupations in her Marple novels, emphasising how traditional divisions of labour enable her social arrangements to 'work'. The received notion of the Christie detective novel is that it deals merely with the life of a leisured middle class. Though this is broadly true, Christie discusses and describes day-to-day circumstances of work much more frequently than in many more self-consciously literary works concerned with such participants. The carrying out of domestic chores, shopping, cleaning, clerical work, looking after the sick, raising children, the hiring and firing of servants; all these activities are recorded in detail. These mainly female pursuits also function as a means of crowding the action of the narrative, and diverting the reader from the 'truth' of the deviant behaviour of the criminal.

Much *Heimat* writing in German has been classified by literary
critics as *Trivialliteratur*, 'trivial' literature. I have never liked this
term with its seemingly *a priori* assumption of triteness and
worthlessness in the object of study. But in an oblique way it does
seem a rather appropriate description of aspects of Christie's St
Mary Mead fiction. The answer to the mysterious in Christie's
secular world can be found in the trivial and humdrum: a conceit
well visualised in the designs for the covers of some paperback
editions. Here, in the manner of Magritte, everyday banal objects,
the clues in the puzzle, take on an enigmatic significance. Such an
interest in the trivial is continued, and takes on a heightened form,
in Ruth Rendell's crime fiction, where Marks and Spencer's pre-
cooked meals and copies of *What Car?* become a way of encoding
social behaviour for her isolated and disturbed characters. In
Christie's novels, though, the enigma of the object relates directly to
the elucidation of the crime. In the Marple novels, the practical and
observant female makes a better detective than the intellectual or
extravagant male – a reversal of the Holmes/Wimsey/Poirot types.
This presumption is further reflected in Christie's own writing. Her
sketches for clue puzzles resemble shopping lists and itineraries.
Her plots are carefully organised and neatly managed. Throughout
her career, her style of writing remained plain, matter-of-fact and
unembellished. As Christie remarks in her autobiography, her way
of writing is eminently serviceable, and she would not wish to
overreach herself by attempting to imitate another writer's.[14]

Attention to the practical and to the small-scale recognises the
frequently unrecorded home life of women, albeit confined to a
specific and privileged class. It is this area of personal influence that
Christie describes with affection in her autobiography, including
such heroism as successfully chloroforming a hedgehog that had
become entangled in a tennis net.[15] Similar everyday, and, on
occasion, exceptional, chores are carried out in the Marple novel
amidst preponderantly female conversation. Planting suggestions,
gossip as a means of supporting and controlling, talking repeti-
tively, often to inanimate objects – all these activities have their
uses.[16] Jane Marple uses all these procedures to discover the
criminal, and also to disguise her own sagacity. After all, she is only
'a harmless old pussy'.

The authorisation of the domestic, and the positive value placed
on female talk, are at once progressive and conservative – progressive, in that they give worth to the circumstances of female
domestic life, but conservative in that the texts limit women's

influence to the domestic. This conservatism is seen strikingly in Christie's creation of Lucy Eylesbarrow in *4.50 from Paddington* (1957). Eylesbarrow has taken a First in Mathematics at Oxford, but has rejected an academic career in favour of becoming a kind of super-domestic. The post-war servant problem means that Lucy is in great demand because of her domestic ingenuity and versatility. By the transference of her powers of reasoning and deduction from the academic to the domestic, Lucy's intelligence is tamed. This is shown not to be the case with Clothilde Bradbury-Scott in *Nemesis* (1971). Her superior education, academic ability and handsome appearance have led her to frustration and insanity. Women who live or work outside the social organisation of home and family tend to come to grief. It is the showgirl, the painter, the dancer, the orphaned servant or schoolgirl who become victims of crimes. Above all, the woman who has married into a different class is at risk. The showgirl or manicurist who has married a doctor or businessman is doubly damned as artificial and *arriviste*.

The other side of this social arrangement, the public world of men, does not, however, get as sympathetic a portrayal as the private domain of women. Although there is usually a romance subplot in the novels, the heroes of the romantic fiction of Christie's day – the doctor, the businessman and his sons – are drawn unfavourably. Women, in the Marple books, are the true inheritors and guardians of hearth and home. Moreover, the businessman and his male relations are viewed as singularly inimical to the stability of the Marple world. Actual economic transactions tend not to take place within the author's preferred class. This 'anti-capital capitalism' means that money is virtually absent from the lives of the good citizens of St Mary Mead. When Miss Marple is left £20,000 by the 'incredibly rich' businessman, Mr Rafiel, in *Nemesis* (1971), it comes as a breach of etiquette. Cash transactions are limited to shop-keepers, entrepreneurs, blackmailers and murderers. In St Mary Mead, which is a community based on rank rather than wealth, the representatives of this miniaturised society – the vicar, the solicitor, the colonel, the doctor, the parlourmaid, the fish shop boy – are all assigned a place. Like the chairs at Bertram's Hotel, they are all individual, but part of the same establishment. As in the *Heimat* narratives, the principal disturbance to this small-scale organisation is often seen to be money, especially excessive wealth in the hands of those individuals who are not organically linked to the community.

The redecoration of Gossington Hall in *The Mirror Crack'd from Side to Side* (1962) is ostentatious, and the grand plans for the garden are unsuitable for an English country house. Marina Gregg, the Hall's owner, is a chronically rootless and exceedingly wealthy American film-star. Her 'improvements' are in contrast to the familiar use and links with tradition that the Hall suggested in Dolly Bantry's days in *The Body in the Library* (1942). Dolly Bantry, Miss Marple's friend, now inhabits the lodge. The idea that the newly rich are unable to employ their money prudently is seen in the completely valueless collection of archaeological bric-à-brac amassed in a Citizen Kane fashion by old Mr Crackenthorpe in *4.50 from Paddington* (1957). The Crackenthorpe money is newly acquired from the manufacture of biscuits, Crackenthorpe's Crunchies and Cracker Jacks, delicacies that Jane Marple, needless to say, has never savoured. The family is doomed to live in the Neo-Gothic pile of Rutherford Hall. In Christie's work, the Victorian mansion, like Timon's villa, epitomises ugliness, impracticality and social pretension, in contrast to the modesty and well-proportioned elegance of the Georgian house. The Crackenthorpe family is a combination of north of England grit, and, as old Crackenthorpe proudly relates, the descendants of kings, going back to before the Normans. This mixed lineage of plebeian and patrician has produced children who do not display the hallmarks of good breeding, such as Flash Alfred, the financial crook, and Cedric, the penniless painter. The motif of the moral and physical decline of the once flourishing business family is not only confined to Christie's texts, of course, but occurs in a wide range of modern fictions, popular and élite, from Susan Howatch to Thomas Mann.[17]

Corruption going hand in hand with business and mixed breeding is delineated much more acutely in *A Pocket Full of Rye* (1953). The Fortescue family's money has been made from dealing with money. The original Fortescues were a cross-breed of Central European Fontescu and English Ramsbottom. There are two sons, Lancelot and Percival, who inhabit the baneful Yewtree Lodge, somewhere in the suburbs of London. Adele, the elder Fortescue's wife, 'was a manicurist on the look-out for big money', whilst Percival's wife, a Mackenzie, was a hospital nurse. Yewtree Lodge is the Fortescue's suburban country mansion, but it is far too much 'city' rather than country, and the whole family is shown to be either unscrupulous or deeply unhappy, as none of the family's members occupies any proper place in society. A sense of displacement is intensified by the unusually Gothic inclusion of the elderly Miss Ramsbottom, who preaches hellfire and damnation to the entire brood from her suite of rooms in the cursed Lodge.

The enemy of a stable provincial society is not just capital in false hands, but also foreign influences. Christie's small-scale ideal is at risk from untoward occurrences within, and also alien elements without. Thus the murderer may dwell in, and be regarded as part of the community, but he or she has a personal history that makes them unsuitable for the host community. The zealot, the possessor of an 'artistic temperament', the intellectually frustrated, the adult warped by a difficult childhood, all feature as criminals. More likely, however, is evidence of a disqualifying blemish in the pedigree – a grandparent was not British, a wife is foreign, the person is adopted and is possibly the result of an alliance with an outsider. In the Marple texts, this insider/outsider model extends in a more overt fashion to the minor characters, who are often nationally determined. Hence, Italians are hot-headed, deceitful and fond of blackmailing; Middle Europeans are tricky and hysterical; the French charming but devious; North Americans exhibit an ingenuous frankness, but sadly lack culture. Nearer to *Home*, Scots are portrayed as sternly practical, phlegmatic and thrifty. However, the imprint of acceptability in St Mary Mead is Englishness, which is constituted as balance, common sense, reasonableness, sympathy, a notion of fair play and tradition and an ability to garden. Those qualities are articulated most fully by Miss Jane Marple, spinster of independent means.

At the end of *The Mirror Crack'd from Side to Side* (1962), Cherry and Jim Baker, who have been grafted from Huddersfield onto St Mary Mead, are invited by Jane Marple into her home as her domestic help. The Bakers are unhappy with the deracinated world of the Development, and are integrated, we presume, into the community through Miss Marple's invitation. Yet, Marple is a woman alone, outside an immediate family. Such a contradictory position in the ideological scheme of Christie's works is almost fully naturalised by her active participation in the happy ending. Marple not only heals the body politic by tracking down the guilty, but also supervises the romance plot by taking on a familial role as both grandmother and fairy godmother. The pregnancy of Griselda in *The Murder at the Vicarage* (1930), Jerry Burton's marriage to the erstwhile *enfant sauvage*, Megan, in *The Moving Finger* (1943), the reunion of the supposedly unhappily married couple in *They Do it with Mirrors*

(1952) are all in part controlled by Miss Marple. Through her, the community is ensured of survival. And, more often than not, the resolution of the Marple book, with its reinstatement of a stable and comfortable life of the bourgeoisie, its mythical 'return to the beginnings', resembles Christie's own portrayal of her snug, pre-war childhood, where her early days are presented as being happy ever before.[18]

In the same way that some German writers lamented alien (*artfremd*) urban influences upon the world of the province, Christie in the Marple texts sees the metropolis as the breeding-ground for widespread depravity and new-fangled ideas. Unlike a broadly constructed idea of pastorality, the countryside is not equated with simplicity and innocence. Without fail, it is made clear in the novels that Jane Marple is well acquainted with wickedness through living in St Mary Mead. Human nature is seen as constant, unchanging, predictable and fixed by birth, whether in the metropolis or in the province. However, it is implied that small-scale social organisations, where individuality is maintained, allow this wickedness to be tracked down and thwarted. Very rarely is human motivation presented as complex, ambiguous and at times inexplicable. Christie makes fun of the 'psychological' writer in her creation of Raymond West, Marple's nephew. Like his aunt, West investigates aberrant human behaviour, but he does not display her decorous gentility, nor her resigned sanguinity about human beings. West, in his modern, difficult, but successful, novels writes about 'such unpleasant people, doing such very odd things'. His work is not to his aunt's taste, versed in the 'official' culture of Shakespeare and Tennyson.

The Marple text itself has been shaped as part of 'official' culture by television and film. Not content with presenting the English person abroad at a historical distance in such products as *The Jewel in the Crown, Fortunes of War* and *A Room with a View*, television and film have turned to the Englishwoman at home.[19] The Christie television adaptations by ITV were first shown on Sunday evenings, with their residual connotations of the 'family hearth'.[20] In 1984 the BBC produced its first Marple adaptation, *The Body in the Library*, which was shown over the Christmas period in three parts. In 1986 and 1987 a Marple text (*Murder at the Vicarage, 4.50 from Paddington*) has been broadcast in a single 'slot' on the very day of the year that celebrates the domestic and familial to the greatest extent, Christmas Day.[21] British television from its early days onwards has assumed a shared sense of citizenship in its viewers; a notion that we are inhabitants of a common, but at the same time pluralistic, culture. This assumed pluralism can be seen in other television detective creations, such as *Taggart, Bergerac, Shoestring* and the *farceur* thriller, *The Beiderbecke Affair*, which make important a distinct regional locality. The presumption of a common culture, though, is nowhere more apparent than on Christmas Day, with our position as subjects of a common realm revivified yearly by the Queen's speech.

The programming of a Miss Marple story on Christmas Day, amidst the various other Christie offerings, has produced new categories of meaning for the 'Queen of Crime's texts. By publishing her novels in October or November, her publishers ensured that her books would be newly available for the Christmas market, and that their author would be associated with the Christmas season in the advertising slogan, 'A Christie for Christmas'. The broadcasting of the Marple text on Christmas Day not only implies continuity and stability, but it also plays on ideas of *Home*. The *Home* element of the Marple novels is brought to the fore in their translation to the screen. The clue puzzle is part of their popularity, of course, and the *bienséance* of her moral and social scheme supports ideas of Christmas as the time of family reconciliation, the 'family hearth' writ large. But, more than anything, I would argue that it is the presentation of *Home* that charms the viewer – *Home* reconstructed through the medium of television as past-ness. The attractive scenes of village life in the opening credits, and the jaunty Percy Grainger-like music underscore this, but it is the location of the texts – the English village with its age-old church, Blue Boar pub, cottages, village green and country house – that has become one of the most potent cultural images of the 1980s. This constructed view of England was also a powerful representation when Christie first began writing, but the historical locations of the BBC Marple texts filmed so far, with their lavishly and meticulously created facsimiles of pre–1960s England, have further provided compelling, and largely invented, visions of peaceful cohabitation and generally lawful behaviour – our recent 'Golden Ages'.[22] The heritage industry has manufactured a desire for the English country house in a harmonious England, which can be seen in the surprising persistence of country house and country living magazines, the quasi-ruralism of urban architecture, the Neo-Georgian, Victorian, and Edwardian trends of interior design.

Outside the heritage industry, the symptoms of a new *Home* with residual features of the past can be discovered in the re-emergence of a servant class of cooks, nannies and parlourmaids, and the retreat from the inner cities to the suburbs and beyond. All these cultural artefacts and practices appear to celebrate the past as the principal hope for the future. Such a celebration of the past also extends to the extolling of the good, old values to prepare for the new order. Marple's (and Christie's) Old Toryism, with its comforting exclusion of the belligerent aspects of Monetarist New Toryism, appears a benign anachronism in the 1980s. It is in this wider context that Christie's works and their reproductions are now partially received. A good deal of the satisfaction offered by the BBC's Miss Marple re-creations is in the invitation they extend to emigrate inwards to a world of the *Home* counties.

Notes

1. See John Cawelti, *Adventure, Mystery and Romance* (Chicago and London: University of Chicago Press, 1976) pp. 111–31; *Agatha Christie: First Lady of Crime*, ed. H. R. F. Keating (London: Weidenfeld and Nicolson, 1977) *passim*; Stephen Knight, *Form and Ideology in Crime Fiction* (London: Macmillan, 1980) pp. 107–34; Julian Symons, *Bloody Murder* (Harmondsworth, Middx.: Penguin, 1974) pp. 102–4, 110–12, 134–5.

2. A comprehensive listing of Christie's many works is available in Dennis Sanders and Len Lovallo, *The Agatha Christie Companion* (London: W. H. Allen, 1984) *passim*.

3. Catherine Belsey uses this helpful description in 'Constructing the Subject: Deconstructing the Text', in Judith Newton and Deborah Rosenfelt (eds), *Feminist Criticism and Social Change* (New York and London: Methuen, 1985) p. 53.

4. Ernst Bloch, 'Philosophische Ansicht des Detektivromans', in *Gesammelte Werke*, Bd 9 (Frankfurt: Suhrkamp, 1965) pp. 242–63. I am indebted to Bloch's distinction between the *detektivisch* and the *detektorisch* aspects of the crime narrative.

5. Rosalind Brunt has commented in a similar way on the image created of and by Barbara Cartland in 'A Career in Love: the Romantic World of Barbara Cartland', in Christopher Pawling (ed.), *Popular Fiction and Social Change* (London: Macmillan, 1984) pp. 127–56.

6. Janet Morgan cites a 1961 UNESCO report, which stated that Christie was the world's best-selling author with her books sold in 102 countries (twice as many as the runner-up, Graham Greene) in her thorough *Agatha Christie: A Biography* (London: Fontana, 1985) p. 326.

7. Sanders and Lovallo, *The Agatha Christie Companion*, p. 434.

8. *Observer*, 27 December 1987, offers an interesting interview with Christie's daughter, Rosalind, about the policies of 'Agatha Christie Ltd'.

9. 'Week's Good Cause', BBC Radio 4, St George's Day, 23 April 1988.

10. Knight, *Form and Ideology*, p. 117.

11. See Heinrich Meyer's introduction, 'Bestseller Research Problems', in Donald Ray Richards, *The German Bestseller in the 20th Century: A Complete Bibliography and Analysis, 1915–1940* (Berne: Herbert Lang, 1968).

12. Peter Zimmermann, *Der Bauernroman* (Stuttgart: J. B. Metzlersche, 1975) p. 99.

13. A much fuller description of *Heimatdichtung, Blut und Boden* and *Trivialliteratur* can be found in the following: Helga Geyer-Ryan, 'Popular Literature in the Third Reich', trans. Kiernan Ryan, Centre for Contemporary Cultural Studies, University of Birmingham Stencilled Occasional Paper, no. 60, pp. 1–15; Henry and Mary Garland, *The Oxford Companion to German Literature* (Oxford: Clarendon Press, 1976) p. 357; Hermann Glaser, *The Cultural Roots of National Socialism*, trans. Ernest A. Menze (London: Croom Helm, 1978) pp. 154–62; Uwe K. Ketelsen, *Völkisch-Nationale und National-sozialistische Literatur in Deutschland, 1890–1945* (Stuttgart: Metzler, 1976) *passim*; Walter Nutz, 'Trivialliteratur Seit 1965', in Paul Michael Lüzeler and Egon Schwarz (eds), *Deutsche Literatur in der Bundesrepublik seit 1965* (Königstein: Athenäum, 1980) pp. 150–63; J. M. Ritchie, *German Literature under National Socialism* (London: Croom Helm, 1983) pp. 8–20, 94–110; Zimmerman, *Der Bauernroman*, *passim*.

14. Agatha Christie, *An Autobiography* (London: Fontana/Collins, 1978) pp. 421–2.

15. Ibid., p. 423.

16. Mary Louise Pratt lists these activities as assumed female verbal procedures in 'Linguistic Utopias', in N. Fabb, D. Attridge, A. Durrant and C. MacCabe (eds), *The Linguistics of Writing* (Manchester: Manchester University Press, 1987) p. 54.

17. Although here glib categories of 'popular' and 'élite' break down, as Thomas Mann's *Buddenbrooks* (1901) was by far the best-selling novel in Germany in the early part of this century (1915–40).

18. Christie, *Autobiography*, p. 13.

19. See the Introduction by Peter Humm, Paul Stigant and Peter Widdowson in their *Popular Fictions: Essays in Literature and History* (London and New York: Methuen 1986), pp. 1–15, for a discussion of how television and film create a fusion of 'great' and 'minor' literature within the realm of the popular.

20. Simon Frith in 'The Pleasures of the Hearth' in *Formations of Pleasure*, ed. Formations Editorial Collective: Tony Bennett *et al.* (London: Routledge and Kegan Paul, 1983) pp. 101–23, discusses how the wireless was seen as a 'radio hearth' for the family, in the BBC's Reithian aims of creating a public service and entertainment for a common culture.

21. Other BBC Marple adaptations broadcast since 1984, outside the Christmas period, are *The Moving Finger, A Murder is Announced, A Pocket Full of Rye* and *Sleeping Murder*.
22. In making such a strong case for the cultural resonance of the country house in Christie's work, I appear to be at variance with Raymond Williams, who argues that her setting is a mere structural device in his *The Country and the City* (London: Chatto and Windus, 1973) pp. 248–9.

10

'Loving and Lying': Multiple Identity in John le Carré's *A Perfect Spy*

TONY BARLEY

In the first chapter of *A Perfect Spy*,[1] the missing double-agent Magnus Pym prepares himself for the painful task of reconstructing the authentic account of his life. Attentive to all kinds of metaphorical equivalent for personal identity, he begins to write when prompted by the sight of his (stolen) briefcase, 'strangely rigid from its steel lining':

> Everybody carried cases, he remembered, as he stared at it. Rick's was pigskin, Lippsie's was cardboard, Poppy's was a scruffy grey thing with marks printed on it to look like hide. And Jack – dear Jack – you have your marvellous old attaché case, faithful as the dog you had to shoot. (p. 36)

The case-history he carries is both legal brief and psychiatric record, its confidential contents kept protectively secure. Pym's well-defended personality none the less stands in contingent relation to others: his dead father, Rick (ostentatious and vulnerable), Lippsie, the surrogate mother and fantasy-lover of his childhood (fragile and unenduring), Poppy, the code-name of Axel, beloved friend, controller and surrogate father (consolingly familiar but self-concealing), and Jack Brotherhood, the reliable, paternal traditionalist (faithful but outdated). Pym's case-history inscribes a network of semi-familial attachments; it includes the four characters who have variously produced and initiated him into identity.

Pym's escape to a childhood haven far away from the dependencies of relationship is a (personal) defection from the real world to a 'safe house' that grants him a sense of comparative autonomy. His father's recent death frees Pym from the one pursuer he could never hide from and he now occupies a provisional space in which he can rewrite his lifetime of betrayal before being found (found-out). With others now present only in memory or imagination, he

152

feels able at last to state his own case definitely. He determines to 'tell it straight':

> No evasions, no fictions, no devices. Just my over-promised self set free. . . . To tell it to all of you who own me, to whom I have given myself with such unthinking liberality. . . .
>   To all my creditors and co-owners, here once and for all the settlement of arrears.   (p. 36)

The psychological contradictions established here are explored throughout *A Perfect Spy*, but with special rigour in Pym's own testimony, where he is shown giving himself away once more, but doing so freely, and thus attempting to repossess himself. The double-agent's 'over-promised', owned, 'given', stolen self, previously sustained through duplicity, identifies the dispersed Pym of social interaction, the third-person hero of his 'I'-narrative: 'What version of himself Pym supplied that day, and had to live with for the coming months, I do not remember. . . . As best he could, he gave you what he thought you were looking for' (p. 276).

The novel's separation of its principal character into a partly disembodied, residual self (the confessing informer who provides an alternative narrative voice), and a plural, refracted Pym who exists *only* within social interactions, instantly offers a challenge to ideologies of the autonomous and self-possessing subject. Almost immediately, however, that challenge seems calmly refused, and then smoothly redeployed in ideological defence: Pym's ever-renewing entourage of identities merely instances the moral disintegration of the con-man. The novel's association of Pym-, or Rick-like multiplicity with delinquency, criminality, political treachery and, as if they were not enough, implied mental illness, invites the obvious conclusion that, of itself, the deviance of Pym-I (and Rick) reinforces the assumed containment of the normal self-contained individual, one who is integrated positively within the larger stabilities of the normal family in normal society. In fact *A Perfect Spy* postpones that simplicity by assigning the dispersed Pym-I to three specific interpretative contexts, each of which stakes its respective claim on him. The first is R. D. Laing's phenomenology of the schizoid individual, the second is Schiller's naïve/ sentimental antinomy and last – inevitably – Freud's conscious/ unconscious distinction.

The ten and more years in which Laing's 'anti-psychiatry'

enjoyed an influence in Anglo-Saxon culture have been succeeded by a period in which even its faintest traces seem to have disappeared. The powerful 'reinstatement' of psychoanalysis was mainly, but not exclusively, responsible for Laing's critical dismissal; both Juliet Mitchell's *Psychoanalysis and Feminism*[2] and Peter Sedgwick's *Psycho Politics*[3] include sharply argued critiques that take issue with his varied methodological assumptions and dispute his radical claims. It is not the place here to try to review the convincing arguments against Laing's analysis of the schizoid state – even though some of them do have a bearing on le Carré's portrayal of his principal character. My aim in citing *The Divided Self* (1960)[4] is not to engage with Laing's analyses as such, but rather with their potential for descriptive comparison. *The Divided Self* depicts and interprets its split 'individuals' in a meticulous detail that provides vivid commentary on the case of Pym-I. The reading of *A Perfect Spy* that follows relies fully on Laing's terminology and attempts to stay within his reflective framework.

In writing to Tom about Pym's time in post-war Austria, the I-narrator refers, as though in afterthought, to his own divided self: 'Austria in those days was a different country . . . and Vienna was a divided city like Berlin or your father' (p. 438). The metaphor is as typical of le Carré as it is of Laing, but perhaps it is more typical still of the period of resumed Cold War in which both writers, at virtually the same historical instant (1960–4), published their first books and first achieved popularity. Le Carré was certainly not alone in exploiting images of political geometry for their relation to individual psychology. *Call for the Dead* (1961)[5] ends with a fatalistic George Smiley suspended 'between two worlds' and contemplating two equally unfeasible alternatives; not East and West it transpires, but 'the pathetic quest for love, or the return to solitude' (p. 156). In *The Spy Who Came in From the Cold* (1963),[6] Leamas endures a comparable alienation in living out his role as an assumed defector:

> while a confidence trickster, a play-actor or a gambler can return from his performance to the ranks of his admirers, the secret agent knows no such relief. For him, deception is first a matter of self-defence. . . . [He] must in all circumstances withhold himself from those in whom he should naturally confide. . . .
> Aware of the overwhelming temptations which assail a man permanently isolated in his deceit . . . he compelled himself to live with the personality he had assumed. (p. 140)

These two schizoid movements even share stylistic resemblances with Laing's individual:

> in the first place, there is a rent in his relation with the world and, in the second, there is a disruption of his relation with himself. Such a person is not able to experience himself 'together with' others or 'at home' in the world, but, on the contrary, he experiences himself in despairing aloneness and isolation; moreover he does not experience himself as a complete person, but rather as 'split' in various ways. (DS, p. 17)

Smiley's dilemma is the schizoid's too – 'the need for one's total existence to be recognized; the need, in fact, to be loved', yet facing 'complete isolation'; dreading a 'complete merging of identity', but fearing equally its 'autistic' alternative (DS, pp. 119, 53). And Leamas's self-protecting deceit is the schizoid defence of 'a false-self system' that operates in any and every interaction with others, role-playing to keep the 'inner' self entirely hidden from view (DS, p. 73).

If such comparisons reflect no more than a common cultural background, le Carré's portrayal of a schizophrenic patient in *Smiley's People* (1980)[7] is clearly indebted to Laing, even to the extent of duplicating the notion that schizophrenia develops in response to the inauthentic compliance demanded within family relationships. 'Not only the mother', writes Laing, 'but also the total family situation may impede rather than facilitate the child's capacity to participate in a real shared world, as self-with-other' (DS, p. 189).

Tatiana's (late-adolescent) psychosis has developed as a result of extreme family circumstances – her father 'Karla' arranged the disappearance (and probable murder) of her mother. Unable to suppress this knowledge, she is deemed 'anti-social' by that larger family that is the State. Now hospitalised and quite dis-integrated, she sees other people as mirror-images of themselves and imagines further fragmenting ways 'of handling what Dr Reudi [R.D.?] called the "divided nature"' (p. 281). Charlie, the young actress-heroine of le Carré's next novel, *The Little Drummer Girl* (1983),[8] evokes similar Laingian echoes in her ambiguous estrangement from her parents, and her state of 'unfinished' adolescence. Like Pym-I, Charlie enacts 'feeble versions of herself' (p. 173); unlike him, she is aware that: 'the divide between her inner and outer world had been a flimsy affair at the best of times' (p. 521).

With *A Perfect Spy*, le Carré represents family interaction directly for the first time, contrasting the domestic normality of Magnus, Mary and Tom with the rogue community of Pym's childhood: a bizarre and intermittently convened extended-family precariously held together by a collective fantasy and a conspiracy of silence regarding its underlying disharmonies. Initially, Rick's fantasy 'Court' is one of festive misrule, aggrandised both by its magnanimous 'King', and by the I-narrator's nostalgic recollection of his childish wonder at its warmth. Rick's *ménage-à-trois* with runaway wife Dorothy and a refugee-lover Lippsie is part of a larger household with its own crooked lawyer, accountant and secretary. Attendant gamblers, helpers and entertainers, and various local 'Lovelies' – there 'to be seen right by Rick and to bathe in his glory' (p. 97) – make up the remaining retinue. For Pym-I, the Court is 'Paradise' until its first disbandment in the 'Fall', which brings Rick's arrest, Lippsie's defection and his own entry into criminal deceit, betrayal, guilt and resentment.

The extravagant image le Carré builds in the 'Court' sections of the novel promotes solid ironies. Festivity covers distress and for all its pleasures, both before and after the Fall, the family assembly expresses damage and hurt. Rick's sexual arrangements prove largely coercive; the six- or seven-year-old child observes the unspoken jealousy between Dorothy and Lippsie, witnesses Dorothy's withdrawal and 'weeping' depression, and overhears Lippsie vainly refusing to become Rick's thief. The wider communality depends upon criminal fraternity. 'Paradise' is a thieves' den; the libertine 'Court' is Lippsie's 'gilded prison' (p. 101), and it heralds future court appearances. The constant threat of Rick's worst crime catching up on him is mysteriously symbolised in the prohibitions attaching to the name 'Wentworth', which becomes, for the boy, 'synonymous with fear and an end to things' (p. 103). Thus situated, Pym-I readily qualifies for membership of Laing's deviant, schizoid élite.

Pym adapts to gratify what he imagines is asked of him by others. The identities he produces *en route* sometimes assume themselves spontaneously, but more often they are consciously adopted because meeting the need to comply requires skilled calculation. The social Pym therefore masters the manipulative techniques of the con-artist and spy; indeed he often plays those very roles. Yet whether or not a given 'version' has been premeditated, and whether or not Pym is impersonating someone else or acting at being himself in his encounters with other people, the identities he assumes are ultimately conditioned by, and dependent upon – in a sense *created by* – the will and the desire of others. Late in the novel, and from his special position of privileged insight, Axel remarks on the results of such circular phenomenology: 'Magnus is a great imitator, even when he doesn't know it. Really I sometimes think he is entirely put together from bits of other people, poor fellow' (p. 501). Quite regardless of his 'true' attitude towards others, Pym overrides private sympathies and suppresses secret contempt in his urge to conform with others' expectations – in marital and domestic privacies as in criminal and intelligence missions, with friends and lovers as in institutions. Even as the eight year old who executes a carefully planned escape from the home of hated Uncle Makepeace (by despoiling the latter's sanctuary), Pym enacts that version of himself ('the young criminal', 'the convict that he was' – pp. 109, 112) that, he senses, Makepeace's moralistic gaze has determined to form.

Produced through empathy, each identity succeeds to the extent that it gratifies; the reward consists more in Pym's delight at pleasing (that is, in being acknowledged and affirmed) than in the satisfactions of expertly conning the unaware (that is, of maintaining complete control over the situation, of confirming Pym's autonomy within the relationship). But such rewards are empty. Any recognition or affection won by pleasing merely affirms the 'false self', immediately negating its authenticating function in respect both of Pym-I and the relationship in which it arose. Similarly, the verification, via pretence, of his independence and self-control also proves hollow. It could hardly have been otherwise. Pym's need to be in control is predicated upon concealing his 'real' or 'inner' self and as such it automatically renders the authentication project impossible. Pym's need to keep 'I' well hidden from others is self-protective: the discovery of 'I' would instantly entail the dissolution of the 'false' Pym, just as the 'inner' self needs insulating against the implosion that would occur were it ever in open relationship with others. The never-ending circularities here are giddying and that sense is compounded in recollecting that Pym is seldom in, or under, control. Although his manipulations are saturated in deliberate pretence, Pym's compulsion to comply with others predominates and, as the I-narrator makes clear, in this state, his indiscriminate craving and (sado-) masochistic responses are ungoverned and ungovernable:

So there's yet another Pym for you, Jack, and you had better add him to my file even if he is neither admirable nor, I suspect comprehensible to you, though Poppy knew him inside out from the first day. He's the Pym who can't rest till he's touched the love in people, then can't rest till he's hacked his way out of it. . . . The Pym who does nothing cynically, nothing without conviction. Who sets events in motion in order to become their victim, which he calls decision, and ties himself into pointless relationships, which he calls loyalty. Then waits for the next event to get him out of the last one, which he calls destiny. . . . It's Pym the Saturday-night juggler bounding round the table and spinning one stupid plate after another because he can't bear to let anyone down for a second and so lose their esteem.   (pp. 195–6)

Aware, determinedly honest, yet helpless, the 'I'-self who so scrupulously relates Pym's chaotic activities does so in changing tones of critical resentment, dissociated sympathy, fear and guilt. Threatened by and weaker than Pym, 'I' typically 'exists' as an 'unembodied' mental state, usually in solitude (*DS*, p. 77). Pym tells Belinda of his someday intention 'to lock myself away and tell the truth' (p. 304), and the I-self finds his domain in the confined privacy of a rented seaside guest-room. This offers safety and control – sufficient to attempt a kind of self-unification in the writing of his testimony. Debarred from real relationships, the I-narrator relates only to 'himself' – to Pym, and, in Laing's words: 'to depersonalized persons, to phantoms of his own phantasies (imagos), perhaps to things' (*DS*, p. 77). Simultaneously the object of others', and of his own investigations, the I-narrator is divided from his 'false' self by self-reflection. Now safely alone, the self-conscious 'I' experiences 'Pym'/'Magnus'/'Titch' – even simply 'he', as remembered or imagined images that can pose no threat to his automony. In whatever remembered role, the false Pyms should be as differentiated from the authentic 'I' as Brotherhood, or Mary, or Kate, or Grant. In telling Pym's story, however, 'I' is also re-creating his own; criticising Pym (and Rick, Pym's model) involves self-castigation, recalling a past encounter automatically involves (within I's imaginary world) entering into a relationship with that other.

From time to time the I-narrator buckles under the pressure, forfeiting control and self-security. Command over tense, person, chronology and location wavers and the I-narrator loses himself in moments of identification with one or other of Pym's multiple selves. Alternatively, when objectivity gives way to remorse or frustration, the I-narrator periodically 'forgets' that he is writing to his son, and switches, temporarily, to address another (Mary or Brotherhood or Rick or himself), invariably adopting an appropriate voice; his self-persecuting text itself becomes schizoid. At one point, the novel's main narrative shows him beginning 'a prisoner's tour' of Miss Dubber's room, then 'glowering at the flames while the shaking grew more violent' (pp. 354–5). Laing summarises: 'The "inner" self becomes itself split, and loses its own identity and integrity. . . . The attempt to kill the self may be undertaken intentionally. . . . The place of safety becomes a prison. Its would-be haven becomes a hell' (*DS*, pp. 161–2). Fear of uncontrol and its destructive effects thus underlies *all* of the individual's experience in Laing's model; its expression as criminal duplicity in Pym's 'false' self finds an overall correlative in the role of theft and its relation to identity. Lacking control over 'who or what comes into him' and over 'who or what leaves him', the schizoid: 'prefers to *steal*, rather than to be given. He prefers to give, rather than have anything, as he feels, stolen from him' (*DS*, p. 83).

Most of Pym's serial betrayals (gifts) are accompanied by the grim and guilty satisfaction of recovering, by theft, something previously given away. When Pym betrays Axel to Brotherhood, he imagines himself back 'in Rick's dressing-room, looking for a way of stealing back the love he had given to a wrong cause' (p. 284). As a rule, the generosity expressed in his betrayals is unreciprocated as the love he requires in return remains unsupplied. But when Axel forgives him – and recruits him as a double-agent – Pym experiences himself 'glowing and exulting', with 'half a dozen' of his identities 'reconstructed', as he embarks on his first act of high treason. This theft, for once, involves no self-torturing equivocation because the transaction it heralds seems an authentic and equal exchange: 'I will bring you gifts as you brought gifts to me' (p. 475). Now, theft signifies love and must be decriminalized: 'Not an invasion. Not a retribution . . . I am here to administer a caress' (p. 477).

The interactions of *A Perfect Spy* operate a dialectic of loving and lying, pleasing and concealing, staying and defecting, giving and stealing. Each term in these pairs at some point merges with its opposite, but the notion of stealing, and being stolen *from*, have a special role in the novel as pre-given functions of identity. When, for example, Pym-I describes childhood photographs of himself in the letter to Tom, he writes: 'All are out of focus; all have a furtive, stolen look about them' (p. 109). Again, Laing illuminates:

> Schizoid phantasies of stealing and being robbed are based on this dilemma. If you steal what you want from the other . . . you are not at the mercy of what is given. But every intention is instantly felt to be reciprocated. The desire to steal breeds phobias of being robbed. The phantasy that one has got any worth that one possesses by stealing it is accompanied by the counter-phantasy that the worth that others have has been stolen from oneself . . . and that anything one has will be taken away finally: not only what one *has*, but what one *is*, one's very self. Hence the common schizophrenic complaint that the 'self' has been stolen. (*DS*, p. 92)

Brotherhood hears that same complaint in interrogating Mary, who reluctantly yields the results of one of her domestic espionage missions. She had found a chart drawn on 'cartridge paper stolen from her sketch block' and had read Magnus's notes for a projected novel, which, like *A Perfect Spy*, slips 'from third to first person'. A draft chapter sketches a frenzied fight between the hero and his creditors

> even with no face left I am doing what I should have done thirty-five years ago, to Jack and Rick and all the mothers and fathers, for stealing my life off a plate while I watched you do it. Poppy, Jack, the rest of you. (pp. 162–3)

Taken in its specific narrative context, this quotation seems to have crucial force in achieving the novel's silent aim of irrevocably shifting the status of its central character from 'innocent villain' to 'innocent victim' – a process that involves dissociating from the I-narrator's guilt, reclassifying Pym's compulsion as socially inevitable and removing him from the deviant category headed by Rick to relocate him in terms of similarity with others. Magnus's injured resentment, as expressed in the rough notes Mary recalls, invites these resolutions precisely because it appears outside the I-narrator's testimony, because its discovery is unintended and because it has been 'disguised' as fictitious. Mary, however, is guilty on all counts: her sight of its contents is a stolen glance, her intrusion a deliberate and professionally executed betrayal intended as punishment and revenge for an adultery she suspects, wrongly, he is currently enjoying. Mary too has a divided self then, and her duplicity damningly pre-dates her time and training with 'The Firm'; in fact it began, just like Pym's, in childhood, but unlike his, it was learned *as a game*, within a family that seems devoid of conflict:

> At Plush when she was a girl they had called it Kim's Game and played it every New Year's Eve along with acting games and Murder and reels. At the training house, when she was supposed to be adult, they called it Observation and played it round the sleepy villages. (p. 160)

A natural spy who lacks Pym-I's determining excuses, Mary has herself lived the inauthenticity of refusing to admit to her know-ledge of Magnus's treachery – just like Kate, the Ollingers, the Lederers, Membury and Syd – other 'innocent' representatives of the worlds Pym-I inhabits.

Notions of divided and *doubled* personality are familiar in le Carré's fiction, not least in the novel that most closely prefigures *A Perfect Spy: The Naive and Sentimental Lover* (1971).[9] The transactions portrayed there between a criminal father and his adult son are the prototypes of many episodes in *A Perfect Spy*, while the movement between heterosexuality and homosexuality, spontaneity and in-hibition, and the interest in competing personal loyalties, are common to both novels. It is no accident at all that Pym resembles 'sentimental' Cassidy in seeking to please, cultivating others and in conforming to social roles. Nor that like Cassidy, the I-narrator yearns for the kind of natural, uncompromised being symbolised in 'naive' Shamus – the 'real' self Cassidy desires. Significantly, le Carré exploits the fantasy dimension of *The Naive and Sentimental Lover* to make Shamus's discrete existence ambiguous.

A Perfect Spy shows le Carré once again borrowing from 'Über naive und sentimentalische Dichtung', the essay in which Schiller describes the alienated self-consciousness of the 'modern' artist as 'sentimental':[10]

> we never see the object itself, but what the intelligence and reflection of the poet have made of the object; and even when the poet himself is that object, when he wishes to represent his own feelings, we are not informed of his condition at first hand; we

only see how it is reflected in his mind and wnat he has thought of it as spectator of himself. ('On Simple and Sentimental Poetry', pp. 296, 306–7)

Parallels with Schiller and his thesis stand out in every chapter of *A Perfect Spy* – even though the entire novel is dense with literary and historical allusion. The Goethe–Schiller relationship from which the essay arose shadows that of Pym-I and Axel, while the treasured, talismanic copy of *Simplicissimus* (their code-book) pointedly invokes the (apparent) supreme naïvety of its eponymous hero. In introducing Pym to German culture, Axel proudly explains that his birthplace once hosted 'Goethe and Schiller' (p. 264), and offers critical opinions on Kleist (p. 269), one of the three sentimental poets Schiller targets, and an obvious forerunner of Pym-I:

> Kleist's poetic instinct leads him far away from the narrow circle of social relations, into solitude . . . the image of social life and its anguish pursues him, and also, alas! its chains. What he flees from he carries within himself. . . . His imagination is vivid and active, but more variable than rich. . . . Traits succeed each other rapidly, without . . . rounding to a form, a figure. ('On Simple and Sentimental Poetry', p. 309)

The very resonance of these (and many other) associations that link le Carré's hero with one or both terms of Schiller's dichotomy must testify against a reading of *A Perfect Spy* that regards Pym-I as portraying the subject's fundamental dispersal. Viewed in the light of Schiller's model, the I-narrator's retracing process features comfortably within the orthodoxies of romanticism, where the divided self seeks to synthesise merely the 'I' that experiences and the 'I' that reflects. It matters little whether or not the division seems 'healable' because, from the outset, it has been posed purely within the terms of a potential unification.

None the less, there is certainly pathos in the fact that the I-narrator's quest for self-integration hopelessly follows the very route Schiller discounts – an attempted return to the lost simplicities of childhood. Pym-I retreats to 'one of his ideal places' (p. 524), the site of idyllic boyhood holidays with Rick; the result is a sad, distracted parody:

> The stairs belonged to the houses of his childhood so he skipped

lightly up them and forgot his aches and pains. The star-of-Bethlehem lampshade on the landing . . . was an old friend from the Glades. . . . When he pushed open the door of his room, everything winked and smiled at him like a surprise party.

(p. 604)

The romantic associations in this are clear: the hero's journey involves rejecting his dependency upon others and retracing the past in order to recover unity with an ideal opposite (childhood 'Paradise'). Previous le Carréan questors are close at hand. Smiley's opposite, Karla, seems to be a figure of ideal evil whom he can only pursue by excluding extant relationships (notably with his wife, Ann), and by reconstructing Karla's past. But, at the end of the quest, Smiley eventually finds mutual resemblance in place of the supposed difference; his own divided self proves mirrored in Karla's dual nature. With Pym-'I', le Carré multiplies the reflections in dizzying planes of recession. Intent on recovering himself from the dependent Pym, the 'I' needs to separate himself from Rick, who, in death as in life, follows him as a loved-and-hated image of his opposite. Yet, paradoxically, Pym-I has always walked in Rick's footsteps and his own history inevitably repeats Rick – and Rick's history – in a hated-and-loved identification. The point of arrival proves to be the point of departure. These quests do not progress developmentally, they regress into circular self-reflection, beginning with the solitary self and ending with it.

Axel is another double, both opposite and identical: opposite in nationality, culture and political affiliation, as surrogate father and as the hero's beloved other; identical in being a secret agent, in his multiple identities, his professed lack of political allegiance and in his loving betrayals. In addition, Axel is the hero's friend and shadow-guide, whose intense reality for Pym-I seems to be conditional on his very indeterminacy. Axel's personal history has the ring of a cover-story, his 'home town' Carlsbad 'no longer exists' (p. 264), while his punning name, which may in any event be false, inscribes a split but no origins. So when the hero introduces himself in his father's name ('My name is Pym'), Axel is just 'Axel', and when pressed for further definition, he supplies only the tautology of repetition: 'Herr Axel Axel. My parents forgot to give me a second name' (pp. 259–60). Axel's domain is extra-territorial, more a place of mind than a place. At one point he tells Sir Magnus: 'We are in no-man's-land here. We can arrest each other' (p. 458) and Pym, in imaginary conversation with him, readily agrees: 'We are men of the middle ground – we have founded our own country with a population of two' (p. 478).

Although for the reader Axel is never simply a cypher or 'figure', for Pym-I his imaginary status is often overriding: 'With Axel so much upon his conscience . . . Pym knew for a fact that Axel did not exist' (p. 456). Neither is he an addressee of I-narrator's auto-biography – as the double that he is, he knows the whole truth already. And as a writer, and as Pym's literary mentor – and rival, Axel is sustained more as a composite of fictional characters than as a 'personality': 'He's writing his Wilhelm Meister autobiography, thought Pym indignantly. That was my idea, not his' (p. 290). True to form, Axel has his 'many-towered castle' (p. 546), a mountain hideaway set aside by the Czech Service for the rest and recreation of treasured agents. Ironically suggesting the tower of *Wilhelm Meister*,[11] it also conjures Kafka's Castle, and Pym's first trip there follows a contact meeting 'in the famous Tyn Church, which has a window looking into Kafka's old apartment' (p. 539); here, he is shown reading a passage from *The Trial*. Axel's principal heritage though must lie in Villiers's *fin-de-siècle* figure, whose 'life of pure reflection and imagination' Edmund Wilson took as the zenith of the Symbolist transformation of Romantic poetry.[12]

From his first appearance then, le Carré's Axel belongs to a category that Jan B. Gordon has summarily described in an essay devoted neither to le Carré nor Schiller nor Symbolism nor even to 'doubles' in literature but – and this completes another circle – to the 'meta-journey of R. D. Laing':

> so many companions of questors en route to one or another of those domed and doomed kingdoms of art in the nineteenth century seem to be but extensions of the solitary wanderer. Such 'doubling' is nothing more than the aestheticization of self-consciousness and comes to be stylistically manifested as the *doppelganger* in stories like *Dr Jekyll and Mr Hyde* or *The Picture of Dorian Gray*.[13]

In terms of the present argument, Gordon's critique of Laing applies equally to le Carré's appropriations of romanticism by implying that the mere operation of the self-reflexive faculty *of itself* enforces no necessary challenge to the belief that every individual comes naturally endowed with their own essential, coherent and consistent self; quite the reverse, in fact.

Of course, it is also the case that the alienation accompanying Schiller's 'Sentimental' standpoint and Laing's 'real', 'subjective', 'private', 'inner' self-consciousness, as well as that prompting the creation of 'doubles', may indeed reflect a fundamental division, but a division of a different kind: 'I believe,' writes Freud:

> that when poets complain that two souls dwell in the human breast, and when popular psychologists talk of the splitting of people's egos, what they are thinking of is this division . . . between the critical agency and the rest of the ego, and not the antithesis discovered by psycho-analysis between the ego and what is unconscious and repressed.[14]

Le Carré takes considerable steps to guard against the psychoanalysis of the dis-integrated subject of *A Perfect Spy*. In the short breathing-space just before he begins to set down his history, the I-narrator scribbles a few lines of 'whatever came into his head' (p. 37), and this free association yields fragments of rhymes, sayings and stories spoken in childhood and now produced 'unconsciously' as thoughts that each double back on themselves, ostensibly inviting psychoanalysis: 'All work and no play makes Jack a dull spy. Poppy, Poppy, on the wall. Miss Dubber must a-cruising go. Eat good bread, poor Rickie's dead. Rickie-Tickie father' (p. 37). Poppy (Axel as 'I') is a mirror-image, that which identifies Pym-I to himself, reflects him narcissistically, suggests a Snow White–Wicked Queen dialectic and gives him sight of a loved father (Pop or Papa, not 'Rick') Miss Dubber is the surrogate mother and, as 'Miss', is simultaneously not-mother but the imaginary ideal opposite of mother; in being subject to his needs, dependent upon him, and only absent in accord with his will ('must a-cruising go'), she reverses his infant helplessness. Just as Axel/Poppy has nicknamed him 'Sir Magnus', thus acknowledging him as father (great sire), so too Miss Dubber names and knights him: 'He could have a knighthood by now for all we know' (p. 18). Rick is the 'murdered' (bad) father ingested and assimilated as 'good bread'; both the cunning snake-killer (castrator) of Kipling's mongoose story, *Rikki-Tikki-Tavi*, and, dead, its (castrated) victim, the killed-snake.

However much this kind of reading seems signposted, the placing of the free-association passage so early in the novel together with the raw, uncontextualised nature of its references obliges the reader to shelve any initial notions of detecting the Oedipal crime. The bewildering density of narrative material and the disorientation caused by shifts of voice and shifting addresses instead forces the attention on to the more pressing business of identifying names and characters and recognising basic plot-connections. In the same way, the complex account of Rick's first arrest and its enormous ramifications in fracturing the already deforming Court/family, and of Magnus's criminal complicity in aiding his father by, significantly, concealing evidence, emphasises conscious perception of the social (domestic/legal/criminal) world at the expense of what is simultaneously an image of the child's unconscious world.

In the Paradise/Fall/Purgatory sections of the novel, the Oedipal crime *is* perpetrated and, so to speak, it is committed with a vengeance. The psychoanalytic description here is superb, but it is kept (perhaps appropriately) hidden, almost as if it were repressed material. Calling his mother and father by their first names and not by role names, and having two mother-figures – one (Dorothy) helpless, the other (Lippsie) a protector and sexual fantasy – the loosely located Magnus finds himself powerless in his desire to rescue and possess either of Rick's prisoners and possessions. His imaginary relationship with both women is guilt-laden and when the crisis of the Fall occurs his desire to save his loved father is mixed with resentment and aggression towards his rival:

> But Rick wouldn't hear him. He was rushing between the papers and the cabinet, loading up the drawers. So Pym went to him and punched him hard on the upper arm, as hard as he could on the soft bit just above the steel spring he wore to keep his silk shirt sleeve straight, and Rick flung round on him and his hand went back to strike him. . . . [Rick's] eyes were scared and crying. (pp. 104–5)

Rick's removal by the police shows Magnus's murderous desire fulfilled, and accordingly: 'a great calm descended over Pym. He felt refreshed and freed of an intolerable burden' (p. 107).

Though still fearing that Rick might return, Magnus now has no obstacle blocking his way to Lippsie, yet Lippsie ran away during his moment of triumph, and Pym is 'furious': 'You hid, he accused her in the secret dialogue he constantly conducted with her.' Lippsie's absence from Purgatory seals this new resentment: 'I guess she was trying to make one of her breaks from me, using

Rick's absence to cut herself off' (p. 108). Lippsie's subsequent suicide ('a judgment upon himself', p. 93) guiltily confirms his punitive desires, just as in earlier days he had somehow 'caused' his mother's depressive withdrawals:

> If Dorothy had been dying Pym could have gone on nursing her for ever, no question. But she wasn't so he resented her instead. In fact soon he began to weary of her altogether and wonder whether the wrong parent had gone on holiday, and whether Lippsie was his real mother and he had made an awful mistake. (p. 110)

Other 'mothers' become 'persecutors' with 'an air of the wardress about them' (p. 109) and Magnus's future betrayals and denials of (or rather, reprisals against) adult women replay these partly *pre*-Oedipal dramas in his father's misogynistic terms:

> [Lippsie's] demise entrenched him as a self-reliant person, confirming him in his knowledge that women were fickle and liable to sudden disappearance. . . . With Lippsie gone his love for Rick became once more unobstructed. (p. 133)

In fact, Magnus's removal of women to the peripheries of his narrative seems to repress Kleinian envies in order to highlight instead the more 'acceptable' father–son antagonism and affection. Disabled from completing the Oedipal stage, Magnus 'faultily' introjects the image of his father and his half-feared but still-despised authority – as 'King' and 'God's representative' and as 'his own' relentless, omniscient conscience. Yet this teasing invitation to pursue a psychoanalytic reading never remains open for long. Throughout the novel, the reader's gaze is controlled so as to deflect or refuse interpretations that might challenge the I-narrator's privileged knowledge.

If the I-narrator is inadvertently 'giving himself away', if he is consciously falsifying, if his account is a distortive self-defence, if his truth-telling is as self-deceiving as the naive Pym, and if his intended suicide attests not to his new-found 'freedom' but to the perpetuation of his aggressive desires, these possibilities have all been anticipated and they remain securely contained by narrator and author alike. 'Freudian' explanations are periodically pre-empted, raised as sufficiently obvious to be taken initially as 'given', yet formulated with sufficient reductive crudeness to ensure their reception as facile and inadequate. Each of the following 'Freudian' interventions, for instance, is set up so as to be speedily brushed aside:

> 'I'm free.' Rick's dead, so Magnus is free. He's one of your Freudian types who can't say 'Father'.   (Brotherhood, p. 83)

> Some men, I think they really want to castrate their fathers all their lives.   (Bee Lederer, p. 412)

> Know why so many defectors redefect? . . . It's in and out of the womb all the time. Have you ever noticed that about defectors – the one common factor in all that crazy band? – they're immature. Forgive me, they are *literary* motherfuckers.   (Grant Lederer, p. 325)

Regardless of the numerous descriptions of Pym's naïve compulsion, the novel's overriding allegiance is not to the unconscious but to consciousness. This is always apparent in the presentation of the I-narrator, whose authority and authenticity, like that of Laing's 'true' self, is never questioned.

The allusive method of the novel is also enlisted to serve the cause of the I-narrator's invulnerability. Le Carré ensures that the dubious veracity attaching variously to many of the works standing within and behind *A Perfect Spy* does *not* attach also to this novel. Thus, for example, Pym's student appraisal of Grimmelshausen's *Simplicissimus*:

> he was pleased to be able to report, in a twenty-page assault on the upstart Grimmelshausen, that [he] . . . had undermined his validity by fighting on both sides in the Thirty Years War. As a final swipe he suggested that Grimmelshausen's false names cast doubt upon his authorship.   (p. 340)[15]

Employing the same tactic he used to immunise against the threat of Freud, le Carré–I evokes a climate of suspicion concerning authorial or narratorial 'unreliability' in the works of his chosen literary precursors: Grimmelshausen, Clarendon,[16] Ford Madox Ford, Hašek, Thomas Mann.[17] By pointing openly to the possible evasiveness and duplicity of the 'autobiographical' texts he admires, the writer quite simply *gains* credibility for his own: warning his readers to doubt his account anticipates and provokes scepticism in order to ease its removal from the agenda.

For le Carré, Pym-I has not been constructed as subject in the way psychoanalysis proposes all human beings are – in opposition to the unconscious – but instead has developed quite idiosyncratically in (hurt) reaction to the crossed and frustrated emotional communications that he actually experienced as an already-individuated child with unmet needs in a perverse family situation. Le Carré's treatment of Magnus's perception of his displacement during childhood is brilliantly observed, but it is predicated on that series of damaging acts that to some extent, alibi Pym-I by evoking sympathies in the reader that keep the I-narrator protected from any more penetrating analytical gaze which might challenge and, even worse, dismiss the privileged, all-aware, nothing-but-the-truth status of his testimony. Forced into his realm of over-sensitive self-consciousness because Pym-as-child ('orphan', p. 160) lacked loving security, the I-narrator stands morally protected from interrogation as the not-guilty product of parents who were not 'good enough' to ensure his healthy development.[18] The exposure of the subject in multiplicity, a potential throughout *A Perfect Spy*, has been ensured against; the open availability of 'I' is already foreclosed. Axel's sympathetic rebuke is based on accurate observation of Pym-I: 'You think that by dividing everything you can pass between (p. 456), but le Carré's subject does pass between his divisions, and he does so unstable yet still whole.

Notes

1. John le Carré, *A Perfect Spy* (London: Hodder and Stoughton, 1986; London: Coronet (pbk), 1987). All quotations from le Carré's novels are taken from currently available paperback editions.
2. Juliet Mitchell, *Psychoanalysis and Feminism* (Harmondsworth, Middx.: Penguin, 1975) pp. 229–92, 382–9.
3. Peter Sedgwick, *Psycho Politics* (London: Pluto Press, 1982) chaps 3, 4. See also Sedgwick's earlier essay 'R. D. Laing: Self, Symptom and Society', *Salmagundi* (Spring 1971), reprinted in *Laing and Anti-Psychiatry*, ed. Robert Boyers and Robert Orrill (Harmondsworth, Middx.: Penguin, 1971) pp. 11–47.
4. R. D. Laing, *The Divided Self* (London: Tavistock, 1960; Harmondsworth, Middx.: Penguin, 1965). Laing's first book, subsequently

abbreviated as *DS* in this chapter, contains in embryonic form his later assertions regarding the role of the family nexus in schizophrenia (see *Sanity, Madness and the Family*, with A. Esterson (London: Tavistock, 1964)); Laing's concentration on the 'individual' person/patient in *The Divided Self*, however, makes this work peculiarly appropriate for comparison with *A Perfect Spy*.

5. John le Carré, *Call for the Dead* (London: Victor Gollancz, 1961; Harmondsworth, Middx.: Penguin, 1972).

6. John le Carré, *The Spy Who Came in From the Cold* (London: Victor Gollancz, 1963; London: Pan, 1964).

7. John le Carré, *Smiley's People* (London: Hodder and Stoughton, 1980; London: Pan, 1980).

8. John le Carré, *The Little Drummer Girl* (London: Hodder and Stoughton, 1983; London: Pan, 1984).

9. John le Carré, *The Naive and Sentimental Lover* (London: Hodder and Stoughton, 1971: London: Pan, 1972).

10. F. Schiller, *The Works*, trans. uncredited (New York: John Williams 1880) vol. IV, pp. 287–309 and F. Schiller, *Sämtliche Werke*, ed. G. Fricke and H. Göpfert (Munich: Hanser, 1965–7) vol. V, pp. 716–37.

11. For a dicussion of the centrality of Goethe's 'Society of the Tower' both to the *Bildungsroman* and the development of the novel, see Franco Moretti, *The Way of the World: The Bildungsroman in European Culture* (London: Verso, 1987) pp. 18–38.

12. Edmund Wilson, *Axel's Castle: A Study in the Imaginative Literature of 1870–1930* (New York: Charles Scribner's Sons, 1931) pp. 259–69, see esp. pp. 260, 265.

13. Jan B. Gordon, 'The Meta-Journey of R. D. Laing', in *Laing and Anti-Psychiatry*, pp. 48–76, see esp. p. 65.

14. Freud, 'The Uncanny', 1919, *Standard Edition of the Complete Psychological Works*, ed. J. B. Strachey (London: Hogarth Press, 1953–74) vol. XVII, pp. 219–52, see esp. p. 235, n. 2. Juliet Mitchell contrasts Freud's distinction with Laing's (*Psychoanalysis and Feminism*, p. 388).

15. In his study of Grimmelshausen's life, Kenneth Negus describes: 'certain [financial] peculiarities that are puzzling, particularly for assessing Grimmelshausen's honesty' and comments that in his writings, 'extensive literary borrowings were blended with the autobiographical elements to form organic wholes that often defy attempts to distinguish between life and art', *Grimmelshausen* (New York: Twayne, 1974) pp. 29, 37.

16. Edward Clarendon's *History of the Rebellion and Civil Wars in England* (Oxford, 1843) provides the major contemporary account of (John) Pym's part in the impeachment of Wentworth; Clarendon's characterisation of Pym applies to both Rick and Magnus: 'the most popular man, and the most able to do hurt, that hath lived in any time' (p. 475). Clarendon sought to combine autobiography with history in his sequel volume, *The Life*, written in seclusion as self-vindication and left for posthumous publication (p. 914).

17. The allusions here are to Ford's *The Good Soldier* (Pym's 'Bible', p. 159), Hašek's *The Good Soldier Švejk*, and Mann's *The Confessions of Felix Krull, Confidence Man.*

18. Compare D. W. Winnicott's appraisal of deprived, delinquent and 'dishonest' children in 'The Concept of the False Self', 'Delinquency as a Sign of Hope' and 'The Child in the Family Group' in Clare Winnicott, Ray Shepherd and Madeleine Davis (eds), *Home Is Where We Start From: Essays by a Psychoanalyst* (Harmondsworth, Middx.: Penguin, 1986) pp. 65–70, 101–11, 128–41.

11

Radical Thrillers

STEPHEN KNIGHT

I

The thriller is usually regarded as so innately conservative a form
that to speak of radical thrillers might seem an unlikely prospect, a
project condemned to dabble in some corner of a genre. But that is
not the case. There are various sorts of radicality in the thriller –
taking 'thriller' as a general description for all types of crime fiction,
and leaving the definition of 'radical' to emerge from the variety of
described radicalities. In some respects the crime novel was born as
a radically new construction; further, its process over two centuries
has included many moments of radicalness. Some of them are
elements of internal strain foreclosed by a simplistic conclusion,
others are deliberate rejections of the usual conservative thrust of
the mainstream thriller. There have also (increasingly in recent
years) been consciously radical thrillers that set out to construct a
left hegemony within a form that most have assumed to be
inherently complicit with bourgeois culture.

The argument about bourgeois complicity has been put with
concise vigour by Ernest Mandel in *Delightful Murder*, a book in
which an expert Marxian continues the tradition of the first of all
pieces of crime fiction criticism, that of *The Holy Family*, in which
Marx and Engels in 1845 stigmatised the Young Hegelians, using
Eugène Sue's early and influential crime story *Les Mystères de Paris*
as a model of bourgeois idealism and repressive cultural politics.

It is not hard to see force in Mandel's statements. There are
evident strands of conservatism in the thriller. In the domestic
crime variety, it can take the pattern of the classic clue-puzzle,
where a wealthy person is murdered and an élite individual
resolves the problem: the poor, the police, the oppressed and the
collective have no place in this particular fantasy. More apparently
modern versions of domestic crime can be just as conservative, like
the police stories of 'Ed McBain', where a group of detectives
operate in the context of big-city realism, but the values remain
fully bourgeois and capitalist. The crimes tend to be against the

172

allegedly free individual, not overtly against the economic structure that throws up that socio-cultural formation – such an analysis is offered at greater length in Chapter 6 of my book *Form and Ideology in Crime Fiction*.

The international crime version of the thriller (the spy story as it is often and misleadingly called) developed in its first phase the racist and nationalist pattern of true Britons confounding the anti-imperial wiles of foreigners of all kinds. Erskine Childers's *The Riddle of the Sands* was perhaps the most nuanced of these novels; the Bulldog Drummond stories by 'Sapper' (H. C. McNeile) were probably the most overtly Fascist. Transmuted as it has been into the quasi-modern discourse of Len Deighton or Robert Ludlum, and often revealing failures of faith or loyalty within the Western camp itself, the international thriller remains firmly attached to the cultural and economic wisdom of the 'free West' – especially if the books are written, usually at turgid length, by people who are apparently no longer employed by the agencies that gave them their special knowledge. Or are they merely in a new section, one for fictional output and disinformational input? Arnaud de Borchgrave is an instructive case: first an editor in the *Time/Newsweek* world, then an author of right-wing fantasy thrillers with Robert Moss, an 'international affairs' expert from Canberra. (They were said to be the favourite novelists of Bob Hawke, Australian Labour Prime Minister.) De Borchgrave became the editor of the Reaganesque *Washington Times*. An illuminating career; but the thriller tradition can remain conservative without the help of such demagogues.

A lot of malign 'isms' are produced and validated in the mainstream thriller, principal among them capitalism, individualism, nationalism, racism and sexism. Yet these constructs are not generated without conflict, without some challenges to their reassuring resolutions. For a start, a perception of threatening radical possibilities is innate to the role of conservative ideology. But the dialectic character of the thriller includes many other radical elements which this paper will explore, in its process stressing the patterns involved more than one particular book or even one particular author.

II

First, and continuingly, it is necessary to recognise the role of formal radicalism in the thriller. After all, the crime story, in its modern form is historically produced in the moment of critique. Three basic texts in the creation of the thriller genre all situate and construct themselves by consciously reversing other patterns, and at varying levels they are consciously politically radical. William Godwin's *The Adventures of Caleb Williams*, published in 1794, is cited realistically as the first mystery novel. It makes central a crime by a socially powerful person, who is pursued by an honest private investigator, Caleb himself; it also reveals the individualist contradiction in which the investigator discovers aspects of criminality in himself. Crime here is not merely a social aberration that can be rooted out by communal means – that was the earlier and conservative character of the *Newgate Calendar* stories. For Caleb Williams, one brain can sense the injustice of crime by the powerful, and, at whatever cost to the investigator, lay bare the truth and the cruelty of power. Godwin was a leading radical, best known then (and still, in France) for his *Political Justice* – a text that has been elided from the British tradition, but one inscribed within his early and distinctly radical thriller.

Edgar Allan Poe's short stories from the 1840s include three about Dupin, the rationally supreme investigator. They too shape in form a dissent from currently hegemonic conventions in Poe's reliance on a reason that goes beyond utilitarian mathematics, and on a perception that breaches the unknowable. Both forces release in story the projected ideology of romanticism, the fully fantasised powers of the individual. Poe develops to a fine point of artistic and notionally self-sufficient power the isolated and self-damaging conflict of Godwin's hero.

The third stone in the arch of the new thriller was Emile Gaboriau's Parisian pattern of the 1870s, in which a highly professional and wisely urban detective (a real and working *petit bourgeois*) traced the past crimes of an aristocracy still trying to restrict the powers of that historically new force in France, the bourgeoisie themselves. The best examples are *M. Lecoq* and *The Lerouge Affair* (also translated as *The Widow Lerouge*). It is quite true, as Ernest Mandel says, that the pattern is fully bourgeois and so, from the late twentieth-century viewpoint, fully reactionary; but in its period it was radical, both in terms of theme and form. With dynamic origination like Godwin, Poe and Gaboriau, it is not surprising that for its later renovations the thriller should continue to find new energy through versions of an innovation and critique that were at once socio-cultural and formal.

III

Radicalism finds strange company at times. There is of necessity a certain element of radical critique built into the pattern of the most conservative writers, because, in order to realise fully a threat that will engage the fears of the audience and so create a pattern that can produce a truly consoling resolution, the text must first dramatise some genuine historical fear and possibility; that is, it must speak with a partly radical voice and realise some aspect of the actual social relations from a period. For example, many early Sherlock Holmes stories present the tensions within the bourgeois family over money, especially the money and probably the body of the unmarried daughter, victim of double desire by the father. Buried within the Holmes stories is a radical perception of the respectable family – consider for example the dynamic combination of step-daughter, snake, safe and penetrated bedroom wall in 'The Speckled Band'.

In a similar way, the two novels that Fergus Hume wrote and set in Victoria, Australia, in the 1880s rely for their disturbing core on a radically accurate perception of contemporary society. *The Mystery of a Hansom Cab* was actually the first best-seller in all crime fiction, written, set and published first in Melbourne in 1886. In many ways it is a powerful piece of work and so is its almost completely unknown successor, *Madame Midas*, set in Ballarat and Melbourne; both novels have recently been reprinted by Hogarth. They draw powerfully on the perilous sense of mushrooming wealth in Victorian Victoria, they perceive the dangerously weak foundation of that society; in particular they activate vigorously the nine-teenth-century anxiety about people of sudden wealth and power whose background is mysterious. The new socio-economic pos-sibilities of great wealth (from the colonies or industry in Britain, from pastoralism or gold mining in Australia) brought with them deep disturbance to the old authority of landed money with its moralised cultural hegemony, and Hume's thriller form helped to create a literary genre out of that drama.

But if most powerful and successful thrillers include such a threat, they also resolve the threat by extirpating its human activators, and so they return the narrative and its audience to a newly established conservative stasis: aspects of strain exist, but are strongly fore-closed. There are much fuller versions of thriller radicalism, which consciously and lastingly criticise the central conservative tendencies of the mainstream thriller. When Sherlock Holmes, that élite avenger of a bungling bourgeoisie, was at the height of his fame in the pages of the *Strand Magazine,* his reflex appeared in the same magazine. Arthur Morrison was a journalist already reputed to be a 'new realist', an Englishman from the Zola mould: his slightly later exposés of poverty, such as *A Child of the Jago* or *Tales of Mean Streets,* became famous. Apparently in deliberate answer to Sherlock Holmes, he produced *Martin Hewitt, Investigator* whose *Chronicles* (the second volume's title) ran for some time, and answered the *Adventures* and *Memoirs* of Sherlock Holmes, texts both idealistic and personalised as those titles suggest.

Hewitt is a very different sort of detective; no deductive posturing, no sudden surges into the night disguised as a Lascar seaman, a drunken groom or some other bogus proletarian. Hewitt stands about a lot, watching; he questions people, bribes them for information. His cases do not depend on illuminating the frailties of the white-collar soul or the amatory foibles of the aristocracy – Doyle's basic early patterns; they are real commercial crimes like a false prospectus in 'The Avalanche Bicycle and Tyre Company'. Hewitt, that is, gives detection back to the detectives and crime back to the criminals, far from Doyle's arias of bourgeois self-analysis. Morrison took critique further through his stories about an unscrupulous near-criminal detective in *The Dorrington Deed Box,* and a similar position was adopted in *The Adventures of Romney Pringle* by 'Clifford Ashdown' – who was apparently Austin Freeman, better known as the author of the unproblematised 'pure science' detection of Dr Thorndyke. Stories by Morrison and 'Ashdown' are to be found in Hugh Greene's collection of *The Rivals of Sherlock Holmes.*

A similar critique, with a different direction, was made by E. W. Hornung when he created Raffles, the 'Amateur Cracksman'. Hornung was Doyle's brother-in-law, but his attitudes to crime and society were different. When living for two years in Australia he developed an interest in the local themes of honourable criminals and hypocritical society: 'Stingaree the gentleman bushranger' was the direct result, but a more successful and immediate version was Raffles – who first took to crime when touring Australia with the MCC (see 'Le Premier Pas'). The Raffles stories are by no means entirely playful; they probe the acquisitive and individual side of respectable society and the hero is made dangerously attractive.

The other example of inherent and low-profile radicalism I want to offer may seem surprising: Agatha Christie. She is often stigmatised as the arch-Tory because of her perfection of the country-house murder, fitted out with moneyed families, clock-work servants and no trace of the depression. That is all true. But radicalism can mean something other than socialism, and Christie's pattern contains a subversive and perhaps fugitive victory for a kind of female (if not feminist) populism.

Her first detective is Hercule Poirot, who goes on in strangely fractured English about his 'little grey cells' and the 'psychology' that seethes through them. This all seems like a version, perhaps parodic, of Sherlock Holmes. But while Holmes's triumphs do quite often depend on some neatly ordered thought, the actual me-chanism of plot-solving in the Poirot stories occupies quite a different ideological terrain.

At a crucial point in *The Murder of Roger Ackroyd*, that brilliantly constructed puzzle that projected Christie into real success, Poirot says 'A good laundry does not starch a handkerchief.' The actual instrumental values of the Poirot stories are not in fact the narcissistic rationalism they offer as a power, but rather the virtues of close attention to material detail, listening to what people say, remembering family relationships, scrutinising personal appear-ances with care, thinking about things like laundries, pot-plants, the position of furniture. That is, the domain of value and functional intelligence is the world of the stereotypical housewife and home-maker, a pattern that challengingly realises the position of a woman like Christie herself who had no formal education at all but had great intellectual capacity. Within the stories is a message of hope-filled fantasy for the housebound housewife, and this is made overt in Miss Marple, a man-less woman (apart from her jejune nephew, author of peacocking mysteries). She solves her mysteries because she uses stereotypically female knowledge as her repertoire of information and judgement.

The model is, of course, politically conservative. Servants remain servants and the moneyed keep taking the dividends, but as with the nineteenth-century initiators of crime fiction, Christie's own reshaping of the form and its values is itself based on some aspects of social radicalism. It may seem passive or ignoble today, but was in its time a firm and in at least some way feminist critique of the sexist heroics of Holmes and his kind. Such a notion is no doubt behind the reprinting in the Pandora Women Crime Writers series of a novel like Christianna Brand's *Green for Danger*, which, for all its acceptance of the values of romantic love, presents that ideology not without irony and sees it firmly from a female position.

There are other versions of subversive innovation within the thriller form. Writing as 'Anthony Berkeley', A. B. Cox broke with some of the clue-puzzle conventions and then, as 'Francis Iles', established the 'Whydunit', where you know in the first page who the murderer is and explore the criminal mind throughout. In a similar move Eric Ambler introduced something like real Europe-wide crime into the feverishly Ruritanian world of E. Phillips Oppenheim. And before retreating into the grand chauvinism (both national and male) of his historical novels, Dennis Wheatley, with J. S. Links, tried in *Murder off Miami* to popularise a dossier story, which, without linking narrative, just provided the clues as a detective would really have them, down to bloodstains and hairs in cellophane packets. The first dossier sold well but the successors largely failed: fact overburdened fiction.

A similar veridical insurgence, of a more controlled nature, is in Len Deighton's colloquial, object-dominated semi-democratisation of the English spy novel, opposing and yet homologous with Ian Fleming's Tory consumerist version of the same form. These interventions were all responses to the conservative ideology in form and content of the hegemonic thriller, and they have aspects of radicalism, albeit muted, inherent in them.

A striking failure to write even a mildly radical thriller, when one might have been expected, is evident in the fictional career of G. D. H. and M. Cole; both were Fabian heavyweights and she (Margaret) was also involved with feminism. They wrote twenty-nine thrillers as a sideline, mostly in the country-house and clue-puzzle style, but some employed a police detective – so mixing somewhat the patterns of Christie and Freeman Wills Crofts. One Cole title is set in a factory during a strike (*Murder at the Munition Works*), but the mystery is established and resolved with traditional clock and alibi techniques. *Big Business Murder* similarly uses a setting observed from their radical work, but offers no economic or political critique at all.

IV

However, some thrillers have been anti-conservative in consciously political terms and so most fully deserve the name of radical; they have been dedicated not just to redirecting the thriller mode but to reshaping public opinion, a political pill in the sugar-coating of a popular genre. That may well have been Godwin's own intention at the very beginning, but in the recent world and in general cognition of thrillers, pride of place as the first big-R Radical must go to Dashiell Hammett.

His work subverted the élitist detective fantasies and the bourgeois values of the mainstream crime novel for two inter-twined reasons: Hammett had worked as a real detective for Pinkertons, whose operations included strike-breaking, and he also held a distinctly leftist political position. *Red Harvest* is a novel with multiple suggestions in its title; both blood and socialism flower in this story of a town taken over by criminals who had been imported by capitalists for their own discreditable reasons. Hammett's radicalism was bleak and ironic; he would unmask the violent and competitive practices of his society and then focus on a symbol of commodity relations like the Maltese Falcon itself or a frail dream of liberation like the glass key. His radicalism was also potently formal; more than anyone else he created the language and plot pattern of 'tough guy' fiction, a materially based discourse that consistently acknowledged conflict between people and between interests. Hammett also treated his own production radically. Each novel is a new departure with a different pattern, interrogating so much the previous versions that this practice may have reduced his impact as a marketable property – he has never been a giant seller.

Hammet's radicalism and auto-critical formal innovations were both absent from the work of the man usually regarded as his successor and sometimes thought of as radical: Raymond Chandler. Elements of urban corruption do appear in his work but by the early novels they no longer explain mysterious events and disturbances as they do in Hammett and in Chandler's early short stories; corruption has become a smokescreen for the real threats that assault the male victims and alarm the detective. Those problems stem from beautiful and sexually active women: it is a fair way from radicalism, either in social or personal relations, as is discussed in Chapter 5 of my *Form and Ideology in Crime Fiction*.

Chandler, with an English public-school education and career as an American executive behind him, realised to the full bourgeois implications of the thriller as Mandel has outlined them; he was also formally conservative, reinforcing in each novel the ideological features of the mainstream private eye thriller. The single and self-

concerned hero, resolving single problems and returning disturbance to stasis – this is an inherently individualist, anti-social and
anti-socialist form. The investigating may become a means of social
enquiry as in *Red Harvest*, but it can hardly realise any positive
radical movements, being so locked into a negative, unmasking
posture.

That inherent negativism has limited the manoeuvres of later
thriller writers whose own political positions have been radical
to some degree. Eric Ambler's international thrillers and Ross
Macdonald's private eye stories probe with vivid power corrupt
authorities and the personal oppressions inherent to the capitalist
world, but the furthest they can go is to present a somewhat
despairing clear eye.

An interesting development of this position is to be found in
Peter Corris's recent novels set in and around Sydney. The context
of plot and action in each novel is a contemporary area of corruption
and extortion – the manipulation of people as well as money alone.
The Dying Trade encompasses political and business corruption,
well before it was a dominant media theme in Sydney, but the plot
also presents a family in disarray and brings in (perhaps a little
underdeveloped) Pacific island nationalist movements. *White Meat*,
the politically sharpest novel so far, deals strongly with the plight of
Aborigines in Australian society; *The Empty Beach* focuses on
corrupt exploitation of old people; *Make Me Rich* explores drug
dealing and its impact, especially on the young. *The January Zone*
defines French nuclear testing as an aspect of criminality. There is a
resemblance between Corris and the successful, now televised,
Boston-based writer, Robert B. Parker. Both use heroes who are ex-
boxers, reasonably educated and critical of urban problems. Parker
is more radical than Corris on the matter of feminism: he confronted it in *Looking for Rachel Wallace* and since then his female
characters have not only been strong but also at times involved in
heavy action.

Corris's radical pattern, restrained as it is by the private eye form,
points towards the position that has been achieved in the other
major modern sub-genre of the crime story: the police-novel. A
radicalism of form and certainly of sentiment was established in
Freeman Wills Crofts's pioneering police novels about Inspector
French; he was a truly plodding bobby, but through meticulous
detection and a host of transport timetables he worked his way to a
success that would have eluded the flashier and more genteel minds
of other thriller heroes, those quotation-dripping, quasi-aristocrats

f what crime buffs have called the 'Golden Age' – Twain's phrase 'Gilded Age' would be more appropriate.

Beyond an anti-amateur pragmatism there was no political critique in Crofts, nor in the fuller developments of the police procedural from Maurice Procter's realistic and populist police sagas through to 'Ed McBain' and television versions like *Dragnet* and *Z Cars*. A collective entity was certainly present in the detective force, but there was no corresponding sense that criminals and politicians might themselves be a structural group, or the deeper perception that crime is a product of a specific socio-economic structure and cannot be genuinely resolved without social and economic reconstruction.

That notion does surface strongly, however, in a set of ten novels written by Maj Sjowall and Per Wahlöo, located in modern Sweden and constructed around a recurring group of police with Martin Beck at their centre. The series was produced for specifically radical reasons, to explore the nature and effect of policing in the allegedly super-democratic Swedish state. Comment cannot replace the impact of reading this rich and absorbing series, the major achievement in recent crime fiction for technical power, conceptual vigour and sustained quality. The last novel, *The Terrorists*, seems in some ways the strongest of all, though *The Laughing Policeman* perhaps best gives the flavour of the whole series.

Essentially, Sjowall and Wahlöo expose modern mechanised and bureaucratised policing as a homologue of the late capitalist state – a technocratic dehumanised creator of many victims, some of whom commit crimes. Against this are set the values of Martin Beck and his friends, human detectives, quite efficient in contrast to the bungling, machine-crazed police gorillas who beset them and the public. There is a positive sense of collectivity here, quite different from the self-seeking sentimentality of the police group in 'Ed McBain'. But this is not a Utopia; the present state of the state prevents that, and there are many behavioural internalizations of late capitalist decay among the human police themselves, especially in Beck's private life, which wavers between despair and sentimentality.

V

Overtly political, relentlessly modern, it sounds as if Sjowall and Wahlöo break new ground by being so self-aware of their radicalism. Actually there was an earlier and largely lost radicalism in the thriller, a period of busy activity in consciously left-wing crime adventures. Few of the authors are remembered and the titles are hard to obtain, but before investigating the recent resurgence of radical thrillers it might be salutary to look at this forgotten past, even to wonder whether it is that period's impact, or our memory, or perhaps the market-controlled access to culture that is the cause of such oblivion.

In the standard books there is an occasional reference, often slighting, to anti-Fascist thrillers of the 1930s. Eric Ambler to some degree, Graham Greene in his earliest work, and perhaps *The Smiler with the Knife* by 'Nicholas Blake', before he emerged from the cocoon of the Communist Party as Cecil Day Lewis, Professor of Poetry at Oxford and then Poet Laureate.

These are not isolated cases of juvenile dementia, as the impression goes. In *Inside the Myth*, Andrew Croft lists twenty-seven titles produced in London between 1934 and 1939 that present Fascism as a powerful threat, mostly in Britain itself – another largely and conveniently forgotten phenomenon. A few novels are set in Germany, like *Hunting Escape* by Montagu Slater and Phyllis Bottome's *The Mortal Storm*, which became a major film for James Stewart in 1940. Some others use a Ruritanian setting to weave a symbolic story about the darkening pattern of European politics, like Eric Ambler's *The Dark Frontier* and Ruthven Todd's *Over the Mountain*. Others deal with Spain, like *In the Second Year* by 'James Hill' – who was actually Storm Jameson, better known now as a writer of what could be called serious romances. But a striking number of these novels see anti-Semitism and Fascism as real forces in Britain itself, like Simon Frazer's *A Shroud as Well as a Shirt*, *The Bad Companions* by Maurice Richardson (a leading post-war crime writer and reviewer) and the intriguing and perhaps well worth resurrecting *Overture to Cambridge* by Joseph Macleod, a satire on Fascist academics.

Few of these are obtainable now, though Rex Warner's powerful *The Professor*, about events in Austria, is not so hard to find, nor is Greene's *The Confidential Agent*, a treatment of Spanish spies from both sides. *The Smiler with the Knife*, country-house in form while apparently radical in content, was reprinted recently by Hogarth, as was *Traitor's Way*, by Bruce Hamilton, a chase story in which the pursuers are Fascists, not the usual mob of foreigners and leftists to be found in Buchan and Sapper.

Such radicalism grew in a time of depression, with a nationalist and pro-banking government, with international affairs increasingly dominated by rearming right wingers – much like the Thatcher–Reagan period; and as if to prove that culture has a socio-economic matrix, the last few years have seen a development of consciously radical thrillers.

Before looking at those, it is worth noting that in Europe at least the leftist thriller is not of recent origin or revival. Mandel mentions Claude Aveline in France and the Swiss Friedrich Dürrenmatt as admirable writers; neither is primarily political in approach but they probe the simplicities of the mainstream thriller and realise both the human realities of crime in society and the oppressive possibilities of policing: there is a line from both towards Sjowall and Wahlöo. A more recent writer of distinctly radical status is Leonardo Sciascia; seeming something like an Italian Hammett, he sees possibilities of penetrating the power of the Mafia, but also shows the debilitating effect of the effort. Like Hammett, he changes his patterns from novel to novel, and may eventually cast doubt on the power of art to do more than toy with the forces he has envisaged – and as Hammett fell to fictional silence, Sciascia has recently restricted himself to investigate reporting.

Pluto undertook an intelligent and admirable project in their avowedly radical crime list and for several years achieved considerable penetration, in all producing twenty-two novels. These included new writers like June Cook (*The Waste Remains*) and Peter Dunant (*Exterminating Angels*) as well as established radical thriller producers like Manuel Vasquez Montalban, author of the admired *Murder in the Central Committee* and *Southern Seas* and Julian Rathbone, a very able writer with some excellent Ambleresque novels like the Spanish-based *Carnival* before his powerful Pluto pair, *Watching the Detectives* and *The Eurokillers*. Some similar titles appeared elsewhere: Chris Mullin, sometime editor of *Tribune*, produced the future imperfect novel *A Very British Coup*; Raymond Williams's *The Volunteers* is both his most successful novel in artistic terms and also the most probingly radical, an intriguing study of long-term moles in a darkening and by no means futurist world.

Gillian Slovo, a Pluto author, presented political radicalism on the topic of South Africa in *Morbid Symptoms*, but she also operated as a part of that strongly developing sub-genre of crime fiction: the feminist thriller; in fact Slovo's next novels, *Death by Analysis* and

Death Comes Staccato, were produced by Women's Press. They also published in Britain two early and influential American texts. Valerie Miner's *Murder in the English Department*, intriguing for more than its inspiring title, showed how new values restructure forms, because this was in no way a whodunit. It centred its problematic on whether the academic woman, who knows quite well who killed her eminently disposable senior (male) colleague, will actually reveal her knowledge or will maintain a feminist solidarity. In a similar reconstructive way Barbara Wilson's *Murder in the Collective* explores the narrator's experiences along the frontiers of gender as well as her criminological inquiries.

Some feminist readers and reviewers have, for all their sympathy with the programme of those novels, found them less than effective as texts, and that criticism has also been voiced about Mary Wings's *She Came too Late*, a thriller more hard femme than private eye, which takes an uncompromising position on lesbian relations, as Wilson does in her recent *Sisters of the Road*. Those who find these writers a little rough, in form if not in topic, have been more approving of the less polemicised adventures of woman detectives like Sara Paretsky's V. I. Warshawski, in *Deadlock*, or Katherine V. Forrest's homicide detective Kate Delafield in *Amateur City*.

Less extensive than the feminist thriller, but equally radical in a different direction, is the related phenomenon of the male gay thriller. Adam Mars Jones has discussed some examples rather sharply in his introduction to *Mae West is Dead*, criticising them for accepting a ghettoised situation. This is not true of the leader in the field, Joseph Hansen, whose series of Dave Brandstetter mysteries (such as *Death Claims*) plays the gay hero quite straight. An insurance inquirer, Brandstetter works as hard and travels as much on his mysteries as ever did Ross Macdonald's Lew Archer, and while his own personal life is dealt with discreetly, the absence of the recurrent sexual tension when the detective interviews women means that Hansen presents much more actual detection and plotting than is usual in the private eye form.

A thought-provoking variant of Hansen's pattern is in the series by Dan Kavanagh, a pseudonym for Julian Barnes with four novels published: the third, *Putting the Boot In*, is a good example. They centre on Duffy, a former policeman and soccer-lover who conducts a moderately successful low-style detective agency in outer London. His sexuality is a little ambivalent; there is a girl-friend, who is still in the police, but little passes between them. Wry, skilfully written but deeply uncommitted, Barnes's novels suggest a considerable difference between American and British approaches to the gay thriller, and indicate that it is possible to be a dissenter and still hardly deserve the name of radicalism.

VI

Though there is an increasing number of thrillers that can be called radical, it might still be asked whether writing thrillers, or indeed writing about thrillers, is in any way sensible or useful for anyone who claims to be radical. Is the genre completely tainted with conservatism? Is the whole concept of crime and detection totally complicit with a society based on property and the individual? Is to talk of radical thrillers just a slender rationalisation of corrupt tastes, a backdoor bourgeoisism? These are substantial questions. If they draw a positive answer, then that is indeed a counsel of despair for cultural studies of radical cast.

My own view is that those questions deserve the answer no; that their premises ignore the dialectical character of culture and society, including bourgeois formations; and that it is valid to write thrillers or write about thrillers and offer that as a political act. Such a view depends on several things. It assumes that culture has its own materiality and that culture is a major producer of ideological attitudes and positions – views that are held today by almost all serious students of culture and society. In that case the terrain on which general ideas in the community are formed and reproduced becomes a crucial force-field into which the left must enter. The huge sales of thrillers in all their forms indicate that this is a major site of ideological production, especially in television series and mass-sale paperback fiction.

It may well be that to write and publicise radical thrillers will at first only appeal to an audience already consciously leftist – which might well have been a limiting factor in the Pluto experiment. That may indeed have the virtue of making it possible for people on the left to explore radicality in fiction as well as other forms of culture, but it does also make possible sales of texts that are artistically unsuccessful, as slackly uncritical and uninformed by dynamism as the poorest of the right-wing thrillers. Few of the Pluto titles were in fact skilful as novels – for one thing, conservatism in them was not as dynamically realised as radical threats often are in the mainstream conservative thrillers.

To survive as a possible form and to construct through that a consciously left hegemony within crime fiction, the radical thriller must adapt for its own purposes the dialectic structure from which comes the power of the conservative thriller and within which inhere the residual radical elements in that tradition. This is certainly possible: Hammett, Ambler, Rathbone, Sjowall and Wahlöo show that potent art in the thriller is just as possible from a leftist standpoint as any other. They have shown that the literature of urban tension, of professional skills, of international drama – the bourgeois thriller, that is – can be redirected radically through a reperception of the conflicts inherent to those categories. What William Godwin started can be continued, and in just as urgent a period; crime fiction can be an instrument of political justice.

References

Ambler, E., *The Dark Frontier* (Sevenoaks: Hodder and Stoughton, 1936).
Ashdown, C., *The Adventures of Romney Pringle* (London: Ward Lock, 1902).
Blake, N., *The Smiler with the Knife* (London: Collins, 1939).
Bottome, P., *The Mortal Storm* (London: Faber and Faber, 1937).
Brand, C., *Green for Danger* (London: Allen Lane, 1945).
Childers, E., *The Riddle of the Sands* (London: Smith and Elder, 1903).
Christie, A., *The Murder of Roger Ackroyd* (London: Collins, 1926).
Cole, G. D. H. and Cole, M., *Big Business Murder* (London: Collins, 1935).
Cole, G. D. H. and Cole, M., *Murder at the Munition Works* (London: Collins, 1940).
Cook, J., *The Waste Remains* (London: Pluto Press, 1984).
Corris, P., *The Dying Trade* (Sydney: McGraw-Hill, 1980).
Corris, P., *The Empty Beach* (London: Allen and Unwin, 1985).
Corris, P., *The January Zone* (London: Allen and Unwin, 1988).
Corris, P., *White Meat* (London: Pan, 1981).
Corris, P., *Make Me Rich* (London: Allen and Unwin, 1985).
Croft, A., 'Worlds Without End Foisted Upon the Future – Some Antecedents of *Nineteen Eighty Four*', in C. Norris (ed.), *Inside the Myth* (London: Lawrence and Wishart, 1984).
Dunnat, P., *Exterminating Angels* (London: Pluto Press, 1986).
Doyle, A. C., 'The Adventures of the Speckled Band', *Strand Magazine* (1892).
Forrest, K. V., *Amateur City* (London: Pandora, 1987).
Frazer, S., *A Shroud as Well as a Shirt* (London: Chapman and Hall, 1935).
Gaboriau, E., *The Widow Lerouge* (1873).
Gaboriau, E., *M. Lecoq* (1880).
Godwin, W., *The Adventures of Caleb Williams* (1794).
Godwin, W., *Enquiry Concerning Political Justice* (1793).

Greene, H. (ed.), *The Rivals of Sherlock Holmes* (London: Bodley Head, 1979).
Greene, G., *The Confidential Agent* (London: William Heinemann, 1939).
Hamilton, B., *Traitor's Way* (London: Cresset, 1938).
Hammett, D., *Red Harvest* (London: Cassell, 1929).
Hansen, J., *Death Claims* (London: Grafton, 1987).
Hill, J., *In the Second Year* (London: Cassell, 1936).
Hornung, E. W., 'Le Premier Pas', in *The Amateur Cracksman* (London: Methuen, 1899).
Hume, F., *The Mystery of a Hansom Cab* (London: Hansom Cab, 1887).
Hume, F., *Madame Midas* (London: Hansom Cab, 1888).
Kavanagh, D., *Putting the Boot in* (London: Jonathan Cape, 1985).
Knight, S., *Form and Ideology in Crime Fiction* (London: Macmillan, 1980).
Macleod, J., *Overture to Cambridge* (London: Allen and Unwin, 1936).
Mandel, E. *Delightful Murder* (London: Pluto Press, 1984).
Mars Jones A., Introduction, *Mae West is Dead* (London: Faber and Faber, 1983).
Marx, K. and Engels, F., *The Holy Family* (1845).
Miner, V., *Murder in the English Department* (London: Women's Press, 1983).
Montalban, M. V., *Murder in the Central Committee* (London: Pluto Press, 1984).
Montalban, M. V., *Southern Seas* (London: Pluto Press, 1986).
Morrison, A., *Martin Hewitt, Investigator* (London: Ward Lock, 1894).
Morrison, A., *Tales of Mean Streets* (London: Methuen, 1894).
Morrison, A., *A Child of the Jago* (London: Methuen, 1896).
Morrison, A., *The Dorrington Deed-Box* (London: Ward Lock, 1897).
Mullin, C., *A Very British Coup* (London: Jonathan Cape, 1983).
Paretsky, S., *Deadlock* (London: Ballantine, 1984).
Parker, R. B., *Looking for Rachel Wallace* (New York: Dell, 1983).
Poe, E. A., 'The Purloined Letter', in *The Gift* (1844).
Rathbone, J., *Carnival* (London: Michael Joseph, 1976).
Rathbone, J., *The Eurokillers* (London: Pluto Press, 1986).
Rathbone, J., *Watching the Detectives* (London: Michael Joseph, 1983).
Richardson, M., *The Bad Companions* (1936).
Sjowall, M. and Wahlöo, P., *The Laughing Policeman* (London: Victor Gollancz, 1971).
Sjowall, M. and Wahlöo, P., *The Terrorists* (Harmondsworth, Middx.: Penguin, 1976).
Slater, M., *Haunting Europe* (London: Wishart, 1934).
Slovo, G., *Death by Analysis* (London: Women's Press, 1986).
Slovo, G., *Death Comes Staccato* (London: Women's Press, 1987).
Slovo, G., *Morbid Symptoms* (London: Pluto Press, 1984).
Sue, E., *Les Mystères de Paris* (Paris: Gosselin, 1843).
Todd, R., *Over the Mountain* (London: Harrap, 1939).
Warner, R., *The Professor* (Boriswood, 1938).
Wheatley, D. and Links, J. S., *Murder off Miami* (London: Hutchinson, 1936).
Williams, R., *The Volunteers* (London: Hogarth Press, 1985).
Wilson, B., *Murder in the Collective* (London: Women's Press, 1984).
Wilson, B., *Sisters of the Road* (London: Women's Press, 1987).
Wings, M., *She Came too Late* (London: Women's Press, 1986).

Index

This index refers primarily to authors. For references to characters or novels, look under the relevant author (e.g. for 'Philip Marlowe', see under Raymond Chandler; for *The Maltese Falcon*, see under Dashiell Hammett etc.). Individual italicised titles refer to TV series, newspapers, magazines or films mentioned in the main body of the text.